"Relevant for our times. Possibly prophetic."

Dewey Clark, PhD, MBA, chair, C12 Business Forums

"An insightful and entertaining story of market dynamics."

Rael Gorelick, head of investments, Biltmore Family Office

"Engaging narrative showcasing the power of
applied technical analysis."

Charles Raymond Shimer, III, CFA, senior portfolio manager,
Level Four Capital Management

"Colorful drama with Southern charm."

Jimbo Perry, JD, attorney-at-law, Perry Law Firm

"Practical reflections of sacred truths. Having a better understanding of
how money works is wise, and to ignore these words is reckless."

Matt Evans, MDiv, pastor, Christ the King Church

STOCK BROKEN

STOCK BROKEN

BILLY HEMBY & JAN HEMBY

pinwheel press

Raleigh, North Carolina

STOCKBROKEN

Billy Hemby & Jan Hemby

Library of Congress Control Number: 2025935996
Publisher's Cataloging-in-Publication
(Provided by Cassidy Cataloguing Services, Inc.)

Names: Hemby, Bill, author. | Hemby, Jan, author.
Title: Stockbroken / Billy Hemby & Jan Hemby.
Other titles: Stock broken
Description: Raleigh, North Carolina : Pinwheel Press, [2026]
Identifiers: LCCN: 2025925996 | ISBN: 9798993687001 (paperback) | 9798993687018 (Kindle) | 9798993687025 (ePub)
Subjects: LCSH: Investment advisors--North Carolina. | Stock exchanges. | Financial crises. | Murder. | Profit. | LCGFT: Thrillers (Fiction) | Christian fiction. | BISAC: FICTION / Thrillers / General. | FICTION / Southern. | FICTION / Christian / Suspense.
Classification: LCC: PS3608.E4733 S76 2026 | DDC: 813/.6--dc23

This book is dedicated to curious readers and
market enthusiasts who ask,
"Is this the new roaring '20s?"

AUTHORS' NOTE

Stockbroken is written to both entertain and inform. At times, the story explores the mechanics of financial markets and includes more detailed discussions of investing and market dynamics. Readers who enjoy the technical side of trading and investing may find these passages especially interesting.

For those who are primarily here for the story, feel free to skim these sections and continue with the narrative. The plot will carry forward either way.

Our hope is that readers will find something to enjoy—whether in the story itself, the ideas behind the markets, or both.

It has been said that history repeats itself.
This is perhaps not quite correct; it merely rhymes.
— Theodor Reik

CHAPTER ONE

From his office in the lower Manhattan Financial District just a few blocks from Wall Street, Bo Parrott stared in disbelief as his phone rang . . . again.

With decades of experience as an investment advisor, Bo was no stranger to the long hours required to answer the barrage of client calls that defined his workday. The call volume typically increased whenever the storm clouds began to gather, signaling a stock market downturn. He was no stranger to that, either. But today it felt different. The phone had been ringing nonstop since he stepped through the door two hours earlier.

"What the hell is going on, Parrott? Did you see this coming?"

Bo recognized the voice as belonging to a client known for his strong personality yet weak command of genteel discourse. Howard Lanning may never have gotten a stomach ulcer, but he was more than capable of giving one to someone else. Bo studied the report streaming across his screen. Despite Howard's abrupt delivery, his words echoed Bo's own concerns.

"I'll find out, and I'll call you back as soon as I can."

Spencer T. Barnes, Bo's young assistant, sat across from Bo's desk. "Howard Lanning?" he asked, raising an eyebrow.

Bo nodded. "Yes, but he's not the only one. Our client base comprises a significant percentage of savvy investors, and many of them have caught wind of a potential shift in the stock market that could negatively impact their earnings. With over three thousand clients worldwide, that's a lot of phone calls! They've been pouring in all morning."

Bo powered up his laptop. Despite feeling unsettled about the possible rate hike from the Federal Reserve, he managed to smile as the charts began to populate his computer screen. He asked Spencer to move his chair closer for a better view.

"The indicators really are something to behold, especially when you consider what they represent. The lines are like a kaleidoscope with a panoramic effect and a beauty all their own."

Realizing how that last statement might have sounded, Bo quickly backtracked as he darted his eyes in Spencer's direction. "If you like that sort of beauty."

Twenty-five years Bo's junior, Spencer chuckled as he ran his hand through his side-part haircut. A few streaks of brown blended with his golden mane. "It's growing on me."

Bo continued, "A seafoam-green background serves as the canvas for the market indicators. They appear like an artist applying dabs of paint squirted onto a palette board."

Spencer leaned in closer as Bo pointed to several images on his computer screen. "Each colorful line tells a story. Some lines have more relevance at specific coordinates on the chart's workspace, and some have less. At zenith moments, the chart system behaves like a supernova: Brightness increases when the star explodes and releases most of its mass. When the mood is right in the stock market, the drama is something to behold."

"What about today?" Spencer asked.

"Today, the mood appears dark and foreboding. Figuratively speaking, this chart represents a network of capillaries that have burst.

Blood is gushing profusely. Unless a tourniquet is applied soon, the victim could die."

Spencer leaned back in his chair. "Wow, it's one thing to see these stock market configuration indices in multicolor. It's another to interpret what it all means."

"It really is," Bo responded. "Movement occurs in real time. Even the most well-intentioned investors stumble badly when making decisions based on the *evidence* of market activity displayed before them. In fact, I've heard it said that market trading is more of an art than a science. An element of intuitiveness is required to get it right. The successful players *see movements in advance* and sniff out the ensuing development."

"Easier said than done," Spencer said as he shifted in his seat.

"Exactly. The road to profitable trading is littered with the remains of deceased sojourners. For some, it's because they lost confidence. Others simply weren't willing to do the work required to achieve mastery. Those who go on to achieve mastery do so by spending relentless hours in the inconspicuous workspaces that house the technology required to track market activity."

"Like that office in your house with the forty monitors?" Spencer asked with a wink.

Bo's face relaxed into a smile. "There are only six monitors, but yes, like that office."

"So," Spencer said as he jotted down a few notes on a legal pad. "You'd say that hindsight in the market is *easy*, which is what most media commentators engage in."

"Correct. What's *complicated* is real-time sparring in the arena. The role of the stockbroker resembles that of a gladiator; basic financial survival is on the line. There is a correlation between the media news feed and the technical charting that occurs during market hours. As stockbrokers, we must corroborate this with the calculus that goes with investing. This enables us to measure what may be considered a fair price for securities purchased.

"All three—the story, the charts, and the math—must be factored into the split-second decision-making needed for timely executions mandated by successful investment management."

Spencer slid his pencil behind his ear and leaned back in his seat. "What is your strategy regarding the potential rate increase by the Federal Reserve and how it could affect the market?"

"If the pattern follows past rate increases—" Bo paused as his cell phone vibrated from his desk. He checked the caller ID.

"It's Selby. Can we continue this a little later?"

Spencer nodded and picked up his legal pad and pencil. "No problem. I've got a list of phone calls to make myself. Give Selby my best," he said as he quietly stepped out of Bo's office.

Bo gave Spencer a thumbs-up and then answered Selby's call.

"Selby, how's your day going?"

"Hi, sweetheart! Probably better than yours!"

Selby's cheerful greeting struck a stark contrast to the fearful and angry salutations he'd heard from his clients all morning.

"I'm surprised you answered. Isn't there supposed to be a big announcement from the Federal Reserve? I'll bet your office phone has been ringing off the hook."

"That it has," Bo responded, shuffling a few folders on his desk.

"I won't keep you. I just wanted to remind you not to work too late. Our move is only two days away. I need you to be alert for that drive to North Carolina."

"But you're the one driving. You get all cagey being the passenger."

"Which is why I need you to be alert. How quickly we forget all the speeding tickets I've received over the years!"

Bo laughed. "Trust me, I haven't forgotten." Then he heard his phone beep. "Hey, I've got another call coming in. I'll see you this evening, and yes, I'll try not to work too late."

Dreading yet another irate client demanding answers he couldn't provide yet, Bo was pleasantly surprised when he looked at the caller ID. The number belonged to an older gentleman who typically didn't call unless there was an issue with his account and, right off the top of his head, Bo couldn't recall one. Either way, he was looking forward to catching up with his very first client, Edmond Brockett.

"Well, they come crawling out of the woodwork when there's a Federal Reserve rate hike," Bo laughed as he leaned back in his office chair. "How are you doing? Are you still enlightening young minds down in Eastern North Carolina?"

Bo could hear Edmond laugh on the other end, but it wasn't the hearty laugh he was used to hearing. Edmond sounded weak.

"I've been better, Bo. That's why I'm calling."

Bo sat up straight in his chair. "Edmond, I'm sorry. What's going on?"

"Lung cancer, and it's progressing quickly."

Bo's breath caught in his throat. Edmond was one of the locals back home who had helped him get his investment advisory practice up and running. With only a few years under his belt as a professor at a local college and a hefty amount of student loan debt, Edmond didn't have much to invest with Bo. Then, he received a substantial payout from an investment company with which he had partnered. That initial deposit, compounded with others over the years, had grown into a sizable nest egg that would allow him to retire comfortably.

Edmond and his wife, Regina, loved to travel and had explored most of Europe. Edmond's dream was for them to visit central Asia when he retired. Closer to home, he aimed to improve his golf game. Bo's heart sank as he realized that neither of those plans would come to fruition now.

He cleared his throat. "Edmond, is there anything I can do? You name it."

"I do need your help, but it's a big request."

"Okay, let's hear it."

"I've been teaching history and economics at the local college for nearly forty years. I'd do it another forty if my body would let me." He laughed weakly and then let out a heavy sigh. "But that's not the case.

I'm turning in my letter of resignation. I want to spend as much quality time with Regina as possible."

Bo swallowed hard. "I understand. That sounds like the right thing to do."

"I told the college board of directors that I wanted to pick my successor, someone who has a passion for learning—as well as teaching—and who won't use the lectern to promote one political view over another."

Bo could hear him stop to take a ragged breath before continuing. "At this point in my career, I'm only teaching one night a week, but that class is important to me. Those *students*—and the ones who will follow—are important to me."

Bo felt a twinge of anxiety. "So, how can I help?"

"When I heard you were moving back to North Carolina, I thought I was dreaming. I can't think of anyone better to be my replacement. You're a walking history textbook, and you have forty years of experience as a stockbroker. Most importantly, you're a man of integrity who shares my values. As I said, it would only be one night a week and shouldn't interfere with your daytime work schedule."

Bo turned in his office chair to face the window. "I'm honored that you'd consider me, Edmond. Your shoes would be big ones to fill. Before I give you an answer, I'd like to discuss it with Selby, if that's okay."

"Of course," Edmond replied. "I look forward to hearing from you soon."

Bo's mind raced. His first instinct was to turn down the offer. After all, his goal for the upcoming season was to lessen his responsibilities, not increase them. Yet the thought of having a platform from which to share the knowledge and experience he'd gained over the years appealed to him. It could be an idyllic way to ride into his retirement sunset, so to speak. He could already picture himself wearing a cardigan sweater and khakis, a crusty old college professor. Maybe he'd grow a beard and start smoking a pipe?

Beyond that, the offer stirred up a deeper longing, one he couldn't quite put his finger on, at least not yet. He would need to discuss the matter in detail with Selby; that is, if he survived today's market turbulence. The Federal Reserve had just announced a half-percentage-point rate increase and would also sell bonds on the open market, which would tighten the money supply. The stock market wouldn't like it.

He checked his watch. As much as he dreaded doing so, he needed to make numerous client calls, beginning with Howard Lanning.

He sighed, picked up the phone, and started dialing.

***

"He didn't say yes," Lutz Osswald said flatly as he folded his arms and leaned back on a wall in Edmond's office.

Today, Lutz made sure to wear an expensive, tailored black suit, complete with a starched white shirt and a designer tie. In this and similar situations, his goal was to keep his audience feeling uncomfortable as he struck a balance between a style inherent to a successful businessman and that of an undertaker. His hair was always meticulously styled to lie just above his forehead. The shade of blonde was an exact match in color to his eyebrows, which enshrouded dull hazel eyes that rarely displayed any emotion. All in all, these well-planned optics produced an atmosphere of intimidation, one which, over the years, he had nearly perfected to a science.

"He didn't say no, either," Edmond responded.

"Yeah, but you didn't sell it hard enough," scoffed a younger man whom Lutz had referred to as Mark and who stood by Edmond's office door. He wore a tight-fitting black T-shirt displaying oversized biceps that looked like they'd been coated in wax.

"I agree," Lutz replied. "You could have thrown in grant money talk and, you know, how his presence at the college could serve the community. All the things that"—he paused and used his fingers to make air quotes—"*people of integrity* want to hear."

"I didn't want to *oversell* it." Edmond shook his head as his gaze fell to the floor. "I still can't believe I'm doing this."

"You didn't really have a choice," Lutz quipped. "You don't want the word to get out that Professor Edmond Brockett invested dirty money, now do you? Although I do commend you for choosing the right financial advisor at the time, Bo Parrott was still wet behind the ears and had no idea what—or who—he ultimately was dealing with."

"Bo is a good man," Edmond said, his words communicating both conviction and regret.

Lutz rolled his eyes. "You've got until the end of the week. Offer him more money. Promise him a grant. Do whatever it takes. Just get him to accept the position."

Edmond's voice shook as he asked, "What if he turns it down? How can I reach you?"

After exchanging glances with Mark, Lutz responded, "I'll be flying back to Europe in a few days. You won't be able to contact me. But rest assured, I'll be in touch."

Once outside in the hall, Mark shook his head and pointed toward Edmond's office. "Lutz, please tell me you're going to do something about him. He knows too much. Simon will act if we don't."

Lutz leaned forward to push the button for the elevator. "It's all been arranged."

"What about Kathryn?"

"My, aren't you bloodthirsty," Lutz said as they stepped into the elevator. As the doors closed, Lutz smiled and answered, "All in good time, my friend. All in good time."

CHAPTER TWO

Selby Parrott hated moving.

She had endured the mind-numbing process of packing and unpacking numerous times in her forty years of marriage to Bo Parrott. Now, she begrudgingly found herself in the process once more.

However, as she wrapped yet another coffee cup in newspaper and tucked it into a box with the rest, she couldn't help but smile. As much as she loathed the moving process, it did bring back fond memories of her and Bo's early years together. Each relocation wasn't just a change of address; it was a significant milestone in their journey.

The first was when a much younger version of Bo and Selby hauled their small collection of hand-me-down furniture from cramped married-student housing to a cozy studio apartment near campus. They had planned to stay there until Bo had finished his MBA and they had saved up enough money to buy a house. That plan changed a year later when Selby discovered that she didn't have a lingering stomach virus, but was pregnant with twins.

For her and Bo's next move, Selby watched from the sidelines as Bo, an excited dad-to-be, single-handedly transferred their belongings to a larger apartment and then stayed up late at night assembling two of everything when it came to the baby furniture. Five years later, when their twin daughters, Alicia and Amelia, were old enough to start kindergarten, she and Bo finally bought their first house—a modest home located within walking distance of the school.

With Alicia and Amelia married and living back in North Carolina, she and Bo had decided it was time to exchange the noise and expense of New York City for a quieter and less complicated life back home in North Carolina. Bo planned to retire in a few years and couldn't think of a better setting in which to wind down his career.

Selby opened the kitchen cabinet doors to see if she'd forgotten anything. Sure enough, she spotted a few stray wineglasses and an assortment of plastic containers. After securing the wineglasses in bubble wrap, she got a lump in her throat when she recognized the plastic containers as the ones she'd used years ago to pack school lunches for Alicia and Amelia.

Besides ensuring the twins had their lunch boxes before they left for school, Selby was also at the helm helping them with their homework, signing report cards, and sewing sequins onto their ballet costumes. Bo, meanwhile, was working long hours building his investment advisory business. He had relied on members of the local community to entrust their savings accounts, property settlements, and 401(k) plans to him for management. Even after he had built a sizable client base and achieved a level of success in the industry, he never forgot his roots or the people who helped him get his start.

Selby reluctantly tossed the plastic containers into the recycling pile. As she glanced around the kitchen at the stacks of boxes and collection of packing materials, she thought about how this move shared a common denominator with all the others in terms of the endless sorting and cleaning. However, she hoped it would be different in that it would be their last. Meanwhile, her role in the process remained what it had always been: the monotonous task of packing and unpacking, and so on.

"Okay, Selby," she said to herself as she took a sip of coffee and then set the cup on the guest room nightstand. "The final frontier: the guest room closet." She leaned over and began pulling out storage boxes and other items she and Bo had crammed in there. The first box she opened contained several rolls of Christmas wrapping paper. Another was full of clothes marked for donation. Aside from these, she tossed out a few stray pairs of shoes, two umbrellas, and a shrink-wrapped shower curtain liner she forgot she had purchased.

In the corner of the closet was a box that contained high school annuals and a few college textbooks. Selby was about to tape it up like the others when she spotted a manila envelope. Curious, she unfastened the clasp and looked inside. The envelope appeared to contain items Bo had saved: a few photos from their senior year of college, movie ticket stubs, and the restaurant receipt from the night he proposed to her. Selby was about to close the envelope when one item caught her attention.

She picked up the weathered piece of yellow legal-pad paper. The numbers written on it were barely visible. It was one that Bo had saved from the first time they met. She thought about how countless people had seamlessly entered her life over the years, slipping in so quietly and unassumingly that she might find it difficult to pinpoint her first interaction with them. That was not the case with Bo Parrott. He noisily barged into her world with a brand of eccentricity that she'd found both annoying . . . and irresistibly charming.

It was the last semester of Selby's college senior year. She had stopped by her favorite coffee shop and diner for a large dark roast with whipped cream topping. As usual, Lionel was working behind the counter. He had a daughter about Selby's age and never seemed too busy to offer her a word of encouragement . . . along with her caffeine fix.

This morning, the sound of the front door creaking opening interrupted their conversation. Selby turned around to see a young man wearing headphones, carrying a book bag and what appeared to be a gym bag with a tennis racket sticking out of it. He was singing off-key to whatever music he was listening to.

Selby rolled her eyes and turned back to face Lionel. "Here's a dollar for the coffee and one for the reassurance that I'll survive those final exams. I needed both this morning!"

As she made her way over to a table, the young man behind her called out, "I hope you didn't pay two dollars for that cup of coffee!"

Selby frowned. If that was a pickup line, this guy seriously needed to work on his game. Not only did he question her judgment, but he also insulted Lionel, and she was not okay with either.

But he wasn't finished.

After fumbling with a pocket on the outside of his jacket, he retrieved a Walkman and, after turning it off, slipped it back inside. "There's a grocery-store brand that tastes just as good, and you can make an entire pot of coffee for less than that." The young man paused for a moment and squinted his eyes as if he were doing the math in his head. "In fact, if one quarter-cup scoop makes one pot and there are twelve serving scoops, you can make each pot of coffee—which is eight cups—for around thirty-two cents. You just paid an extra five hundred percent for that one cup of coffee." Then his eyes lit up, and he broke into a smile. "Do you want to know how much you could save in a year?"

Selby suddenly realized that he was serious. He really wanted to help her.

That didn't make her feel better.

Lionel, on the other hand, was leaning on the counter, looking at this young man as if he were a rare exhibit at the zoo. With a raised eyebrow, he asked him, "Are you going to order something?"

"Uh, yes, let me check out my options," he said as he studied the menu posted on the wall behind Lionel.

Selby shrugged her shoulders as Lionel shot her a questioning look.

"Okay," he said, "I'll have the large breakfast sandwich. I can eat half now and the other half for lunch. It will save me—"

"About a buck and a quarter," Lionel said flatly as he stood upright and stepped over to the griddle.

The young man nodded and glanced over his shoulder at Selby. "He's right."

Selby's eyes grew wide. "*I know*," she said. Quietly, to herself, she mumbled, "Geez! I would need more than coffee to deal with this guy."

Unzipping her book bag from where she had set it on the floor next to her chair, she pulled out her literature textbook and a yellow legal pad with a mechanical pencil clipped to the front. Then she heard a chair scrape against the floor. She raised her eyes to see the same young man about to sit down at her table.

"May I?" he asked.

Selby silently protested. *No, I need to study, and I haven't even had my coffee yet!* But she decided to be polite. "Sure, have a seat."

After setting his book bag and gym bag onto the floor, he extended his hand across the table. "I'm Bo Parrott."

Selby hesitated but shook his hand and said, "Selby Brookstone."

"Selby?" He repeated as he placed the wax-paper-wrapped sandwich onto the table.

"Yeah." Selby responded as she pointed to his headphones, "You could hear me better if you took those off."

Bo smiled sheepishly as he removed the headphones and let them rest against his shirt collar. He slipped his arms out of his coat and hung it on the back of his chair. Taking his seat, he said, "You're right; it's not a good look for me." He leaned in and lowered his voice as if he were telling her a secret. "My ears are my best feature."

Selby unsuccessfully suppressed a chuckle. Bo's face lit up in response. When it did, Selby noticed that it was a handsome face, complete with a pair of deep-set denim-blue eyes. He had dark brown, wavy hair that appeared overdue for a trim and curled slightly on the ends.

"No, I heard you loud and clear, I was just wondering about your name, Selby. It's . . . different. Is it a family name?"

"Yes, it is, *BO*," she retorted. "What's that short for? And please don't tell me it's Beaureguard . . . or Bozo." She smiled as she took a sip of her coffee.

This time, it was Bo who laughed. He pointed in her direction. "Good one. No, it's short for Beaufort."

"North Carolina or South Carolina? Wait," Selby said as she paused to think for a moment. "It's pronounced differently in South Carolina, right? Like Bu-fert. So, that would mean you have roots in North Carolina. I'm assuming it's a family name."

"That's right. Tar Heel born and bred. How about you?" Bo asked as he unwrapped his sandwich and took a bite.

"Selby was my mother's family name," Selby said as she looked out the window. "I was raised right here in Chapel Hill." She turned back to Bo, eager to continue the conversation, when she remembered his "I hope you didn't pay two dollars for that cup of coffee" comment.

"Hey, what was with that crack you made about my coffee purchase?"

She watched Bo's countenance fall. He quickly wiped his mouth with a napkin he retrieved from a silver metal container on the table. "Oh, I didn't mean to be rude. It just bothers me when people overpay for stuff."

"But it was a CUP OF COFFEE. It wasn't like I was mortgaging my house to buy a sports car."

"I get it. It's just that most people don't stop and think about how they spend their money. That includes both small and large purchases. It all adds up. As my grandfather used to say, 'It's not how much you make, it's how much you keep.'"

"I take it you're a finance major?"

"Double major in history and business with a concentration in finance, so, yeah, sort of," he said before taking another bite of his sandwich.

"I'm impressed."

"Don't be. I'm just doing what I love, learning about history—especially the history of money—and the stock market. I know it sounds painfully boring, but it's actually kind of fascinating."

Selby put up a hand in protest. "I'll take your word for it!" She took another sip of her coffee. "What else do you love to do?" She leaned over and pointed past him to his gym bag. "I'm assuming, tennis?"

Bo turned around to look in the direction she was pointing. He nodded. "I've been playing since I was a kid." He turned back to look at Selby. "My mom introduced me to the game. She's in her fifties and still plays."

Selby internally swatted at the butterflies fluttering in her stomach as Bo gazed intently into her eyes. She felt as if he were studying her. "So, what do you love, Selby Brookstone?"

Then, as if he realized that he was coming on too strong, he cleared his throat and pointed to her textbook. "*Insights Into Eighteenth-Century Literature*? I take it you're a literature major. Do you love to read, or are you a writer?"

"Both," Selby responded without blinking or breaking eye contact. She leaned back in her chair and folded her arms across her chest. "You're quite the hybrid, Bo Parrott. When you walked through that door a few minutes ago, I had you pegged as the biggest nerd I'd ever seen in my life. Yet, while having an IQ almost as high as what I paid Lionel in cash this morning, you're athletic, and you have great people skills. Is there anything you can't do? Besides singing, that is." She started laughing. "You sounded terrible!"

Bo joined in, laughing with her. "In my defense—"

Selby interrupted him as she looked down at her watch and gasped. "Oh my gosh, I need to get to class." She picked up her pencil and jotted something down on the corner of her legal pad. She tore it off and slipped it into her coat pocket.

The chair made a scraping noise as she stood and picked up her book bag, stuffing her textbook and legal pad inside.

Bo quickly stood up and grabbed his coat and two bags. "Wait, can I walk with you?"

"Not necessary," Selby responded, in between taking a few sips of her now-lukewarm coffee before tossing the cup in a trash can by the door. "It's all the way across campus."

"But how do I get in touch with you?" he asked as he followed her.

Once outside the diner, Selby stopped and turned to face him. "Bo Parrott, let's get one thing straight. I don't go out with guys I don't really know."

Bo's head dropped. He stared at the sidewalk and nodded. "I understand."

Selby slung her book bag over her shoulder. "But here's the crazy thing. I feel like I've known you for years." She smiled, and once again, Bo's face lit up.

"I feel the same way."

She reached into her pocket and gave him the piece of yellow legal-pad paper.

"What's this?"

"It's how to get in touch with me." She grinned. "Just don't call after ten. My roommate goes to bed early."

Bo's face spread into a big smile. "Got it!"

As she turned to walk toward campus, she called out to him over her shoulder, "Hey, Mr. Finance Guy."

"Yeah?"

"You left a buck and a quarter back on the table."

"Huh?"

She grinned. "Your lunch."

For a second, Bo looked panicked, and then he burst out laughing. "I'll talk to you soon, Selby Brookstone."

"Oh, one last thing," she said with a wink before she made her way down the sidewalk. "Your ears aren't your best feature."

Selby shook her head to dispel the old memories. *Where had the past forty years gone? Why hadn't she ever pursued her dream of becoming a writer?* She knew the answer. Although she had occasionally entertained the thought, Bo's career demanded an unwavering commitment from them both. Yet she felt no resentment; instead, she took immense pride in their shared achievements. Choosing to be a stay-at-home mom was a decision she would not trade for anything in the world.

She slipped the piece of paper back inside the envelope, placed the envelope in the box, and taped it shut. With the smaller items from the apartment packed, all that was left was the furniture, which the moving company would handle. She picked up her coffee cup and glanced around the room. "Next on the agenda is locating my cell phone."

The sound of a text message alert coming from the kitchen at least told her in *which room* she had left it. With the countertops cluttered with newspapers and bubble wrap, she eventually spotted it behind a cardboard box near the sink.

She checked the message and saw that Bo was letting her know he'd probably have to work late tonight, due to the Federal Reserve rate change. After placing the phone back on the counter, she sighed in frustration. "I hope things will be different when we move."

She picked up her coffee cup and took a sip. "But for some reason, I have my doubts."

CHAPTER THREE

With the apartment packed up and the obligatory farewell parties and handshakes behind him, Bo was excited to return to North Carolina, especially to his hometown of Wilson. This thriving community, located just east of Raleigh in the upper coastal plains, was where he grew up. It was also where his father, Beaufort Hardy Parrott Jr., had founded the CPA firm Parrott & Watson. Before Bo's father retired and then passed away a few years ago, he had served the local community for nearly fifty years. But Bo's true inspiration for the world of finance came from his grandfather, who had worked as a stockbroker during the Great Depression.

Bo's assistant, Spencer, and his wife, Carrie, would return to North Carolina later that same week. Like Bo and Selby, they each had grown up in the area and were grateful for the opportunity to move back. Spencer's father, Toisnot Barnes, was a well-respected banker whose family had long been recognized as one of the town's first families. The financial institution that Toisnot started eventually expanded throughout the region, providing an essential pillar for the local economy.

As much as Bo enjoyed conducting business within the friendly, close-knit culture of Eastern North Carolina, he was proud to have received a promotion within the firm, which had allowed him to move to New York City and take a key role in sales management. The agreement was for him to work on Wall Street for five years to help drive business development. While in New York, he would maintain his North Carolina client base and then return to that local office to finish out his career.

The North Carolina office was a short distance from his and Selby's home back in Wilson. Bo had made it a point to travel there once a month to meet with clients and check on the house. Those trips were brief, but he made the most of them as everything dear to his heart was there: family, church, and a sense of belonging he would never experience anywhere else.

Spencer had accompanied Bo to New York for the five-year stint, with the understanding that he would return to North Carolina with Bo and continue his apprenticeship of supporting client account management. It would be several years before Spencer would be ready to assume Bo's responsibilities entirely, but he could learn from the more seasoned advisors and grow into his advisory role.

Bo and his family's years in New York had been the experience of a lifetime: Broadway plays, ice skating at Rockefeller Center at Christmas, and—Amelia and Alicia's favorite—celebrity sightings. There was little that the city didn't offer in terms of places to go and people to see. But what it couldn't offer, at least for Bo, was the feeling of home. He was a small-town boy at heart, and today, his heart was happy to be returning to his roots.

His and Selby's drive out of the city eventually took them into Virginia, where their view transitioned from lifeless concrete to open skies and green fields. The scenery provided Bo with a sense of peace and tranquility.

The climate inside the car was a different matter. For most of the drive, Selby had remained uncharacteristically quiet. This didn't happen very often, but when it did, it made Bo nervous since it typically meant she was upset with him about something.

Bo preferred dealing with issues quickly. Selby didn't always operate like that. More often than not, she needed time to "collect her thoughts," as she described it. He equated her quiet "thought collecting" to a military commander strategizing his next attack. Bo remained ill at ease until Selby finally spoke her mind, a process that could not be rushed. As painful as it was, he always gave her the space—and time— she needed.

This time, however, he was losing patience.

"Are you going to give me your feedback or not? I don't have to take this teaching position. I communicated to Edmond that I was interested, but I certainly haven't given him a clear answer yet."

"Maybe not," Selby said, "but it's clear to me what your answer will be."

Bo drew his head back. "How do you know what my answer will be when I don't even know?"

The corners of Selby's lips curled slightly. She momentarily took her eyes off the road and looked over in his direction. "Maybe because I know you better than you know yourself?"

Bo shook his head in frustration and turned to look out the window.

Selby took a deep breath. "The way I see it, your head is telling you that you shouldn't take the job. The plan was to work less and spend more time at home. You always have a plan, Bo."

"That's a good thing, right?"

"It is until something comes along that's not part of the plan. Then you have this tug-of-war between your head and your heart. Your head is telling you to stick with the plan, but your heart is telling you that Edmond needs you, and you'd love to have the opportunity to teach these students information they're not going to get from anyone else."

Bo didn't respond.

Selby grinned. "I'll bet you've already pictured yourself with a beard and wearing a cardigan sweater, the kind with the leather patches on the elbows."

"You left out the part about me smoking a pipe," he said sheepishly as he cut his eyes over to Selby.

"I see you with a pipe as a prop but not actually smoking it. You're too much of a health nut."

Bo chuckled. "But seriously, it's important that people are taught how our country's economic system works. And they can't do that without learning the history that goes along with it. Otherwise, there will be gaps. We've talked about this before, you know, how my grandfather began teaching me about money when I was a child. Our conversations whetted my appetite to learn more. I was the weird kid reading while the other kids were playing outside. That's one of the reasons my mother introduced me to tennis. She had to get my nose out of a book and into the fresh air."

"Did it work? Was tennis a healthy distraction at the time? I mean, obviously, you fell in love with the sport. We had to rent a second moving van just for your trophies."

Bo laughed. "That's not true. Just half of the moving van. The other half contains your Christmas decorations."

"Touché," Selby quipped as she reached over to turn the heat up in the SUV.

"But to answer your question, it did. And when I began to work on my finance studies, I saw how success in tennis bore similarities to success in investment management."

"How so? I mean, I've heard most of this before, but refresh my memory."

"Well, for one, a tennis player should never compromise a sound method just to score a few points in the short term. Sacrificing those points is a small price to pay for developing the discipline, skill, and instinct required to hit the ball well."

"Okay, that makes sense. What else did tennis teach you?"

"What it *didn't* teach me is a better question. Let's see . . . that certain fundamentals remain timeless, but some techniques that worked in the past may not work now. To avoid being left behind, you have to incorporate change. So it is with navigating—and winning—with the investment market. Trust me, the training has proved brutal both on and off the court."

"Speaking of brutal, didn't you miss a college tennis match because you had a hangover?"

Bo groaned and briefly cut his eyes over at Selby. "You had to bring that up, didn't you? Yes, it was my first frat party as a sophomore. I wasn't keeping up with how many times the upperclassmen were refilling my cup. It was all fun and games until I found myself hovering over a toilet bowl for the rest of the evening. Needless to say, I didn't feel much like playing tennis the following morning."

"So, you were overserved, which kept you from *serving* the following morning? Sorry, but I couldn't help but notice the double entendre."

Bo smiled. "Actually, you can overserve or overextend in tennis, which can result in an unforced error. An experienced player—"

Bo stopped mid-sentence. His mind raced as he recalled the current stock charts he'd studied. Correctly deciphering market movements typically brought him a deep sense of satisfaction. In recent weeks, however, those same future indicators had caused him deep concern. The tennis analogy just brought into focus what they could mean. Unfortunately, it wasn't the interpretation he was hoping for.

"What are you thinking about? The noise from those wheels turning in your brain is distracting my driving."

"I just realized how this could apply to the current economic environment."

"Explain."

"Do you remember learning about the Roaring Twenties?"

"Of course! It was the time when women wore those fancy flapper dresses with matching fascinator hats. And they used those long cigarette holders. Did you know that, in addition to serving as a fashion accessory, those holders also kept ashes from falling on their dresses?"

Bo shook his head and chuckled. "No, but it doesn't surprise me that *you* do. With all that was going on in that decade, you *would* focus on the fashion trends!"

"Well, somebody in this marriage has to think of something other than the stock market!"

Bo's smile faded, and his expression grew serious. "There are times I wish that wasn't my role. But the stock market affects our everyday lives more than people realize. Just like the Roaring Twenties, the economy is like one big party right now. People are enjoying a wide range of goods and services. Monetary policy is accommodative, characterized by low interest rates and ample money flow. Fiscal policy is also conducive to vigorous activity and escalated asset prices at almost every level."

"I have no idea what you just said, but please continue."

"The money flow has found its way into elevated stock prices. Individual retail investors are routinely discussing *which* stocks to buy rather than *whether to buy at all*. Institutional investors are feeling pressure to accept investments and allocate funds to new purchases. Corporations are ramping up buy-back operations for their stock, while many corporate insiders are selling their holdings to take advantage of historically high prices."

"English, please?" Selby quipped as she pulled up to a stoplight.

"Think of it as a party that seems like it will never end. But I have a growing sense that the scenario of my college drinking fiasco is about to be played out again, but in economic terms: a short-term high preceding an unpleasant experience to confirm an inability to tolerate indulgence. This could easily result in a malaise followed by an extended period of incapacity for the economy and the stock market."

"So, you're predicting a market crash?" Selby asked as she quickly glanced in his direction.

Bo's eyes widened. "I'm impressed!"

Selby raised an eyebrow. "You realize you could have said that without using fancy finance jargon, right?"

Bo knew that one of his biggest foibles was his tendency to overexplain. Since Selby's first encounter with him in college, she had come to accept this character flaw and actually found it endearing. Admittedly, Bo was well aware of how frequently he got lost in his own world. When he found his way back, however, he often brought with him insightful solutions to the problems at hand.

Bo grinned. "Point taken."

"Playing devil's advocate, I'm not hearing any of what you're predicting when I watch the news. In fact, I'm hearing just the opposite."

Bo gazed out the window. "Yeah, me, too. But these new schools of thought that rationalize it by saying 'it's different this time'? It rings hollow to me."

"So, what's your plan, Bo Parrott?"

"Obviously, I've got to start taking defensive measures for my clients and my loved ones. The problem is that no one wants to be the first to leave the party in terms of getting out of the market." He paused for a moment and then added, "But no one wants to be the last either."

"I agree, but that's not the plan I'm talking about."

Selby took his hand, and, in response, Bo turned in his seat to face her. She smiled. "What's your plan for telling Edmond that you're going to take that teaching job?"

Bo's eyes widened. "You're not mad at me about it? You did that quiet thing earlier in the drive."

Selby shook her head. "I wasn't mad at you. I was just tired. Packing up the apartment really took a toll on me. Then again, I'm not as young as I was the last time we moved." She shook her head. "Five years older, in fact."

"Does being five years older also make you *colder*? It's like a hundred and twenty degrees in here. Can I turn the heat down a little?"

"If you let me stop for coffee up ahead," Selby said as she pointed to a Starbucks sign at the next exit. "A girl's got to stay warm—and caffeinated—if she's going to keep driving."

"Deal."

"Another part of the deal? You call Edmond while I'm getting my coffee."

Selby pulled into the Starbucks parking lot and turned off the car. Grabbing her purse, she opened her door and glanced over at Bo. "Can I get you anything?"

Bo grinned. "How about a cardigan sweater? You know, the kind with the leather patches on the elbows?"

Selby shook her head. "Nope, this stop is just for coffee. Besides, I'll bet Edmond has one you can borrow."

Bo watched as Selby made her way into the coffee shop. He picked up his cell phone from where it was charging on the center console. He paused for a moment and then took a deep breath.

"Siri, call Edmond Brockett."

CHAPTER FOUR

Kathryn Romanov left the basement of the secluded Eastern European warehouse where she had just attended a covert meeting. The rush she experienced from working with such a storied group never got old. Though she'd evolved over time, she remained categorically different from the rest of the members. Each of them had always enjoyed seemingly unlimited wealth while maintaining an invisible footprint. She, on the other hand, had lived modestly for years as a news reporter, despite earning global recognition.

Her high heels crunched against the gravel parking lot as her mind drifted back to her freshman year of college. The journalism school she attended was recognized as one of the most prestigious in the world. Her scores going into the acceptance interview were average but not stellar, and the interview itself went well enough; however, she wouldn't call it a home run. Yet, somehow, she got in.

Similar to her getting accepted into a college that many only dreamed of attending, career opportunities abounded for Kathryn. It was almost as if an invisible force was propelling her forward. After earning her journalism degree, she became a featured speaker for several financial media outlets, with a following that grew exponentially.

After a couple of years of working in that capacity, the media company's executives extended an offer for her to study at Europe's Marquis Military Academy. Her credentials from the military academy—combined with her journalism degree—opened even more doors for her. She landed a political cabinet post and parlayed it into a prominent role in the inner council. In a few short months, she was elevated to deputy marquis. Not long after she began serving in that role, the premier mysteriously died, leaving a vacant spot that she was asked to fill. The backing from all the right people swiftly ushered her into the number two position in the country.

Serving in that role felt like an exercise in paying her dues; she did what she was told by those in power and gained favor as a result. But she had a driving hunger to be the one who called the shots. That hunger was satisfied two years ago when she was sworn in as the premier.

When she first took the position, she had to demonstrate to certain world leaders that, while her country was small, it wasn't weak, and she was a formidable opponent. Flexing her political muscles resulted in orchestrating close calls when it came to the stability of their empires. She earned their respect—and their submission.

Kathryn spotted her executive limo, with its flawless black finish sparkling under the parking lot lights. As she approached the car, she watched as the driver immediately got out and opened the door for her. She settled into the back seat and marveled at how far she'd come in such a short time. She had started out working as a news reporter who didn't have two nickels to rub together. Now, she possessed treasured artifacts. She sipped tea from fine china once held by monarchs. An army of attendants stood at her beck and call to see to her every need with fastidious care.

She had everything. Well, *almost* everything. The leader of The Circle was the most coveted of positions, and the current leader, Lutz Osswald, remained untouchable. Kathryn knew she wasn't powerful enough yet, but in time, she planned to engineer an overthrow so she could acquire a seat at the table. For now, she maintained a level of trust with him that accompanied a necessary level of *mistrust*. Likely, they would eventually double-cross each other. The question was who would emerge as the victor. She had a track record of beating the odds. She bet on herself.

As the limo stopped at the road to let traffic pass, Kathryn noticed that the vehicles belonging to The Circle members hadn't moved. She had expected that, by now, the members would be trickling out of the building. For a moment, her stomach knotted. *Why are they meeting without me?*

All The Circle members were dispensable, quite literally. She had witnessed it. But if she was in good standing with Simon, she needn't worry. She ultimately took directions from him.

Simon. Now, there was a true leader with a brilliant mind. She'd never met anyone like him. As her limo exited the parking lot, she recalled her last meeting with him.

As she approached the outdoor café, she spotted him looking through the latest edition of Paris Match. *His bored expression was like that of a CEO reading his own company's performance reports; he reviewed it with a strange type of anticipated outcome.*

"On fait quoi?" Kathryn asked. "Or should I say it in English . . . what shall we do?"

Simon quickly replied, "Hmm. I really don't know!"

They both chuckled as Kathryn took a seat across from him at the small wrought-iron table. Her question begged the response he gave. It engendered the mood of contrived ennui. The irony was not lost on either of them, as their aspirations were anything but. They both planned on playing lead characters on the world's stage, a deep desire Kathryn had cultivated for as long as she could remember.

She suspected that Simon had cultivated it even longer than that.

Kathryn couldn't put it into terms of months and years, but she sensed he'd been at his craft for a long time. He had boasted of having worked with the most renowned individuals in the world. His words were few but poignant. He made it a point to never lose in the campaigns he conjured up for his followers. His fee was prohibitive, but his clientele—including Kathryn—considered his services to be priceless.

Simon raised a cup containing a beverage she couldn't identify. "Congratulations, my Kathryn. You are now a world-class bitch. You have arrived!" The flattery seemed to ooze from him. Kathryn marveled at how his words were precisely what she wanted to hear. She took a moment to drink it all in.

She nodded and smiled. "Perhaps, but it is a mixed bag. I am respected but hated at the same time. A small price for power, n'est-ce pas?"

Simon displayed a half smile. "Indeed," he replied. The nihilistic look in his eyes exuded a sense of meaninglessness. His eyes were not merely dark brown; they were as black as the darkest night. His pallid complexion showed he was not one for the outdoors. Wherever he spent his time, it was not in the light of day. His voice was like the lure of the siren's song, his rhythmic speech patterns hypnotic. Somewhere deep inside, Kathryn knew she should turn a deaf ear to it. But she found it difficult—no, impossible—to resist.

She also found it impossible to resist ordering another demitasse. The waiter knew her favorite choice of French roast.

"For you, madame."

"Merci, Claude." Kathryn allowed herself to be distracted for a moment. It temporarily broke the spell.

She took a sip and then set the cup down on the table. She looked off into the distance as she spoke. "You do know there is more to me than what appears on the surface." She briefly glanced back at Simon. "Much more." Once again, she gazed off into the distance. "The world is about to discover just what a once mild-mannered journalist can do."

Simon leaned forward. "The laughable thing is that The Circle thought you were their pawn—a tool—an emissary merely sent to do their bidding." He leaned back in his chair and pointed to her. "You were young when they recruited you. They could see a fire inside of you, a burning ambition. Once upon a time, they possessed it, too. Then, like you, they became jaded. As I did for you, I took each of them to their dark side. There is power there. And *inspiration. They thought you would create a vassal state for them to develop into a cash cow. Time is all that remains before we turn the tables on them."*

As the limo headed out onto the highway, Kathryn shook her head, smiled, and said out loud, "No worries, Kathryn. You are Simon's favorite. He has opened all the right doors for you, and he will close all the wrong ones. No one can touch you."

CHAPTER FIVE

Bo glanced out the living-room window as a strong breeze evicted the three or four leaves still clinging to the maple tree in the front yard. Dry and lifeless due to harsh winter temperatures, they submissively drifted down to the hardened ground.

It had been several weeks since he and Selby had moved back to North Carolina. Before immersing himself into a busy schedule, Bo had set aside a little time to refamiliarize himself with the area and become better acquainted with the local college where he'd be replacing Edmond Brockett.

Tomorrow, however, he would be back in the saddle, meeting with clients at the office during the day and then making his teaching debut that evening. This afternoon was not only about completing market research and finalizing lesson plans, but also a time for him to mentally prepare for the shift.

One thing Bo anticipated as he adjusted to living back in the South was a change in the weather patterns. He developed a habit of checking the app on his phone to compare the conditions in the two states. Even though the city had seen more snowfall, the winter temperatures hadn't varied all that much—at least not this year. He remembered one North Carolina Christmas years ago when the mercury in the thermometer reached a balmy eighty degrees. Warm weather fans couldn't have been happier. Others—like Selby—didn't share their enthusiasm.

"If I'd wanted a tropical Christmas, I would have traveled to the tropics!" she had complained while fanning herself on the back-porch swing.

Bo knew how much Selby wanted to experience a white Christmas at least once. When they relocated to New York, he hoped she'd finally get her wish. Yet, despite living there for five years, she only witnessed one or two light dustings. The one year Mother Nature decided to dump six inches on Christmas Eve, they missed the event. As luck would have it, they had traveled to North Carolina to spend the holidays with Bo's family.

This past Christmas had been a blur, weatherwise and otherwise, with Selby and Bo getting settled back in North Carolina. The holiday festivities included a brief but enjoyable visit with Alicia and Amelia, as well as their respective spouses, Carl and Hunter.

Alicia and Carl made their home in Kitty Hawk on the Outer Banks. Amelia and Hunter settled in Blowing Rock, a quaint town nestled in the Blue Ridge Mountains. Whenever Bo and Selby traveled to visit them, they experienced the best of both worlds.

The grandfather clock in the far corner by the fireplace kept time with the clicks of the computer mouse as Bo conducted market research and put the finishing touches on his first lecture as Edmond's replacement. His father-in-law had assembled the clock years ago. The heirloom was like Warren Brookstone, Selby's father: detailed and reliable.

Bo remembers Selby saying, "They don't make them like that anymore; I'm referring to the clock *and* my dad. When that great generation dies out, an era will have come to an end. They saved the world once. I wish they were still here to save us again."

Bo agreed. Yet, the torch *had* been passed. To effectively address and help solve current issues, Bo and Selby's generation had to emulate those like Warren, who had gone before them to blaze the trail with selfless acts of service and sacrifice.

Bo felt that his contribution to the greater good was through his work as a stockbroker and now with his part-time teaching position at the local college. Both required research and planning, which is what this Sunday afternoon was for.

His thoughts were interrupted by the sound of Selby milling around in the kitchen . . . and the spicy aroma of hot apple cider.

Bo smiled as Selby set a cup full of the steaming liquid on the coffee table. He looked up at her eyes, which were a lighter shade of blue than his own. Her shoulder-length brown hair displayed streaks of gray that seemed to have appeared overnight. While gray hair for Selby (and hair loss for Bo) displayed the passage of four decades of marriage, certain features appeared sheltered from time's exorbitant tax rates. One was the sparkle in Selby's eyes, which was especially evident when she smiled.

Bo caught a glimpse of this as Selby cheerfully tossed one of the couch pillows aside and settled beside him on the couch.

"Market research or lesson plans?" she asked as she craned her head over to look at his computer screen.

Bo blew at the steam rising from his cup before taking a sip. "Both, and I feel like they're connected."

"What do you mean?"

"With other research I've conducted regarding past events and how they affected the stock market, there is always an overlap. For my first lecture, I'll be addressing the historical and political significance of *The Wizard of Oz.* My research has uncovered a deeper meaning in the story and, more importantly, its relevance to current events in the global economy. I admit there's a lot I don't know, and I won't have all the answers."

"No one has all the answers."

Bo gazed out the window once again. "Or they *do*, and they're not coming forward with them."

"Now you're sounding conspiratorial." Selby pointed in his direction as she picked up her cup once more.

"There are lessons from history we shouldn't ignore. That much I *do* know." He smiled and stroked her cheek with his index finger. "Thank you for always being so supportive."

Her eyes sparkled, and she winked. "All I did was bring you a cup of cider."

Bo took a sip and then pouted his lips. "How about another when I finish this one?"

After having solidified his presentation for the following evening, Bo decided to turn in early. But sleep wasn't coming easily. He stared at the bedroom ceiling, remembering Edmond Brockett's words that he wanted someone to replace him *who had a passion for learning as well as for teaching*. Bo knew that when he stood behind the lectern, he would assume a dual role as teacher and student. Despite working in the finance industry for over four decades, he still had questions that begged for resolution.

One question continued to gnaw at him: Why didn't the government directly issue currency backed by its sovereign authorization instead of having a coin from a banking organization inconspicuously named the Federal Reserve Bank?

Bo had always found it amusing that the entity's name included the word *federal,* which provided an implication of being a governmental entity. Yet, it wasn't listed in the blue pages of the Washington, DC, phone book, in the section for government agencies. And, despite the rest of the name, no reserves might exist there after all.

The Federal Reserve repaid its earnings to the US Treasury after paying a 6 percent dividend to shareholders and compensating employees. The payments to the national banks that sell Treasury bills to the Federal Reserve are then loaned out through fractional reserve lending—at a rate of ten times the amount of money received from the Federal Reserve.

Bo marveled at how this was like free inventory for a business. Most businesses must buy the inventory to promote their products and services, thereby gaining a spread of net profit over cost. Banks, on the other hand, got money to loan on an exponential basis from the Federal Reserve. Bank capital was extended ten times beyond its supply inventory through fractional reserve lending.

He also wondered how the behavior of the stock market and a seemingly inexplicable turn of the global economy formed a consistent pattern over time. It further advanced the smart money at the expense of everyone else. One thing was for sure: The central bank, global and national banks, and the Treasury routinely played a role in each inflection point of the investment markets and the economy.

Beyond the tactile, Bo pondered how money seemed to have the power to expose the best—and worst—of humanity.

Selby must have known that he was having a difficult time falling asleep. As she slipped under the covers next to him, she nestled her head on his shoulder.

"I'm sorry that God didn't provide an off switch for your brain."

Bo smiled and pulled her closer. "Yeah, me, too. But there's still a solution."

"Which is?"

"If something doesn't have a switch, you simply unplug it to get it to stop working. And that's what I'm ready to do tonight. Unplug. In fact," Bo said as he leaned over and picked up his cell phone from the nightstand, "I'm silencing the ringer."

Selby's jaw dropped, and she sat up in bed. "You have international clients in, like, five hundred different time zones. You never turn off your phone."

Bo chuckled. "True, but I'm going to be retiring at some point. This will be good practice."

After changing the settings, Bo placed the phone back on the nightstand and pulled Selby close to him once again. Her presence always brought him comfort.

Just as Bo was drifting off, his phone silently lit up. The caller ID displayed the name *Edmond Brockett*.

Bo instinctively reached for the phone but then stopped. *"He's probably just calling to wish me well at my first lecture tomorrow evening."* Having reassured himself that the call most likely wasn't of an urgent nature, he turned over and fell asleep.

CHAPTER SIX

The following morning, Bo awoke to the aroma of coffee brewing. He fumbled around on the nightstand for his glasses, and after putting them on, he picked up his cell phone. Evidently, Edmond had left a voicemail when he called the night before. Bo clicked on it and turned up the volume on his phone.

"Hi, Bo. It's Edmond. When you have a moment, please call me. I have something important to discuss with you."

He sat up in bed, took off his glasses, and rubbed his eyes. This wasn't what Bo was expecting. Edmond didn't quite sound like himself, which made Bo wonder if he had suffered another health setback. He immediately dialed his number, but the call went straight to voicemail.

After a few minutes of stretching, he lumbered down the hall in the direction of the kitchen. As he stood in the doorway, he projected his voice over the sound of cabinet doors opening and closing.

"Who needs coffee this morning? You slamming those doors is enough to wake the dead!"

Selby remained focused on a higher shelf in the cabinet, not turning around as she spoke. "Adjusting to being back in this kitchen has been challenging. I find myself instinctively reaching for items in the places where they were stored in our New York kitchen."

"It's not like someone stocked these cabinets for you," Bo managed to say through a long yawn. "Didn't you place everything where you wanted it?"

"Yes, but that doesn't necessarily mean I'm going to remember!" Selby quipped as she climbed up onto the counter. "Ah, here it is!" she said after parting a row of glass stemware. "Your favorite coffee cup."

"You went to all that trouble to find a *coffee cup?*"

As Selby stepped down from the counter, Bo smiled at the sight of her hair pulled back in a ponytail. Her eyes displayed an early-morning softness, indicating remnants of sleep that hadn't faded just yet. As much as Bo appreciated it when she wore makeup and styled her hair, this was one of his favorite looks. That, and when she was in a rush to leave the house and threw on a baseball cap.

Selby pointed in his direction. "Not just any cup. It's the UNC Tarheel ceramic mug I gave you for your birthday the first year we dated." She turned it from side to side. "I don't know how it has survived our forty years of marriage and six moves without so much as a chip."

Bo smiled as he took the cup and stepped over to the coffee pot located on the other side of the kitchen. He picked up the carafe. "Maybe it's tough . . . like we are. But that doesn't answer my question of why you went to so much trouble to find it this morning."

"I woke up thinking of how today would be a departure from the normal for you. It's your first official day back at your old office *and* your first evening teaching at the college. Maybe having something familiar with you would help, even if it *is* just a coffee cup."

"That's very thoughtful of you, but it's not like I haven't been back at this office since we moved to New York."

"True, but a trip once a month to check on your clients isn't the same as clocking in every day." Selby folded her arms as she leaned against the counter. "Not to mention, it's going to feel different driving to work instead of having someone drive you. *And* did I mention that it's your first lecture at the college?"

Bo nodded as he took a sip of coffee. "I guess you're right. Speaking of my new teaching position," he said as he set his cup down on the counter, "evidently, Edmond tried to contact me last night. I tried reaching him this morning, but the call went straight to his voicemail."

Selby picked up her coffee cup from where she had set it on the counter and took a sip. "Maybe Edmond sets it to Do Not Disturb when he goes to bed. I know it's still a foreign concept to you, but people do occasionally turn off their phones. It's not even mid-morning; he probably just hasn't switched it back to where he can receive calls."

Bo shook his head. "That would be a first for Edmond. He's always been an early bird. If he had a question about his account, he called me first thing. Of course, that was when he was in good health."

"Why don't you stop by to see him on your way to work? A visit from you might cheer him up."

"That's a good idea. It might be just a few minutes out of my way, but it would be worth it to see him in person."

"Speaking of *going out of one's way*, would you mind picking up my iron supplement prescription from the pharmacy?"

"Sure, but that's not out of my way. The pharmacy is just a few doors down from my office."

"I know. I was talking about *me* going out of *my* way. It will save me a trip across town," Selby said with a wink.

"Are you starting to see any results? I know you said that it takes a while for iron to get into your system, but how long has it been?"

"Long enough," Selby said with a heavy sigh.

"Should you get a second opinion?"

"This *was* the second opinion. I touched base with Dr. McGill. She was my family physician before we moved to New York."

"I remember her. Is she still practicing?" Bo asked while rummaging around inside the refrigerator. A few seconds later, he emerged with a plate of leftovers.

"Yes, she was just starting out back then. I was one of her first patients," Selby responded. She pulled two plastic containers from a cabinet near the stove and handed them to Bo. "She wants me to take the iron supplement for a couple more weeks. If she isn't satisfied with my blood count by then, she'll do more tests. I hope she doesn't think it's something serious."

Bo's stomach twisted, but he forced himself to smile reassuringly. "I'm sure she's just being thorough."

Selby turned to rinse her coffee cup in the sink. "That's what she said."

Bo looked up from transferring the leftovers into the plastic containers to see Selby quickly wipe her cheek with the back of her hand. He took a step over to put his hand on her shoulder when she abruptly turned around.

"If you're going to stop by to see Edmond, you need to leave soon," she announced with a smile that appeared mechanical.

If Selby was worried, she had just made it clear that she didn't want to discuss it any further. So, Bo would drop the matter for now.

"You're absolutely right. I'll take a quick shower, and then I'll be on my way. But can you do one favor for me, I mean, since I'm picking up your prescription for you?"

"Sure, what is it?"

"Make sure I have plenty of coffee in that mug! I don't want to leave home without it."

Selby's face relaxed into a genuine smile this time, and she nodded. "I'll put on a fresh pot right away."

Bo rehearsed his presentation for the evening's class as he drove through a maze of winding streets that emptied into a private estate secured by a large iron gate. Inching his car closer, he was surprised when the gate creaked open automatically. He cautiously made his way up a long, paved driveway lined with meticulously manicured bushes on both sides.

Cresting the hill, he spotted flashing lights from an ambulance, a firetruck, and several police cars parked in front of a French Tudor-style house. His eyes narrowed as he said to himself, "What are they doing at Edmond's house?"

He pulled forward a few feet toward the scene. A uniformed officer standing nearby put his hand up and approached the car. Bo lowered his window.

"Is everything okay? I'm Bo Parrott. I'm here to see Edmond Brockett."

When Bo looked to see who the officer was, he recognized him as Vince Porter, a childhood friend.

"Vince," Bo said. "It's good to see you. It's been a long time."

"It sure has," Vince said. "I heard you had moved back. I wish I was seeing you under better circumstances."

Vince glanced away for a moment, then leaned in closer, his voice low and earnest. "I know I probably shouldn't tell you this, but given your friendship with Dr. Brockett, I feel you deserve to know. I'm truly sorry, Bo. Dr. Brockett has passed away."

Bo's breath caught in his throat. "What? What happened? I know he's been battling lung cancer."

"It looks like a portable kerosene heater overturned. We see this kind of thing a lot with the elderly when the temperatures plummet. It's tragic, but not uncommon."

Bo's heart raced. "What about his wife? Is she okay?"

Vince shrugged his shoulders. "It doesn't look like Mrs. Brockett was at home when this occurred. Now, I'm going to have to ask you to move your car so you're not blocking any of these emergency vehicles."

Bo nodded and numbly pushed the button to raise his window. He turned his car around and headed out the way he came in. He drove through the estate entrance and, when he was back on the main road, pulled over into a parking lot to collect his thoughts.

He fought back the tears as numerous questions flooded his mind. *Could this have been attributed to a caregiver's negligence? If not, how could*

Edmond have been so careless? Did he recently experience a sharp cognitive decline? If that was the case, why wasn't Regina there with him? Then Bo felt a stab of guilt. *I shouldn't have turned off the ringer on my phone! Is that why he tried to call me last night? Could I have helped in some way?*

Regardless of what happened—or why—the fact remained that Bo had lost a dear friend and a loyal client. He had also just lost the battle with his emotions. His shoulders shook as he cupped his hands over his face and cried.

CHAPTER SEVEN

It took several minutes of regrouping and a phone call to Selby before Bo felt composed enough to move on with his day. He could have used more time but wasn't afforded that luxury. He had a nine o'clock appointment at his office, and if he hurried, he might make it in time.

After pulling into his parking space in front of the office building, he darted into the bathroom to splash some water on his face. As he entered his office for the first time in weeks, he settled in behind a desk constructed of grained cherry and flame mahogany. It boasted a cordovan leather inlay that softened the hard lines of the wood.

In many ways, it reflected the persona of its prior owner: classic but with a flair. It had been a gift from Charlie Randolph, an older broker in the firm, who took Bo under his wing and helped show him the ropes when Bo was just beginning to establish a client base.

Charlie made painstaking efforts to ensure that Bo got off to a good start, even letting him set up shop in his office when he retired. He insisted that the desk stay, asserting that every stockbroker needed a quality desk. Bo equated it to a mother carefully dressing her son for the first day of school.

As Bo sat behind this desk today, he thought about how he would pass it down to Spencer when he himself retired—if that ever happened. With the trends he was seeing in the market and the work that would be required to protect his clients' accounts, he wasn't so sure.

Bo was grateful that his nine o'clock appointment arrived a few minutes late, allowing him time to further rein in his emotions. While engaging in small talk was integral to developing a favorable rapport with his clients, it was the last thing he wanted to do this morning.

Nevertheless, he took a few minutes to catch up with the newlyweds, Kyle and Nancy Campbell, before reviewing their current investment positions and year-to-date yields from a trust left for Kyle by his grandfather. As the meeting concluded, Kyle and Nancy leaned forward as Bo offered some parting advice.

"Food, housing, and clothing represent the obligatory cash outlay for the middle-income American family. However, meeting societal expectations requires a heftier bankroll. For example, you'll need to allocate money for your children's extracurricular activities, such as team sports or dance, and later on, for college tuition. Finding a house in a safe neighborhood is a top priority, along with purchasing a reliable car. And, if you have a daughter one day, don't forget the cost of a nice wedding." Bo winked and said, "I've been there—twice!"

Kyle and Nancy chuckled.

"It can feel overwhelming," Bo said as he set his laptop aside and smiled. "But I'm here to help you make it happen."

Kyle stood and extended his hand. "Thank you for scheduling the meeting earlier in the day to accommodate our work schedules."

The springs inside Bo's chair squeaked as he stood to shake Kyle's hand. "You're welcome."

Bo walked them to the front door and then watched as they crossed the parking lot over to where their car was parked. Many of the financial terms he had used today probably sounded like a foreign language to them. Having been young once himself, he recalled what it was like trying to map out finances—and life in general. Kyle and Nancy's concerns mirrored those of millions of their contemporaries. At the end of the day, they just wanted to make it all work.

Making it work for Bo meant finding people with resources and an interest in investing so he could help them meet those essential goals. It was all a product of capitalism, where each party stood to mutually benefit from the efforts of the other. No world economic system was perfect, but ultimately, it was capitalism that succeeded at creating wealth.

Bo had learned that the market, in some ways, was a world unto itself, one he ventured into every day to study and explore. It was through those expeditions that he discovered, in particular, how shorting the market was practiced frequently and had a more significant impact on the global economy than most people realized.

Following his appointment with Kyle and Nancy, Bo powered up the flat-screen monitor for a brief virtual meeting with Martin Beargrass, a registered assistant who worked at an office located about an hour's drive east. For training purposes, Bo had asked Spencer to join them. Spencer arrived just before the meeting was scheduled to begin, carrying a steaming cup of coffee that sloshed as he set it down on Bo's desk.

"Sorry I didn't get here earlier," he said. He slid a chair up closer to Bo's desk. "Carrie is still unpacking, and I had to drop Silas off at daycare."

"It's no problem," Bo said, forcing a smile. "I was running late today, too." His smile quickly faded, and he paused for a moment before continuing, "I stopped by Edmond Brockett's house on my way in."

"How is he doing?"

Bo stared down at the floor. "I was greeted by a police officer who informed me that Edmond had passed away."

"I'm so sorry. I knew Dr. Brockett had cancer. Wait, a police officer?"

Bo let out a heavy sigh as he looked back up at Spencer. "Evidently, a kerosene heater tipped over. It's been so bitterly cold the past few nights. With his illness, I suppose he was just trying to stay warm."

Spencer shook his head. "That's awful."

"It's going to take time for me to fully process it. At first, I didn't know if I could come to work. Now, I think it's providing a welcome distraction. Speaking of which," Bo said as he glanced at his watch, "our meeting with Martin is about to start. One of the reasons I scheduled it was to teach you about the client initiative of selling short."

After Martin joined online, the three of them spent a couple of minutes exchanging pleasantries. Afterward, Bo officially began the meeting.

"Martin, I know you're familiar with this concept, but I'm going to take a little extra time to explain it to Spencer." Turning to look at Spencer, he said, "The clients we're going to be focusing on are those who want to benefit from a downward market but don't want to go through the often-complex processes of borrowing shares of stock from the brokerage firm to short-sell them. They will be utilizing an inverse ETF or an exchange-traded fund."

Spencer scribbled down notes on a yellow legal pad as Bo spoke. Without looking up, he said, "Remind me again how *short selling* works."

"Shorting the stock means selling stock shares by borrowing the stock shares. I realize it sounds odd to sell shares without owning them. It requires purchasing back shares in the future to cover the positions. The borrowed shares are returned to the brokerage firm. The hope is that stock prices will fall and be lower than when the stock was sold earlier."

Martin chimed in, "It's an intriguing process."

Bo smiled and added, "With an equally intriguing origin. According to legend, the term *short sell* originated from a bakery in New York. They were experiencing a high demand for a particular strawberry cake dessert; so high, in fact, that they couldn't keep it in stock. So, they took orders and confirmed them even though they didn't have enough cakes on hand to fill those orders. The cakes were delivered later to meet the order demand. The bakery was *short* of cakes yet sold them anyway."

Spencer raised an eyebrow. "So, I take it that's where the term *strawberry shortcake* came from?"

Bo chuckled as he picked up a water bottle from his desk and took a sip. "No, it comes from the dessert's ingredients. But it serves as a great example of short selling."

Martin chuckled. "Hey, Spencer, if nothing else, you now have a new icebreaker to use at parties!"

"Who has time to go to parties?" Spencer said as he threw his arms in the air. "All I do is work!"

They all laughed, and then Bo said, "Okay, let's review the list of clients cleared for these inverse exchange-traded funds."

Martin read the list aloud. "These are set, right?"

"Yes. Go ahead and place the trades. Thanks, Martin."

CHAPTER EIGHT

After the online meeting with Martin had concluded, Spencer sighed and shook his head. "I still feel like I'm missing something with the concept of selling short. I understand how it worked with the bakery, but how does it work in real time in the stock market? Do you have a few minutes to explain it a little more in depth?"

Bo paused to collect his thoughts. Spencer wasn't just an employee; he was slated to be part of the succession plan when Bo retired. Therefore, more was riding on his training than merely a transfer of information. Bo wanted to ignite in Spencer a passion for a career that many would consider devoid of such.

Indeed, to the casual observer, the financial world could appear as a collection of lifeless charts, complicated math, and news anchors droning on about this outcome or that. But in Bo's experience, it was a living organism whose tentacles could reach beyond the physical realm of dollars and cents. A person's self-worth—as well as their net worth— could become collateral damage. Money could be friend or foe, and a careful study of its inner workings would determine which.

Bo leaned back in his chair and smiled. "Once you grasp it, it's quite fascinating. Can I borrow your legal pad?"

"Of course," Spencer said as he slid the legal pad in Bo's direction.

Bo picked up a pen from the desk and began illustrating as he spoke. "An investor can sell a stock without owning the shares and can borrow from the brokerage firm at interest. The trade aims to sell the stock at a higher price and repurchase shares at a lower price.

"During the transaction, selling pressure escalates in the market. Volume increases, driving markets lower. Then, a chain of events can occur. Artificial intelligence and machine-programmed trading generate additional market activity with participation by institutional investment firms and individual investors. The market rewards those who arrive at the party on time. The trade is wound up, and positions are covered."

Bo looked up at Spencer. "Are you with me so far?"

Spencer squinted as he studied Bo's drawings. "I think so."

"A modern approach to the process is to purchase exchange-traded funds. The personnel of the financial company offering the ETF conduct short covering activity. It makes for a more efficient and flowing market for convenient account execution."

Spencer shook his head. "That's a lot to digest—"

Bo interrupted, "Which is why you're not ready to execute this activity or even discuss it with clients."

Spencer smiled. "Duly noted."

Bo leaned forward in his chair and folded his hands on his desk. "Here is the historical backdrop: In Wall Street lore, banking titans from the Great Depression era pulled together just before the stock crash of 1929 to sell their stock at the market's peak. One account alleges that renowned Wall Street financier Bernard Baruch had made a fortune by investing in stocks from 1924 until October 1929. A few years before what was known as Black Tuesday in 1929, he began shorting stocks in anticipation of a significant stock market correction. He had refused to participate in a pool of bullish investors after the Labor Day market peak in 1929."

Spencer's brow furrowed. "What happened to this Bernard Baruch guy?"

"Wall Street heralded him as a market titan. American humorist Will Rogers credited Baruch for timely advice before the crash. Rogers said to Baruch, 'I did what you told me, and you saved my life.'"

"That's incredible," Spencer remarked as he took a sip of his coffee. "I really appreciate your taking the time to explain all of this to me."

Bo nodded. "Well, I appreciated my grandfather taking the time to explain such matters to me. It created an allure that whetted my appetite to learn more. I just want to pass it down to you and all my team members. It's what gives us a competitive edge."

Spencer raised his coffee cup as if offering a toast and said, "And we can all use that!"

Bo chuckled. "True. But just as important as the information itself is *who* you get the information *from*. My grandfather was a man of integrity and held himself to a high standard of ethics." Bo raised his eyebrows. "Not everyone in our industry is like that. Trust me."

Spencer tilted his head to one side. "I have a feeling you have someone in mind."

"Unfortunately, I do: an investment advisor named Jacob Wiley. I've run into him several times over the years at financial seminars and conventions. He represents the other end of the spectrum; short selling and putting in monster trades are nothing new for his organization. His firm has initiated short positions multiple times in the last few decades. Then, with a meaningful measure of success, they stack the trades to add more."

"Is there a historical backdrop to this as well?" Spencer said with a twinkle in his eye.

A smile tugged at the corners of Bo's lips. "I'm glad you asked. Years ago, before the advancement of modern technology, an investment firm's principal could manually enter orders to accomplish this. Now, algorithms network with astonishing precision triggered by a cluster of moving average calculations that converge during the trading day." Bo shook his head. "Though sovereign states, institutions, and individuals reach the brink of financial ruin, it is just another profitable day at the office for brokers like Jacob.

"I was at a conference dinner several years ago. Jacob was standing at the bar bragging to some of the younger associates. He told them that they had to play ball with the system. He said, 'Throw them a bone to allow them to digest orders at the open and then row the market up and down in the first hour of trading. Wall Street calls this Amateur Hour. So, get a piece of that!'"

Spencer shuddered. "I'll definitely stay away from that guy. What happens after that?"

"The action builds. Jacob's activity establishes the direction of trades that determines whether the market trends up or down. Trading builds more prolifically, allowing the *axe*—these traders seeking to overwhelm the market—to have their way with their trades. This creates losses for other traders."

"Jacob would consider himself to be the axe as he seeks to exploit the weaknesses of inexperienced and unassuming investors, right?" Spencer asked.

For Spencer to arrive at this conclusion was quite impressive. It reflected his capacity to learn and, hopefully, Bo's ability to teach—something he needed reassurance about with his first lecture just hours away.

Either way, Bo's heart swelled with pride, and he responded, "That's correct. In the end, it's not really a matter of good versus evil. It is just market forces at work. But it does represent a more sophisticated type of weaponry in the battlefield of market activity."

For a second time today, Bo was reminded of why he did what he did: to help people. It's why he chose this profession.

Or did it choose him? Every now and then, he wondered.

CHAPTER NINE

When Bo arrived on campus that evening, his first stop was the men's restroom closest to the lecture hall where he would be speaking. There were no stalls or urinals available, which, although inconvenient, suggested that his class would be well attended. He overheard brief conversations among the students that indicated a wide range of political views. In just a matter of minutes, these diverse perspectives would populate his classroom, making Bo wonder if he had his work cut out for him after all.

Something else that proved more difficult than Bo had anticipated was stepping behind the podium where Edmond Brockett once stood. It was all he could do to push past his grief. Still, he forced himself to begin his first evening as Edmond's replacement. "Good evening!" he said as cheerfully as possible.

The class responded with a collective "Good evening."

Bo looked around the room as he spoke. "My name is Bo Parrott. As many of you know, Dr. Brockett recently retired and asked if I would take over his evening class for him."

A few of the attendees nodded.

Bo took a deep breath. "What you may not know is that Dr. Brockett passed away earlier today." He lowered his head and waited until the anticipated gasps and quiet conversations had tapered. "It was going to be hard enough to step into shoes that would prove challenging, if not impossible, to fill. Now, I have the responsibility"—Bo swallowed hard, and his voice cracked—"no, the *honor* of carrying on the legacy of a friend who, even though his health prohibited him from teaching, still valued learning . . . and would want all of us to do the same."

After a brief pause, which felt appropriate, Bo decided to lighten the mood a little. "I have to assume that the wind was blowing in the right direction a few months ago, and Dr. Brockett caught the scent of a history and finance major going into retirement. Evidently, he felt that it was his civic duty to provide him with something to fill up his time."

The sound of laughter filling the room did little to ease Bo's heartache. He continued, "I have been a stockbroker for over four decades. I started my practice in Eastern North Carolina as senior managing partner before moving to New York, where I have served as a partner at the Crawford Webb and Parrott investment firm for the past five years. My wife, Selby, and I recently returned to North Carolina to wind down my career in a place that will always feel like home to me."

Bo could tell by the attendees' facial expressions that his small-town roots, combined with his highbrow financial-firm credentials, brought something to the table that appealed to a broad and diverse audience. Even though he was just now realizing this, he felt sure that Edmond factored it in when he chose Bo as his successor.

If he had to guess, the older students represented either local businesspeople pursuing an MBA, or avid investors auditing the class. Regardless of which of the two categories they fell into, they were giving Bo their undivided attention. However, the younger college students, taking the class merely to fulfill a course credit requirement, expressed apparent disinterest by repeatedly glancing down at their phones or smartwatches.

Such is the life of a teacher, Bo thought.

"Now, let's delve into what I am excited to explore with you tonight: an interpretation of the symbolism found in L. Frank Baum's book *The Wonderful Wizard of Oz*. When this literary classic was adapted into a film, the title was shortened to *The Wizard of Oz*."

Bo raised his index finger as he spoke. "Perhaps the story wasn't simply about a tornado and a young girl and her dog. Perhaps L. Frank Baum was communicating a deeper financial theme in the landmark publication."

He took a deep breath. His lecture on *The Wizard of Oz* would demonstrate if he had the chops for teaching. He had certainly put in untold hours of research. But aside from communicating useful information, what would define success for him would be imparting his passion for learning about money and how the financial system works. Beyond that, his goal for this and all his presentations would be to make Dr. Edmond Brockett proud.

He cleared his throat. "Let's get started. A fiery debate over gold, silver, and the national currency influenced the politics of Baum's era. Legendary political figures, including William Jennings Bryan, were outspoken about the role of precious metals and their preeminence in national and global economics. Baum unassumingly tucked sweeping political commentary and significant symbolism inside the nationally beloved children's tale.

"Does anybody know who gave the Cross of Gold speech at the 1896 Democratic National Convention?"

A young man who was sitting in the front row raised his hand. "William Jennings Bryan. He ran several times but never won the presidency. However, he did serve as secretary of state."

Bo nodded his head. "Good answer."

The young man cupped his hand over his mouth as if he only wanted Bo to hear his next comment. "My name is Perry Godfrey. I'm writing my honors paper on Bryan."

Bo smiled and gave him a thumbs-up. "As Perry just correctly answered, on July 8, 1896, Democratic National Convention presidential candidate William Jennings Bryan delivered the famous Cross of Gold speech. The speech reflected the prevailing mood regarding the controversy surrounding the means of currency in the US. The Coinage Act of 1873 resulted in a pivot toward a gold standard and away from silver.

"Skeptics referred to this as 'the Crime of 1873' and viewed it as partial to the big banks. Before this, anyone could take silver to the Treasury Department to have the metal struck into a coin. After the act was passed, silver was no longer an acceptable medium of exchange. Congress engaged in a heated debate, and sharp division ensued between political parties. An interesting fact: In that same year, L. Frank Baum was only seventeen but was already publishing a local newspaper.

"Now, does anyone know what color Dorothy's shoes were in the book? I'll give you a hint: They weren't red. Later, in the Technicolor movie version, the producers changed the shoes to a bright ruby color."

A woman in the back of the classroom raised her hand. Bo recognized her as Melanie Sue Williams, a former classmate from high school. Not wanting to create a distraction, he decided to wait and greet her after class. Meanwhile, he called on her to answer.

"It's just a guess, but since you've been talking about silver, I'm going to say that her shoes originally were silver."

"That's right. Most likely, Baum was using symbolism to communicate his viewpoints on the topic. The original writing emphasized the favorability of silver adorning Dorothy. She represented the public. It's possible that *gold* symbolically comprised the yellow brick road. Hang on to that thought. We'll come back to it a little later.

"The Cowardly Lion represented William Jennings Bryan, who was nicknamed 'the Lion of the Free Silver Movement' because of his bold oratorical skills and strong advocacy of precious metals. He had originally supported the Populist cause to defend the individual citizen's ability to hold silver for value. However, Bryan's political opponents later criticized him for appearing indecisive. They considered him spineless for no longer supporting the cause with the same conviction and zeal he had previously shown, hence the Cowardly Lion story character.

"Let's move on to the Tin Man. What do you think the Tin Man represents?"

No one answered.

"Most likely, he portrayed the American factory worker. The mechanization of assembly work had desensitized him, leaving him with a limited capacity for healthy human emotion. Therefore, he claimed he needed a heart.

"The Scarecrow depicted the American farmer who thought he lacked intelligence because of an absence of formal education. Yet he possessed a high level of common sense that was well suited to the agricultural industry. It was equally valuable; he just couldn't see it.

"In the end, the Wizard only reaffirmed what each of the travelers already had in their possession.

"The demise of the antagonist character, the Wicked Witch of the West, came about by simply injecting liquidity into the situation. It was mere water that destroyed the villain in a pivotal moment of the story. Liquidity here has a double meaning and is symbolic of free cash flow in the economy.

"Like the man behind the curtain in the story, making the issue plain took away the obscurity that prevented the characters from seeing it clearly. An image defined by mystique fueled the illusion of grandeur. Of course, those who perpetrated it stood to gain from it. Specifically, if they could convince the population that an elusive, high-finance structure was necessary, Main Street would never be able to comprehend Wall Street. It placed the ordinary citizen in a subordinate position. The lesson is that basic currency and commonsense economics are better than a complicated financial system."

Once again, Perry raised his hand. "What about gold?"

Bo smiled and pointed at him. "You read my mind. Let's get back to how gold fits into this narrative.

"Many conservative monetarists advocate that gold is superior to paper money in that it is issued with the full-borrowing backing capacity of the US government. This debt-based model, combined with paper money, results in a dollar with less value over time. Either goods and services become more expensive, or the dollar has less worth. The argument is made against a fiat currency and its potential to become *worthless*—not merely *worth less*.

"But an emphasis on gold as a currency could provide the exact opposite of a true solution, as a second golden rule may apply: *Whoever has the gold makes the rules.* A concentration of gold tends toward a narrower power base, which ironically would *not* result in a more equitable distribution of wealth or economic stability. Baum's sublime message could involve advocating for a currency that provides liquidity rather than gold. That way, greater portions of the population can gain access."

Bo paused. "Are there questions or comments?"

A hand went up. "Wouldn't we be better off with a gold standard? At least gold provides a tangible store of value and a time-honored system of exchange."

"What's your opinion?" Bo asked.

"I think we *would* be better off. At least something of proven value would be the medium of exchange instead of simply paper. Gold has always had recognized value. It's God's money, right?"

"I've heard that said," Bo responded. "Perhaps the best money systems are found in early American history. Before the American Revolution, the colonies thrived on Colonial scrip."

Without raising his hand, Perry asked, "What made their systems better?"

Bo's eyes lit up. "Excellent question. There was *no inherent debt* associated with this paper; it was backed by an accepted issuer of the collective colonial government. It worked well until England wouldn't accept it and insisted on payments in gold. That effectively took gold out of the colonies and spoiled the backing of the money supply."

Bo pointed in Perry's direction and said, "Don't confuse Colonial scrip with the Continental dollar, which was the currency issued during the Revolutionary War." He then addressed the rest of the class. "That currency didn't have the strength to maintain a consistent medium of exchange; it ultimately collapsed. One factor that led to this collapse was the British flooding the colonies with counterfeit money, which drove down the value.

"George Washington was said to have lamented the loss of value in the Continental dollar and exclaimed that a wagonload of money would scarcely buy a wagonload of goods." Bo smiled. "The first president of the United States had insight into the value of money.

"Fast-forward to the Civil War. President Lincoln sought financing to fund the Union army. High-profile banks offered to loan him the money but with usurious lending rates. So, rather than borrow against a currency, Lincoln issued greenback dollars and referred to them as US notes.

"These worked well as direct obligations of the US Treasury. They differed from the modern dollar, which is issued by the Federal Reserve and backed by borrowing capacity.

"In other words, *it's based on debt.*

"The US Treasury issues Treasury bills, Treasury notes, and Treasury bonds. Most money is now digitally created and not printed or coined. All of this maintains a measure of the national deficit.

"This finance system creates a position of sovereign weakness that remains overextended. The Contraction Act of 1866 mandated the retirement of the greenbacks in circulation, thereby removing a considerable percentage of the money supply. Lincoln's system of government-based currency played out when his administration ended."

Bo glanced at his watch. The alarm he had set was about to ring, so he needed to wrap this up.

"In summary, a consistent theme emerges, and that is fear and greed. Smart money makes the first move, which determines the direction of investment markets. And if you want to learn more, come back next week!"

The chuckles in the classroom occurred just as the alarm on Bo's watch sounded, letting him know he had ended the class on schedule.

Afterward, the room was filled with the hum of brief conversations and the sound of backpacks unzipping and zipping. Bo perched on the corner of his desk, signaling that he was available to entertain questions or comments. The only student who stayed afterward was Melanie Sue Williams.

Bo found it noteworthy that the question she had accurately answered involved Dorothy's shoes. While Melanie Sue's weren't ruby slippers, they were crafted by designer Christian Louboutin and featured his signature red soles. Selby had dreamed of owning a pair but didn't want to spend the money.

One thing he knew for sure about Melanie Sue: If she had any concerns at all, money wouldn't be one of them.

With bouncy blonde hair and striking blue eyes, she hailed from an affluent family and, back in high school, was the girl every boy in town had a crush on—including Bo. She ended up marrying a prominent cardiologist named John Broughton Williams, who had recently become one of Bo's clients. Bo had just spoken with John last week; he hadn't seen Melanie in over five years.

She approached Bo where he was sitting on the edge of his desk. The scent of her designer perfume arrived before she did.

"Bo Parrott, it's been a long time!" she said cheerfully as she extended her hand to shake his.

"Five years, to be exact!" Bo responded. He smiled as she shook her hand, grateful that his inner teenager didn't show up with a batch of leftover goose bumps.

"You did a great job with your presentation tonight, and your tribute to Dr. Brockett was moving. I am deeply sorry to hear of his passing. I attended several of his lectures in recent months. Having a husband who is a cardiologist," she said, shaking her head and rolling her eyes, "all I hear about are valve repairs, ablations, and bypasses. Beefing up my knowledge of history and economics has become sort of a hobby for me, not to mention a nice change of pace." She winked as she leaned forward. "From now on, you might want to start taking roll before class starts. You never know who might wander in!"

Bo laughed. "Well, for tonight, I'm glad it was an old friend. And Selby could say the same about me talking nonstop about the stock market! But speaking of your husband, I've enjoyed working with him recently on a few of his investments."

"Oh, John can't say enough about how much he appreciates your input and how much he's learned from you in such a short period of time."

Bo felt humbled by the compliment. "That's high praise coming from someone as brilliant and accomplished as Dr. Williams." He scrunched his nose sheepishly. "I'm sure there's a lot he could teach me, but I wouldn't be able to understand most of it!"

Melanie shook her head and laughed. "You're too modest, Bo. Now, while I have you here, I'd like to invite you and Selby to a luncheon we're hosting next month to celebrate our son, John Jr.'s, engagement to Sarah Beth Edwards. We decided to have the event at our house on Evans Street in Morehead. I hope you'll plan on attending!"

If Bo had to pick a *Southern Living* magazine–worthy event to depict the epitome of Eastern North Carolina society, it would be this one. He had a split-second decision to make. "We'd love to come."

"Great! Tell Selby to expect a call from me to provide all the details. And be sure to give her my best."

Bo smiled as Melanie and her red-soled shoes left his classroom. He knew that Selby would cash in on being invited to such an exclusive event with just a few weeks to prepare. He chuckled as he gathered his belongings and turned off the lights in the lecture hall.

"Melanie, I don't need to give Selby your best," he said out loud to himself as he closed the door behind him. "She'll be getting the best of my checking account soon enough."

CHAPTER TEN

Bo was used to Selby turning on the television for background noise while she prepared her morning coffee. She rarely worried about the volume; Bo was a sound sleeper. However, this morning, he awoke earlier than usual. The stock market projections he heard blaring from the news anchors only served to fuel his anxiety about the start of today's trading session.

The fact that a cold rain was falling outside didn't help matters, especially since Edmond Brockett's funeral would be held today. Before heading into the kitchen, Bo stepped over to his closet, pulled out a dark suit, and draped it across the bed.

The sound and smell of the coffee pot coming to life greeted him before Selby's routine good-morning kiss. He spotted steam rising from the electric tea kettle, indicating that she also had assisted him with his new morning routine: a cup or two of tea. Trying to curb his caffeine intake, Bo had taken his daughter Alicia's advice and started replacing his morning coffee routine with tea. According to her, tea contained less caffeine, and its effects were more time-released. Time would tell if it woke him up or not. He selected a mug from a kitchen cupboard and poured the water.

"I see you have the news channel going this morning." Bo said as he repeatedly dipped a tea bag into his cup.

Selby pulled out a chair from the kitchen table and took a seat. She glanced in his direction. "I thought it would be a better use of my time than the Home Shopping Network."

Bo tossed the tea bag in the trash compactor and scoffed, "You don't watch the Home Shopping Network."

Selby's eyes twinkled from behind her coffee cup. "Just checking to see if you're awake." She set her cup on the table. "It might have been *better* for me to start my day with the Home Shopping Network." She shook her head. "There is so much unrest in the world. That being said, what's going on in *your* world? You had a fitful night's sleep."

Bo took a sip of his tea and joined her at the kitchen table. "I suspect there will be a change in the market in an attempt to mount a move to the upside." He shook his head as he raised the cup in the air. "Not that there isn't plenty of anxiety to go around already." He took another sip and continued. "My years of experience are telling me that this could be a money-making opportunity. But the elevated concerns of my investment clients make me lean toward proceeding with caution."

"What's the plan?" Selby asked as she added a splash of coffee creamer to her cup. She looked up at him and winked. "I know you have one."

Bo smiled. "Well, for more sanguine investors, I'll confirm buy orders to add positions at prices twenty percent to forty percent lower than they were a few months earlier. The jury is still out as to whether this will merely be a stock market correction or . . ." He stopped short of saying the dreaded words. So Selby said them for him.

"A crash?"

Bo's brow furrowed. "I think so."

"I understand that the stock market is beyond your control, but have you noticed any change in the number of hours you're working? Our move back home was so that you could wind down your career. From where I'm sitting, it looks more like it's ramping up."

Bo raised his eyebrows and nodded. "It's starting to look that way to me, too. With Edmond's funeral, my schedule won't be quite as busy . . . at least for today."

"Speaking of which, would it be okay if I didn't go with you? I read in the paper that it's going to be a graveside service, and this cold rain is already chilling me to the bone. I'd love to throw a couple of logs on the fire and research some new iron-rich recipes to try. If I have to eat another serving of chicken liver, I think I'll scream."

"You did your part by ordering a flower arrangement from us. And I'm thinking about working from home this afternoon, so you might have some company by that fireplace. I don't have any in-person client appointments scheduled; I just need to make a few phone calls. Mostly, I need to finalize my lecture plan for this evening's class. I'll be able to focus on it a little better if I'm not at the office." Bo took one last sip of his tea and then winced. "Not as many distractions."

Selby dramatically put her hand to her chest. "Why, Bo Parrott, are you saying that I'm not a distraction?"

Bo grinned, placed his teacup on the kitchen table, and then took her hand into his. "You are what I love most in this world and are—by far—my biggest distraction." He kissed her hand. "I wouldn't have it any other way."

Selby giggled and then pointed to his teacup. "What you don't love is tea, am I right?"

Bo's eyes widened. "It's terrible. But please don't tell Alicia. She was so excited to outfit me with the electric tea kettle and enough tea that, even if I drank it three times a day, I'd still have an ample supply to pass down to our grandchildren one day."

"You can always use the kettle to heat water for the French press."

Bo smiled a broad, toothy smile. "As in coffee?"

Selby grinned. "Help is on the way. There's a stash of French roast in the freezer."

Regina Brockett forced herself to open her eyes. She sat on the side of the bed and reached for a bathrobe neatly folded across a custom-designed chaise lounge covered in douppioni silk. She stepped over to her dresser, where she studied her reflection in the mirror. The compliments she'd received over the years wafted across her consciousness.

"You never age! What's your secret? Boy, did Edmond rob the cradle!"

While the mirror did, in fact, reflect the results of her most recent facelift, what she saw was a woman who, out of necessity, had dedicated most of her adult life to maintaining appearances. Cosmetic procedures aside, she had invested a significant amount of time and energy in gentrifying her otherwise country-girl persona to blend in with a culture that had proven both foreign and intimidating. Yet, gentrify she did, evolving into a model wife to a college professor who had also earned the title of history department dean. She became a gracious hostess to the other professors' wives, most of whom had also earned prestigious degrees themselves.

She sat down on the stool in front of her vanity. Her eyes welled with tears as she allowed herself—for just a moment—not to be Regina Brockett, but Regina Anderson: a twenty-year-old girl with a high school education happily working as a secretary at the local college. Her longtime boyfriend, Joey, had turned what had begun as an after-school job at a local mechanic's shop into full-time employment. Regina and Joey were head over heels in love. Joey was working overtime to try to earn enough money for a down payment on Regina's engagement ring. Life was simple back then. Regina had dreams of starting a family with Joey.

Of course, that was before the college hired a new history professor.

Edmond Brockett was handsome, funny, engaging, and, most importantly—to Regina's family, at least—could provide Regina with a lifestyle that Joey couldn't. Even though she did grow to love Edmond, she would later question how much of her acceptance of his marriage proposal was due to the pressure her family had applied. Over the years, she began to see that, perhaps, their relentless persuading wasn't as much for her benefit as their own. She lost track of how many times she and Edmond loaned them money, loans that were rarely, if ever, paid back.

Tears streamed down Regina's face as she remembered how heartbroken Joey was when she broke off their engagement. But life moved on, and so did Joey. A few short years later, he married a girl from out of state. The last Regina heard, they had relocated to her hometown in South Carolina. Of course, that was twenty years ago. From time to time, she wondered if they were still married and if they had any children or grandchildren.

The tissue made a swishing sound as Regina retrieved it from a silver-plated holder on her vanity. After wiping her eyes, she slowly opened the middle drawer. Shifting a few items aside, she lifted the liner to reveal an old black-and-white photo.

After picking it up, she used her fingers to gingerly outline the image of a baby girl holding a teddy bear. The argument she and Edmond had concerning her future took place years ago, but Regina remembered it as if it were yesterday.

"We don't have a choice. You don't know what these people are capable of. There's no limit to what they might try."

"Well, since they want to take our daughter, I guess I do know!"

"We will get to visit her. They will pay us handsomely."

"I don't care about the money!"

"She will have opportunities beyond what we can provide. She'll be trained by the very best!"

"What kind of training? And why our *daughter?"*

Edmond had been right about two things: First, they did pay handsomely. Edmond invested the money, and the interest and dividends alone allowed Regina to quit her job at the college. Beyond that, they were able to pay cash for an elaborate private estate.

However, he was wrong about the visitation rights. Each time they tried, one of their family members would get into a serious car accident or experience some other unexplained catastrophe. It didn't take too many close calls before Regina realized that the second thing Edmond had been right about was that these people—whoever they were—were capable of anything.

Her thoughts were brought back to the present by a polite knock on her bedroom door, followed by her assistant, Authur, asking, "Mrs. Brockett? Do you need me to help you get dressed? We have to leave in about an hour."

She cleared her throat and called out, "No, thank you, Authur. I'll be out shortly."

Before putting the photo back, she studied another one that maintained a permanent spot on her vanity. It was of her and Edmond at a country club golf tournament a few years prior. She reached for a clean tissue as, once again, tears streamed down her face.

She shook her head. "It didn't have to end this way, Eddie," she whispered. "It *shouldn't* have ended this way."

She took the photo, placed it back in the drawer, and then proceeded to get dressed for the funeral.

CHAPTER ELEVEN

As Bo approached the cemetery, he noticed that a large crowd had already gathered. The steady cadence of the rain provided a background track to the muffled conversations taking place beneath raised umbrellas. He spotted several familiar faces, including a few students from his class. They nodded in acknowledgment when they saw him.

After a few minutes, the conversations hushed as a black limo drove up. The driver got out and opened two of the doors to allow family members to exit. Regina led the way, escorted by a young man dressed in what appeared to be an expensive suit and overcoat. The heel of her shoe got caught in the gravel once or twice, and he was quick to steady her.

The sound of their umbrellas collapsing followed as the handful of family members took their seats underneath a large tent bearing the funeral home's insignia.

The officiant stood before a bronze casket with silver trim; Bo would later describe it to Selby as understated yet distinguished. The style reminded him of Edmond, and Bo wondered if Edmond himself had picked it out when he learned that his cancer was terminal.

The service began with an opening prayer and a reading of a few familiar New Testament passages. The officiant then invited attendees to share any special memories of Edmond. As one of Edmond's former students stepped forward, Bo struggled to stay in the present. His mind kept analyzing and reanalyzing what could have caused the heater to overturn and, more importantly, what could have prevented it. It was like trying to solve a math problem for which there was no solution. Perhaps what Selby had said in their phone conversation that fateful morning was true.

After pulling his car into the parking lot, he dialed her number.

"Selby, you're not going to believe this, but Edmond is dead."

"Oh my. I'm so sorry. The cancer must have been more progressed than he realized."

Bo's voice cracked as he said, "That's just it. The cancer didn't kill him, at least not directly."

"What do you mean?"

"Evidently, he was using a kerosene heater, and it overturned. He was either asleep or too weak to get out of the house."

"Bo, that's so tragic."

"That's the word the police officer used. But it doesn't make sense."

Bo could hear Selby sigh. "Tragedies rarely make sense. That's what makes them so, well, tragic."

"He tried to call me last night. Maybe he needed help?"

"If he had needed help, he would have called 911. He was probably just touching base to wish you well with your first lecture the following evening."

"I guess you're right."

Bo forced himself to focus on the stories Edmond's students were sharing. After all, this was a time to honor Edmond. Bo wasn't doing that by letting his mind wander, even if it was to try and understand how such a kind, generous, and upstanding member of the community could face such a tragic—if not senseless—ending to his life.

The last attendee to raise his hand was a man who appeared to be in his early forties. He recounted a humorous story of how, as an undergraduate student, he overslept one morning and was going to miss class. Dr. Brockett was going to provide notes for the upcoming exam during that class, and he needed those notes. So, he got his twin brother to go in his place. Unfortunately, Dr. Brockett recognized that it was his twin. The following day, this man assumed that Dr. Brockett would be upset with him, but instead, he applauded his ingenuity.

The man concluded, "I was impressed that Dr. Brockett knew his students so well that he could tell me from my identical twin, something even our own family members struggled with." He paused as a chuckle rippled through the crowd. "What I learned from that experience—besides what I needed from those notes to ace my exam—was that Dr. Brockett cared enough to be keenly aware of everyone who walked through his classroom door."

Bo's thoughts immediately traveled back to a comment Melanie Sue Williams had made a few weeks prior. *You might want to start taking roll before class starts. You never know who might wander in!*"

Bo swallowed hard. What if someone had wandered into Edmond's classroom—or his life, for that matter—with ill intentions? Should Bo be more vigilant about making sure that the students who attended his lectures were, indeed, registered with the college? Professors typically did this at the beginning of a semester, but since Bo was new to this position, perhaps he should attend to it at his next class.

After a few closing remarks and a prayer, the officiant ended the service. Bo was about to file into the long line of attendees waiting to offer their condolences when one of his students, whom he had recognized earlier, stopped him.

"Excuse me, Mr. Parrott? Can I ask you a question about your lecture?"

The exchange only took a couple of minutes, but it put Bo at the end of the line for visitation. By that time, the wind and the rain had picked up, making his umbrella virtually useless. On top of that, it felt colder than it did when he first arrived, as if the temperature had taken a significant dive. He decided to keep his interaction with Regina brief so that she and the rest of the family could escape these less-than-ideal weather conditions.

As he approached the tent, he noticed the tag on a stunning arrangement of lilies and roses that read, "With deepest sympathies, Bo and Selby Parrott."

He smiled. *What would he do without Selby?*

As the person in line in front of him stepped away, Bo saw that Regina looked just as lovely up close as she had from a distance. She'd changed very little since he'd last seen her, and that was several years ago. Her hair was still colored the same shade of blonde and styled to rest on her shoulders. Her deep-set brown eyes perched above cheekbones that displayed youthful skin and belied her actual age. Still, even the best skincare and cosmetic procedures couldn't alter the effects of stress and grief: Regina's smile appeared robotic, and her eyes dull and tired.

Bo squatted down in front of her chair and took her hands into his. "Regina, I'm so sorry."

Her eyes softened and welled with tears. She squeezed Bo's hands. "Thank you, Bo. And thank you and Selby for the beautiful flowers."

Bo had attended numerous client funerals over the past forty years, and it never got any easier. After dealing with the pain of the loss, the next challenge was finding the right words to say to the bereaved. It made communicating about a market downturn or a poorly performing investment seem trivial.

Bo smiled. "You know, Edmond was my very first client."

"Yes, I remember," Regina responded but, to Bo's surprise, didn't return his smile. Instead, her countenance fell, and she looked off into the distance. After a moment, she looked back up at Bo. She opened her mouth as if she wanted to say something but then stopped as if she'd changed her mind.

The young man who had escorted Regina earlier put his hand on her shoulder. He looked at Bo and gave a polite smile. "I'm sorry to interrupt." He then turned his attention to Regina. "It's starting to sleet. We need to get you home."

Regina nodded. "Thank you, Authur."

The young man extended his arm to help her get up from the folding chair. As she stood and started walking toward the car, Bo felt as if he needed to say something in parting. He ran up behind her. "Regina, you know I'm here if you need anything. Anything at all."

Regina stopped. She paused before turning around. When she did, her eyes, once again, welled with tears.

"Be careful, Bo."

Bo stood in the gravel and watched as the limo drove away, sleet pellets bouncing off his suit jacket. He got the sense that Regina wasn't just talking about being careful on the roads that were beginning to ice.

So, what *was* she talking about?

CHAPTER TWELVE

In her executive suite in Minsk, Kathryn paused for a moment to take in the grandeur of the decor with its gilded mirrors, priceless artwork, and furniture preserved from past empires. She stepped over to where the blue-and-gold window treatments puddled stylishly on the marble floor and delicately ran her fingers down the pleats.

There were times when she still couldn't believe that she held the office of premier. Most of the people serving under her had only been acquainted with her since she rose to power. They weren't there during her humble beginnings and knew very little about who she was back then.

How could they? She had her own questions about who she was. Only recently had some of those questions been addressed. But there was more she wanted to know, which is why she was anxiously awaiting a call from Simon.

She jumped when her cell phone rang. "Simon?"

"Kathryn, I have bad news."

Her heart raced. She stood up and began pacing her office. "Has something happened to my parents?" she asked in a demanding tone. "Tell me now!"

"No, Yulia and Dimitri are fine," Simon responded. His words communicated what she wanted to hear, but his tone annoyed her. It sounded condescending, as if he considered her concern to be silly or childish.

She took a deep breath. Her next question was equally important. "How about my birth parents?"

"I'm sorry to have to tell you, but Dr. Edmond Brockett has died."

She gasped and steadied herself by putting her hand on her desk. "We were too late. It was the cancer, yes?"

"No, he died in a fire. I am sorry."

Once again, Simon's words should have comforted her, but his delivery fell flat and emotionless.

She stepped over to the other side of her desk, where she all but collapsed into her office chair. She swiveled it around to where she could look out the window. Wiping the tears from her eyes, she allowed herself a moment to digest this news. As devastating as it was, it might not be the worst that Simon had to deliver. Kathryn braced herself as she posed the question she most dreaded asking. "Was it an accident?"

Simon was quiet for a moment and then answered. "It was made to look like one."

Kathryn's hand went to her chest. She could hardly breathe but forced herself to speak. Through gritted teeth, she asked, "By whom?"

Simon sighed. "Who do you think? Lutz Osswald, of course. Most likely, he was concerned that Edmond knew too much."

"But Edmond has kept quiet for forty years! Why would he say something now?"

"Because he no longer had anything to lose. He was dying, Kathryn. His days were numbered. Lutz was probably concerned that he would want to set things straight before his time ran out."

Kathryn's stomach turned, and she felt like she would throw up. But she willed herself to transition into business mode. After a brief pause, she stoically asked, "How do we deal with this?"

"You leave that to me. You have enough to deal with right now."

"Such as?"

"Keeping *yourself* alive. Lutz is hungry for power. He will attack anyone who stands in his way. His weakness? He thinks he sees the big picture, but his vision is limited. You and I are part of the grander plan. Be smart in your dealings with him."

For the first time in their conversation, Simon's response seemed sincere.

"I will," she responded.

"If there's nothing else—"

"Wait," Kathryn said as she sat up straight in her chair. "What about my birth mother?"

"Regina? She is alive and well."

Kathryn breathed a sigh of relief. "I only have one other question."

"Which is?"

"When can I see her?"

"It's being arranged. I'll be in touch."

As Kathryn ended the call, she reflected on what Simon had said about Lutz. She recalled her last meeting with him and the other members of The Circle. She never completely dismissed her suspicion that they had talked about her in her absence. Could Lutz have been plotting against her? Could he somehow know of her aspiration to become not only a member of The Circle but also its leader? Would he stoop so low as to kill a world premier to eliminate the competition?

She would follow Simon's advice and be careful in her dealings with him. Better yet, she would avoid contact with him altogether.

CHAPTER THIRTEEN

In the days that followed Edmond's funeral, Bo continued to replay Regina's words in his mind—and to Selby, who finally threatened to tape his mouth shut if he brought up the topic again. Her take on the matter was that Bo was talking to a grieving widow whose emotions were all over the place.

"Having just lost her husband, maybe she had fresh insight into just how fragile life really is. Her advice was for you to be careful as you make your way along. *Or*, she could have noticed the worn tread on your tires and expressed concern about you driving on the ice!"

Bo wanted to believe that Regina's words were as innocuous as Selby had suggested, but his gut told him differently. Regardless, they added another question to his growing list surrounding Edmond's death.

One thing was certain: After attending Edmond's memorial service, Bo felt even more committed to honoring his memory. Namely, he would endeavor to teach material that the students needed to hear, even if it made them uncomfortable listening to it—or him uncomfortable delivering it.

Arriving a little early for his next lecture, Bo ducked into the registrar's office to get an official list of the students who had signed up to take his class.

The receptionist smiled when she handed him the roster she'd just printed. "Looks like you're drawing a crowd!"

His eyes lit up when he saw that, in addition to the students who had registered before the semester began, several new names had been added since his first presentation.

A few minutes later, after the students had taken their seats in the lecture hall, Bo performed an old-fashioned roll call. He inwardly breathed a sigh of relief as everyone in attendance had registered to take the class, with only two absentees. Their names, Dimitri and Yulia Romanov, stood out as they could possibly be of Russian origin. Bo had hoped they would be in attendance as he was anxious to meet them and learn about their background.

But, for now, he could better focus on his lecture, having checked to see that everyone in attendance had, in fact, registered for the class. After taking a sip of water from a plastic bottle located inside the lectern, Bo looked out across the room, where almost every seat was filled. He cleared his throat and began.

"Theodor Reik, one of Dr. Sigmund Freud's first students, stated in an essay that 'history repeats itself.' This is perhaps not quite correct; it merely rhymes.

"With that in mind, last week, when the icy weather mandated that I—and probably most of us—work from home, I decided to sort through a box in storage that contained items belonging to my grandfather Beaufort, who was a stockbroker back in the 1920s and 1930s. Not only am I his namesake, but he was the one who fostered in me a fascination with the history of economics and the stock market.

"While rifling through numerous photos, personal records, and a collection of odds and ends, I came across an old, leather-bound book with faded pages and faint scrawl. After thumbing through it, I realized it was my grandfather's journal."

From where he had it open on the lectern, Bo picked up the journal and showed it to the class. As he did, he noticed an older couple quietly entering the room and walking toward the back, where the only available seats were located. Since two students were absent when he took attendance, he assumed these were the two. He didn't want to interrupt his lecture, especially if they *weren't* registered. He'd rather take care of that when the class concluded.

After placing the journal back on the lectern, he continued. "I gingerly opened the diary, careful not to damage its aging pages. As I began reading, they transported me back to a different time.

"Or was it really all that different? Let's start reading."

For stockbrokers in 1929, we received market-related updates over a news wire called the Squawk Box. On the morning of October 29th, the news we heard was riddled with mixed messages.

I can remember how, otherwise, the day started like any other. I arrived at work a little early to catch up on the paperwork from the previous day. As I began shuffling the folders on my desk, I glanced down at my watch. It displayed a few minutes shy of eight o'clock.

I'm grateful that the firm where I work maintains a solid reputation for dealing fairly with the public. Members of the community hold our stockbrokers in high regard as savvy businessmen and civic leaders. Several of our team members serve on advisory boards, ranging from nonprofit organizations to prominent banks and corporations that provide the lifeblood of our small city.

The city itself is close enough to—and far enough from—Raleigh, where our firm's regional office sits. I've established a rapport with regional management, as well as with several members of the national leadership team at the home office in New York. I never know when those connections might prove vital.

When I'm not working, I enjoy a round of golf. It helps me unwind and, at least for a few hours, escape the pressure and responsibilities of my profession. Last Sunday provided the ideal setting to do just that. With clear skies and temperatures in the mid-seventies, it was a perfect day to spend out on the fairway with a few of my contemporaries.

Afterward, we congregated at our favorite gathering place, the 19th Hole Bar and Grille. The conversations that take place there typically cover a wide range of topics, not the least of which is who finished the course with the lowest score. Most of it is locker room-type bluster, but occasionally something of substance is discussed.

On this day, I was standing at the counter waiting for my usual—a Reuben on rye—when I overheard a conversation at a nearby table. Two local businessmen were discussing market news. Of course, it piqued my interest.

"My broker in Charleston is dramatically selling my positions," Gene Porter said as he dipped his spoon into a bowl of vegetable soup. "I don't know what to think."

"That's nothing," Rand Fowler said as he wiped his mouth with his napkin and leaned in with both elbows on the table. "My broker contacted me and told me to sell everything. He said I needed to take a short interest to profit from a dropping stock market. Rumor has it that the big shots up North are already doing that. Right now, they look foolish because they haven't made any money yet." He leaned back in his seat and tossed his napkin on the table. "Who knows?"

"I bet you know." The comment was directed at me. It came from a man sitting at the counter a few seats down from where I stood. Even though the open newspaper he was holding concealed his face, I recognized his voice. It was my longtime friend and client Rob Groves.

Rob lowered the newspaper to reveal his face and a glass of Scotch he'd been nursing. He keeps his favorite stock in the liquor locker in the clubhouse.

"What are you hearing?" Rob asked as he picked up his glass and took a sip.

"Mixed messages. Some say it is the top of the market and time to go," I responded. "Others say it is only a pause before the next leg higher."

"What do you think?"

I shook my head. "Something feels like it's off. I can't put my finger on it."

"When was the last time you felt like that?" Rob folded the newspaper and set it aside. I assumed he wanted an unobstructed view as I attempted to answer his question.

I hesitated, knowing my response would trigger painful memories for him. I took a deep breath and said, "The high school conference baseball tournament. The sports press had picked us to win, but several of our players had sustained injuries. We knew we wouldn't be able to give it one hundred percent. We just hoped the other team wouldn't be able to figure that out."

Rob took another sip of his Scotch and stared ahead at nothing in particular. "We had our chances. And we were stacked for talent."

My heart sank as I remembered Rob's disappointment when our team lost in the final game that year. The top college recruiters, who had been courting Rob for a baseball scholarship, seemed to evaporate after that. I hated to bring up the topic, but the analogy still best described how I felt about the state of the market.

My thoughts were interrupted when Roy, one of the cooks on duty, handed me a lunch-size paper sack containing my order.

"That will be one dollar even, Mr. Parrott."

I counted out a dollar and fifty cents and placed it on the counter. Roy's liquid brown eyes expressed gratitude for the tip. I smiled and nodded.

I recalled those conversations as I jotted down a few notes for the clients I wanted to contact on the morning of October 29th.

By 8:30, it was time for our daily office meeting. The usual cast of characters made their way into the conference room with Joe Johnson, our top producer, leading the parade. I've almost outperformed Joe a couple of times, but he has a way of coming through in the last quarter. It's clear that he craves the recognition he receives, and regional management makes sure to satisfy that craving each year at the awards ceremony. They can't afford to have their golden goose waddling off to another firm.

Tobacco smoke had filled the room by the time the meeting concluded at nine a.m. I was one of the few team members who wasn't holding a lit cigarette. I did, however, understand the preeminence of the golden weed in the North Carolina economy. Many of my clients grew it in the county. Several portfolios I oversaw maintained large stakes in the major tobacco companies. Year in and year out, those companies consistently generated profits and offered attractive yields. Some clients lived on the stock dividends of those companies. It was just part of the local culture.

Before we all made our way back to our desks, Joe stood up to make one of his usual boasts about landing a big account.

"Yep, I just bought ten thousand dollars of stock in a prominent national bank. I'm really going to clean up. I plan to reach out to all my clients and suggest that they consider selling their utility company shares. Who needs boring stocks like that?"

According to Joe, the fast money was in bank stocks. I wondered if the term "fast money" applied to his clients—or to Joe. I felt uneasy about the discussion points from the meeting, but I kept it to myself. I did, however, write it down in this diary entry as I sign off as Beaufort Hardy Parrott.

"My grandfather's concerns would soon prove valid. The 1929 Depression would hit America like an economic tsunami. Many families would suffer from poverty, unemployment, hunger, and the lack of everyday resources. Oddly enough, certain individuals would thrive and prosper. How could that have happened?

"More importantly, what did they know that the others didn't? Let's see if the next entry provides us with any answers."

Business activity had slowed down considerably following the autumn of 1929. With less to do at the office, I decided to use the extra time to become a better stockbroker. I sought to gain an understanding of current market conditions to determine how I could become a source of a solution rather than just another part of the problem.

I checked with some of my friends in New York about the circumstances leading up to the stock market crash in October. A number confirmed that, from what they understood, several Wall Street insiders had sold positions in the months preceding October 1929. The smart money had simply considered that they had done well enough by that point in the year. They cashed in to book their profits.

Large institutions and major investors initiated short interests to hedge their existing positions. Still, the falling prices that followed resulted in significantly increased gains for them. Rumors abounded about an intentional effort to crash the market at its height to profit from the steep drop that was to occur.

"Is this the bottom?" The question was posed by the office's branch manager and registered principal in the autumn of 1929. The conference room table was full of wide-eyed stockbrokers who were wondering the same thing.

"Stock prices are down. It may be a good time to find new investment opportunities. We are behind in our goals, and the New York office is putting pressure on us. The firm fired the branch manager in Charlotte, and I hear rumblings of more cuts. I hate to be the bearer of bad news, but we've got to get going."

I could smell the sweat in the room. Grown men's livelihoods were on the line. One of the brokers, Carl Thompson, stood up and said, "That's it. I'm out. My father needs me back on the farm. It will take every family member to tend the crops. The land has been in the family for generations, and we're not about to see it go over to the bank. I'll miss working with you, gentlemen, and I wish you well."

My heart went out to Carl. Prices were at a near-term low. That was true for stocks, and it was also true for other assets. Land values plummeted as foreclosures mounted. I just hope to be able to endure with the rest of the population and hope for better days."

Bo thumbed forward a few pages. "Here is an entry from the early 1930s."

Exciting and controversial historical events are happening that center around the precious metal gold. The Gold Reserve Act of 1933 requires US citizens to submit their gold to sell at a standard price of $20.66 per troy ounce. It's now illegal for individuals to maintain gold, as some have done. On April 5th, 1933, President Roosevelt issued Executive Order 6102, "forbidding the hoarding of gold coin, gold bullion, and gold certificates within the continental United States."

After confiscating the gold and gold certificates of the population, the US government raised the standard price of gold to $35 per troy ounce. Conspiracy theories abound. I'm trying to make sense of it all. I'm surmising *the matter is in good faith, but I'm never sure if I can do so and rightly discern the nature of the winners and the losers; there are undoubtedly both.*

Bo paused and looked around the classroom at his students' faces. He expected to see a variety of expressions, including disinterest, boredom, and those politely paying attention while stealing an occasional glance at a smartwatch or cell phone. Tonight? His heart swelled as he noted that every eye in the lecture hall was glued to him.

"In closing, the challenge remains to use my grandfather's insight to better discern the times we currently live in. I'm committed to the same pursuit as my grandfather nearly a hundred years ago: finding a method to the madness. Theodor Reik may have been right in saying that history doesn't repeat itself, but merely rhymes." Bo paused and smiled as he looked around the room once more. He raised an index finger and said, "But that doesn't mean it's going to make sense. Thank you all for attending."

As the room came to life with conversations and the sound of laptops closing, Bo spoke over the din. "Next week's class will be held in the main auditorium. The college is hosting the Carolina Economic Forum, which is included in your tuition. Two of the speakers are internationally acclaimed, and then, well, there's me."

The sound of laughter added to the noise over which Bo had to project his voice. "And lunch will follow!" he concluded, not knowing if anyone heard him or not.

Bo remembered the two students who had arrived late to class. He excused himself past those still milling around until he finally spotted them.

"You must be Yulia and Dimitri Romanov."

They both nodded, and Dimitri extended his hand. "Yes, it is nice to make your acquaintance. It's been a long time since we took any classes, but we are eager to learn about how the American financial system works. We are sorry for arriving late. We move a lot slower these days!"

Bo chuckled. "I'm just glad you were able to attend! I look forward to seeing you next week."

As the remaining students filed out of the room, several of them stopped to thank Bo and compliment him on his lecture. Once the room was empty, he took advantage of the quietness and allowed himself to decompress for a moment. He felt satisfied with how the lecture went, but he couldn't take all the credit.

He picked up the journal from the lectern, looked heavenward, and said, "Thanks, Grandfather."

CHAPTER FOURTEEN

Back in their hotel room, Yulia and Dimitri sat on the bed as Yulia dialed Lutz's number. She adjusted the volume on her cell phone speaker so Dimitri could hear their conversation.

"Bo Parrott is very knowledgeable," Yulia said, glancing at her husband, who nodded in agreement. "When it comes to understanding what makes the American economy function, there is no one more qualified."

Lutz sighed impatiently. "I'm just frustrated with your archaic method of gaining information. The plan was to place recording devices in the lecture hall and possibly in his office. Remember, we not only need the information he provides. We also need a recording of his voice to replicate by artificial intelligence, if necessary. There are easier ways to do this. It *is* the twenty-first century, you know."

Yulia leaned in closer to her phone as she spoke. "And, in the twenty-first century, there are ways to *detect* recording devices and be arrested for invasion of privacy. If the authorities were to dig any deeper, God only knows what else you could be charged with. But Dimitri and me? Two middle-aged immigrants from Belarus eager to learn more about American history and culture? It's our best chance."

"Well, since you financed the trip yourselves, it's no skin off my nose. I will need updates to report back to Simon. How often does the class meet?"

"Once a week. There will be two additional speakers in addition to Bo Parrott next week. All knowledgeable. In other words, three for the price of one."

Lutz chuckled. "I can't help but be amused at the irony we're dealing with here. Mr. Bo Parrott has profited from American capitalism by establishing clients worldwide. And yet, it's that international reach that exposed his expertise, which we will now use to disrupt the notion of capitalism on a global basis."

"That is, if the plan works," Yulia said as she cast a worried glance at Dimitri.

"Oh, it will work," Lutz said flatly. "Meanwhile, keep me informed and keep a low profile."

Yulia ended the call and looked over at Dimitri, who had taken her hand into his. With his other hand, he brushed her gray hair back from her face. He smiled kindly and said, "Such a beautiful face etched with so much worry."

She frowned. "It is not a beautiful face." She raised her index finger. "Kathryn? Now, *that* is a beautiful face. It is a miracle we passed for her parents all those years."

"Of course we did. Everyone thought Kathryn favored her handsome father."

Yulia raised an eyebrow. "Have you looked in the mirror lately?"

Dimitri chuckled. "Beauty is not always defined by what we see in the mirror. And you, Yulia, are beautiful to me inside and out. You do worry too much, though. But there is no need to worry about this. No one will suspect anything."

"And by no one, you mean Lutz?"

Dimitri scoffed. "Lutz isn't as smart as he thinks he is, and he certainly isn't in charge. We will report to Lutz the information he needs, and we will report everything else to Simon."

Tears welled in Yulia's eyes. Her voice cracked as she said, "What about Kathryn? Who will tell her the news?"

Once again, Dimitri took her hand. "Simon will inform Kathryn."

"And who will pay?"

Dimitri's eyes narrowed. "Whoever is responsible."

CHAPTER FIFTEEN

Bo awakened with a start and looked over at the clock on his nightstand. Even though it was a Saturday, he chided himself for oversleeping. He had intended to get an early start to review a manuscript that his writer friend, Casey Balan, had emailed him. The two were scheduled to meet for lunch, and Bo wanted to ensure he had ample time to review the material beforehand.

After a quick breakfast, Bo topped off his coffee and headed back upstairs. As he took his seat in front of his laptop, he basked in the warmth of the morning sun. Disrupting two days of cloud cover, it poured in through the arched window of his study. The space he now used for work had formerly served as a walk-in attic, where he stored history books and family records that he frequently referenced. It had been laden with dust and insulation particles that, when illuminated by the sun, mimicked a steady flow of molecular traffic on the jet stream.

When Bo and Selby embarked on the remodeling project before moving to New York, they had the old window recast. It now sported a fan-shaped design that added curb appeal to the front of the house. The rest of the area reflected compromise—decor-wise, that is.

Bo favored a traditional Queen Anne sofa and chair with a ball and claw design and heavy dark wood legs accenting a deep blue Chatham fabric design. Yet, such a classic ensemble could not coexist with the contemporary ergonomic desk chair that anchored the writing surface of the drafting table where Bo now sat. Function won over taste in this context, and the furniture Bo selected displayed a more modern look.

As Bo opened the email from Casey, he reflected on how their friendship remained strong through the years despite their opposing political views. Lunch on the first Saturday of the month was the time they set aside to engage in a verbal jousting match, and both were skilled debaters. Bo contended that they each left these exchanges with their swords—and minds—a little sharper and open to consider alternative views. And, for Bo and Casey, friendship always triumphed over political differences.

Bo was all too aware that Casey wasn't fond of the current president—or his policies. Yet Casey was confident he had cracked the code on his thought processes. Bo took a sip of coffee as he opened the document and began reading.

Although often unpredictable, the current president aims to project a larger-than-life image. This approach unsettles his political opponents but fosters the chaotic atmosphere that seems to surround him.

He's also adept at creating distractions that enable him to accomplish many of his objectives, particularly those related to economic recovery. Washington, DC, has not seen a president like this one—at least not in a long time.

Bo and Casey agreed that this president shared characteristics with a predecessor from a couple of centuries ago, who was also an outsider and a fighter. He continued reading.

Though different in many ways, the current president and Andrew Jackson are similar in spirit. Andrew Jackson arose as a controversial figure and was no ally of the popular press. Old Hickory was not afraid to take on multiple enemies simultaneously.

Perhaps Jackson's ultimate nemesis was the central bank of his day. By the time he was elected president, the central bank was in its second iteration in America. The first was the short-lived Bank of North America, which the Continental Congress chartered in 1781. A second, the First Bank of the United States, was chartered in 1791. Both were private national institutions.

The Central Bank became a magnet for controversy and conflict. Key critics included statesmen Benjamin Franklin and Thomas Jefferson. Controversy shrouded the origins and ownership of the bank, and concern abounded regarding foreign influence that could pose a threat to American security.

Bo took a sip of his coffee, adjusted his glasses, and found his place on the Word document.

Congress renewed the bank's charter for its second twenty-year period when Andrew Jackson was elected. During Jackson's tenure, he engaged in numerous heated battles with the Second Bank of the United States, which was chartered in 1816. He ultimately succeeded in his goal of preventing the bank's charter from being renewed.

Someone asked Jackson on his deathbed what he considered his greatest achievement as the leader of the new free world of that era. Jackson had a long list from which to choose. In particular, the nation heralded him as the hero of the Battle of New Orleans in the War of 1812. But of all his possible choices, he stated, "I killed the bank." It was a very telling statement. He was, indeed, referring to the central bank of his time.

The central bank of an earlier time and the current one both stimulated national debt and a currency that facilitated sovereign borrowing at interest. Does easy monetary policy weaken the nation's underlying strength in a way that could make it vulnerable in the future? Could this, somehow, represent a heightened threat from foreign powers?

Bo could tell that Casey reluctantly embraced capitalism. He suspected that, deep down, he nursed a fetish for the mood of ennui and indifference displayed here and there in European culture. Casey's apparent sympathy for certain aspects of socialism gave him a left-leaning quality that sold well to his audience.

Bo checked the time. He still had to shower and change. Arriving late for this lunch appointment would provide Casey with additional ammo, and Bo wasn't willing to let that happen. He quickly read through the remaining paragraphs.

In times of war, debt escalates. A nation will spare no expense and will go to extreme levels to strengthen its viability for the future. During World War II, the nation's debt exceeded its gross domestic product (GDP) by 125 percent. Referring to the COVID-19 pandemic, in 2020, the president commented that America was at war with an invisible enemy that had asserted itself on humanity across the globe.

No one was resisting the excess spending taking place to finance the nation's businesses and citizens' survival. It was creating more debt, and debt had consequences. The president did not appear to want to increase the national debt but saw no choice but to acknowledge an easy-money policy.

Central banks all around the world increased global debt. After all, the whole world was at war with the coronavirus. A nation spared no expense in staving off the massive recession and economic destruction that could have ensued due to the shutdown of global business and enterprise.

Bo closed the document and leaned back in his chair. Based on what he had learned about the role of the money supply and the central bank, he wondered if America was headed down a path that would ultimately prove harmful. The current stock market, gold market, real estate market, commodities market—and almost every other market—was currently elevated and celebrated. He wondered when the bill would come due.

Bo headed back to his bedroom, quickly took a shower, and got dressed. Even without speeding, he somehow managed to arrive before Casey at their lunch spot.

The old diner wasn't much to look at on the outside—just a small, wooden structure that appeared overdue for a power washing and a fresh coat of paint. Yet, for more than fifty years, it had proudly occupied the corner of a downtown street, attracting both locals and tourists for its world-famous hot dogs and chili. Inside, the decor unintentionally harkened back to the 1960s with red vinyl seat covers and Formica tabletops that had not been updated in decades, if ever. The air hung heavy from decades of fried food cooked on a hot griddle, an aroma that seemed to permeate the walls. This same smell typically clung to customers' clothes when they left, serving as a complimentary souvenir.

Bo had just taken a seat when he heard the clanging of old-fashioned bells on the door at the front entrance, and a stocky man in his early sixties entered the diner. Sporting a headful of unkempt brown hair and a crumpled dress shirt, he approached the booth where Bo was sitting.

Bo stood to greet him. "I just finished reviewing the most recent addition to your book. Reads like another bestseller!"

Casey smiled and extended a handshake to Bo. Casey replied, "We'll see. I still have a lot of work to do. As they say, one page at a time!"

Bo watched as Casey slid into the opposite side of the booth. After settling in, he took a sip of water from a clear plastic glass situated beside a plastic fork and spoon wrapped in a paper napkin. "How are things over there on the right of the issues?" Casey grinned as he peered over the pair of half-glasses that had partly slid down his nose.

Bo chuckled. "I think you should eat first before we go there. You're gonna need your strength."

As a formality, the waitress approached their table to take their order. Knowing it would be the same as it had been the previous week and the one before that, she humored them by asking. And they humored her by answering.

Casey spoke up, "We'll both get a hot dog all the way with a side of fries." She smiled without making eye contact and collected the menus from the table.

The meal would be less than nutritious and give them both an offensive case of indigestion. But like their friendship, the meal represented tradition. And neither ever got old.

CHAPTER SIXTEEN

"How was your lunch with Casey?" Spencer asked the following Monday as he popped open a plastic container filled with tossed salad. The smell of sliced cucumbers drifted across the room.

Bo raised an eyebrow. "Are you on a diet? Or did Billy's Burgers go out of business?"

Spencer laughed. "Carrie has evolved into such a health nut. She has both of us taking vitamins and surviving on this rabbit food. She claims it will help build up our immune systems . . . or something like that."

"She's probably right. Selby has been eating differently in recent months. The contents of our refrigerator look like someone robbed the produce section at a Fresh Market. So far, the new regimen seems to be helping her energy levels, but I can't be certain. She doesn't talk about it much. To answer your question about my lunch with Casey, it was full of preservatives and cholesterol but enjoyable nonetheless.

"Now, nutrition aside," Bo said as he glanced down at his watch and then back at Spencer, "I want to show you something I noticed on my charts earlier today. We only have a few minutes before Jackie Trayor's phone appointment."

Bo turned his laptop screen so Spencer could look at it. "I don't like these trend lines. They indicate a market downturn."

Spencer paused from attempting to saw through a lettuce leaf with the plastic knife. "Should we be worried?"

"I'm hoping it's just a false start. No need to jump to conclusions. It's one thing to put new investment money to work by buying shares and establishing new positions. It's another to sell those investments. Our mission is to grow our clients' assets and generate portfolio income for them. Selling investment positions halts the progress of both. You need to have a strong sense of conviction to justify closing a position."

Spencer leaned forward in his seat. "When you do, it interrupts the potential for appreciation and cash flow, right?"

"That's right. In fact, one of our clients just submitted a sizable check from a property sale. In terms of investing it, I want to proceed with caution. The funds will remain in a money market account for the near term since market volatility is on the rise. If there is a market pullback, we can look for a smart entry point."

"Is this what they call trying to"—Spencer used his hands to form quotation marks— "*time the market*?"

Bo rolled his eyes. "That's what the *critics* of our profession call it. But it's our job to safeguard the value of client accounts. It's especially important with the buying and selling of real estate, businesses, and most other assets."

Bo's phone vibrated from where he had placed it on his desk. He picked it up to look at the caller ID. "It's Jackie Trayor—on time as always. I'll put the call on speaker."

Bo refreshed his laptop browser to reveal a screen displaying Jackie's account. "Good morning! How's everything out there in the fruited plains?"

Jackie's voice was strong, much like his temperament. "Well, Beaufort, we've got ample sunshine and rain, so I'd say it couldn't be better."

Bo chuckled. It amused him how Jackie occasionally called him by his given name. Jackie owned and worked a large tract of farmland in the northern part of the county. In Bo's estimation, Jackie demonstrated more common sense than most people with twice his education. In particular, he was observant and took the time to notice details that others missed. Timing was everything with farming, and Jackie also employed a keen sense of timing when it came to the market. He was also known to be a risk-taker, which was why Bo was surprised to hear his following statement.

"Look, Bo, I want you to sell all my positions. My CPA has a running count of tax losses from those land sales that went south."

"Well, your track record is still impressive," Bo responded as he scrolled down to view more of Jackie's account data. "You always land on your feet. A couple of duds haven't tarnished your reputation. But if you want to sell, that's what we'll do. I'll list each trade as unsolicited. Is there anything else I can do for you?"

"Nope. That covers it."

Bo smiled. Jackie was a man of few words.

"Okay. Hey, don't forget to set aside money for taxes if you make another turn on one of your businesses this year. That will use up much of the carried losses that your accountant has confirmed."

"Will do."

Bo made eye contact with Spencer and asked Jackie, "What prompted you to sell your positions?"

"Gut instinct."

Again, a man of few words.

After ending the call with Jackie, Bo unscrewed the top off a water bottle and took a sip. "Have I ever told you about Jackie?"

"No, but I have a feeling there's a backstory."

"Besides farming, Jackie makes money by issuing loans to other farmers in the community."

"What kind of loans?"

"Two kinds—each with a different interest rate. He offers one at ten percent. This is for the applicant who has good credit but needs to borrow money on terms the local bank won't approve. The other is at twelve percent and is for folks who won't be able to get traditional financing due to bad credit history, speculative pursuits, or excess amounts."

"He sounds like a good guy."

"Well," Bo said as he tilted his head from side to side, "he *can* be. It's like my father-in-law, Warren, once said of Jackie, 'He'll give you the shirt off his back if you need help. But he'll take the shirt off *your* back if you default on a loan he has extended to you.'"

Bo continued, "Since Jackie is selling, he most likely has detected signs of distress in his lending, a portent of what is to come. If hard times do arrive, he can rescue other businesses and farming operations if he has cash on hand. In the past, he has achieved this by acquiring a majority stake in a struggling company or property. The current owner maintains a minor stake and can remain in business."

Spencer nodded. "It probably helps preserve a little dignity."

Bo leaned back in his chair. "You're exactly right. Only a few people *in the know* are aware that this is how the businesses managed to survive. But it's a small town—"

Spencer interrupted. "And everyone is *in the know*."

Bo took a sip of his water and then responded, "You got it."

"Let's look at the lines on the screen and see if anything has changed since earlier in the day. What do you see?"

Spencer put on his glasses and leaned in toward Bo's laptop. He pointed to the middle of the screen and said, "It looks like they've reversed and are going up. Maybe this is the reprieve you've been hoping for."

"A reprieve would be nice. Unfortunately, it could be another false start." Bo let out a heavy sigh. "No need to jump to conclusions."

CHAPTER SEVENTEEN

Later that week, Bo did receive a reprieve. However, it didn't involve the stock market; instead, it was related to the party that Melanie Sue Williams had invited him and Selby to attend.

Selby had maintained that appropriately preparing for such a fancy event required months, not weeks. Bo wasn't sure if that was official etiquette or something Selby had made up to justify her shopping trip. Either way, it was a concession on Bo's part. Once the logistics—as well as the budget—had been settled upon, Selby was quite pleased.

Early that Saturday morning, Bo put his and Selby's luggage in the trunk of Selby's car, and they headed for the beach. Their drive would take them through a wasteland of bogs and marshes—a wasteland, that is, to developers and outsiders. To Bo, it possessed a splendor all its own. He loved how the sun reflected off the sand and gravel particles that populated a stretch of well-traveled highway in desperate need of repaving. Caution signs with pictures of farm equipment reminded the wayfarer that the agricultural economy nearby was alive and well.

A cloudless noonday sky greeted them as they arrived at John and Melanie Sue's two-story, cedar-shake-sided home perched gloriously on Bogue Sound. When they stepped inside, they took in all the signature sights and sounds of a well-planned—and well-funded—event.

A uniformed catering staff popped champagne bottle corks for mimosas. Delicately placed celery sticks in heavy crystal hurricane glasses filled with freshly made Bloody Marys were served to guests on the screened-in porch overlooking the sound. The temperature was unseasonably warm, and a gentle breeze eased in while ladies conversed about the rise and fall of television personalities. The men took shots at each other over basketball rivals.

Bo and Selby, along with the other guests, congratulated the engaged couple, who graciously thanked everyone for attending. Bo reasoned that this reception was merely one of many events planned along the way leading to a grand wedding ceremony scheduled in just a few months.

He also considered how, in Eastern North Carolina culture, events like this could produce profitable business mergers. They could also spark friendships that turn into marriages that resemble profitable business mergers. It's for those who can afford life without worrying about the tab. With such a high level of affluence in attendance, money inevitably becomes a topic of conversation. Today, it revolved around the stock market.

Bo listened from just outside the doorway of a wood-paneled room that sported a wet bar. A professional golf tournament was being displayed on a large flat-screen television.

"It's time to sell," John Williams announced as a small crowd of men gathered to refill their glasses. "Prices are high. The market is full of money, and the season is shifting. My broker recommended that I take profits. So, we added a short position for a hedge against the stock that I can't afford to sell because of the taxes." John continued, pointing at the group with his right index finger. "And I sold out of the *money call* options to raise funds to buy *put* options. The call options are two months out in time. I get more money for that, and that's as far out in time as I want to go."

A man in a collared polo shirt and chino pants piped up. "What do you see the market doing in the near future?"

"I think it will trend lower for the next couple of months. The put options are five months and one strike price out of the money. The option premium is less than it is for options already in the money."

The man folded his arms in front of his chest. "Explain."

John set his wineglass down and began using his hand to make an illustration. "I buy one and a quarter times the amount of put option contracts compared to the underlying shares of stock I own. I expect to make more money on the drop in the market because of the magnified movement of the option price. You don't initially see it move in direct correlation with the stock price, but after a short time, it moves faster than the stock price when you're right." He picked up his wineglass from the table and raised it. Before taking a sip, he smiled and said, "My broker is smart."

"That is a pretty investment-savvy statement from a cardiologist," mumbled one of the onlookers.

"Or maybe he's just getting to *the heart of the matter*," another chimed in as he took a sip of bourbon.

With a raised eyebrow, one of the gentlemen pointed at the glass of scotch and said, "Nice. What are you having?"

"Lagavulin . . . 16," he responded.

"Fine choice. But I think you may have started a bit too early today."

The two of them laughed, exchanged friendly backslaps, and then turned their attention to the golf game in progress on the flat-screen television.

Hearing John Williams speak well of Bo's market skills gave him a boost of confidence. Yet, he wondered if he would have what it took to weather the financial crisis he feared was not only possible but inevitable.

In need of a little fresh air, Bo stepped out onto the screened-in porch and stared across the sound. Two low-flying seagulls glided over the water as the afternoon sun began to slip beneath the horizon.

The blinking from a distant channel marker beckoned to him. With a green light that welcomed and a red that warned, it provided guidance for sailors navigating a tameless ocean. The similarity these bore to Bo's stock market charts was not lost on him.

In fact, the scene took Bo back one hundred years to the writing of F. Scott Fitzgerald's classic novel, *The Great Gatsby*. He reflected on the prosperous culture of that era before the 1929 market crash and the Great Depression that followed. While the current market and times reflected a century of change, in some ways, they weren't all that different.

In his first presentation at the college earlier, Bo had pointed out that Oz wasn't all that it appeared to be. Upon further reflection, he wondered if the Emerald City represented Washington, DC, for the answers and allure it seemed to offer. Kansas, where Dorothy's aunt and uncle had provided a loving home for her, was the depiction of *true* value. At the end of the story, the solution for Dorothy had been right at her feet all along—both literally and metaphorically.

Bo had always felt grateful for his small-town roots. But even "home" came with a price tag. His eyes landed on Selby as she walked past him in her new, cream-colored linen dress. She cast a wink his way as she kicked up the heel of one of her shoes . . . revealing a red sole.

CHAPTER EIGHTEEN

The market activity weighed on Bo as he took a few deep breaths and then a few more. He wanted to believe that it would experience an upward trend, but he couldn't shake the feeling that the opposite would happen. News outlets projected both. A conflict always existed between the bulls and the bears. It was what made a market. Which one was right? Time would tell.

"Time will tell." Dr. Andrew Scotsby said as he draped his stethoscope around his neck after listening to Bo's heart and lungs—and cutting in on his daydreaming.

Dr. Scotsby had been Bo's primary physician for years before Bo and the family moved to New York. Upon returning to North Carolina, Bo was delighted to discover that he hadn't retired and scheduled his yearly physical with him.

He also had served as Edmond's doctor. With HIPAA restrictions in place, Bo knew Dr. Scotsby would be limited as to what he could disclose regarding Edmond's death. But, at some point during his visit today, Bo planned to ask anyway.

Bo chuckled. "You're right, Andrew. You know, the lines on your patient charts look like the lines on the stock market charts. The question is: Which one represents a healthier outcome?"

Dr. Scotsby laughed and shook his head. "Bo, can't you think of anything else besides the stock market? Are you still stressing about things you can't control? Don't you know it will all work out in the end? Worrying won't help, and it's not good for your health."

Bo smiled. "Again, you're right." He paused and then asked, "But what about when things don't work out in the end?"

Dr. Scotsby stepped back and took a seat on the stool beside the examination table. "Why do I get the feeling we're not talking about the stock market anymore?"

"I'm referring to Edmond Brockett."

Dr. Scotsby shook his head. "I was sorry to hear of his passing. He was an icon in the community."

"And my very first client," Bo added. "I realize you can't comment on his medical condition, but were you surprised about how he died?"

Dr. Scotsby raised his eyebrows. "I was shocked."

Bo didn't expect Andrew to disclose even that much information. Not wanting to appear overly eager, he calmly nodded in agreement. "Same here. I had spoken with him a few days before he passed away. Besides sounding physically weak from the cancer, he sounded the same mentally: sharp as a tack. Do you think he could have suffered a stroke in those final hours?"

Dr. Scotsby shrugged his shoulders. "As a general rule, it's possible. Lung cancer patients are at a high risk for hemorrhagic strokes." His gaze fell to the floor, and he shook his head. "It's the kerosene heater that doesn't make sense to me."

"What do you mean?" Bo asked, cocking his head to one side.

"I stopped by later that day to visit with Regina. The charred remains of the heater were still out on the side porch where the fire department had inspected it. It's a good thing Edmond had a state-of-the-art security system; as soon as smoke was detected, the fire department rushed over. They didn't arrive in time to save Edmond, but at least they prevented the fire from spreading beyond the bedroom where he was sleeping."

"But what's different about the kerosene heater?" Bo pressed.

Dr. Scotsby looked off into the distance. "It was an older model—*much* older. It doesn't add up that a couple with such a modern security system would use something so antiquated, not to mention hazardous, especially considering Edmond's compromised pulmonary function." He looked back at Bo. "Those old heaters were notorious for emitting pollutants, like carbon monoxide."

"Which isn't good for someone even with *healthy* lungs."

Dr. Scotsby nodded. "Exactly."

Then, as if Dr. Scotsby had regrouped, he raised his palms in the air and added, "But, then again, this was an older couple who had been dealing with a terminal illness. Prolonged stress can cause lapses in judgment. We may never know exactly what happened, but what we *can* know is that Edmond was spared the end stages of lung cancer, which can be brutal." He stood, stepped over to a small table, and picked up a clipboard. He quickly signed a piece of paper and, after handing it to Bo, said, "Be sure to give this to the receptionist on your way out."

Andrew's attempt to find a silver lining to Edmond's death did little to alleviate Bo's growing concern that perhaps Edmond's death wasn't an accident after all.

As he left Dr. Scotsby's office and got in his car, Bo reflected on how the lines on his market charts and the lines on Bo's medical chart both told a story. The lines on Bo's forehead told one as well; Andrew saw new ones each year. They were like the annual rings on a tree. Some represented worry, others simply got etched in as part of the aging process.

Bo wondered what the lines in the stock market charts would indicate in the coming days. Daylight or darkness? Thriving health or grave illness?

Time would tell.

CHAPTER NINETEEN

The following morning, Bo woke up with his stomach churning with anxiety, a feeling that had become all too familiar lately. The disturbing trends he had uncovered in his stock market research troubled him. What concerned him even more was whether his clients and associates would take his warnings seriously. At this point, he felt that he was the only one sounding the alarm.

These concerns made his speaking at the Carolina Economic Forum seem less stressful. Normally, he would have been nervous before such an event. However, with weightier issues on his mind and several lectures under his belt, he was looking forward to it.

The only part he wasn't looking forward to was the possibility of coming up short alongside the other two speakers. When the college initially asked him to fill in for Dr. Brockett, they neglected to inform him that the other two presenters were internationally acclaimed.

At least his biggest fan would be at his side today. Whether he soared to new heights in his accomplishments or fell flat on his face, he could always count on Selby's support. Today, she was seated next to him as he waited for his turn to speak.

She held up the trifold program and pointed to a section on the first page. "Take a look at this: The very first name on the lineup is none other than Beaufort Hardy Parrott III, complete with an impressive array of letters after your name. I'm so proud of you! And I'm glad you decided to invest in a new suit for the occasion. Not only will your presentation be superior to the other two speakers, but you'll also look stylish while giving it. I have no doubt that you'll impress everyone here!"

Bo chuckled. "Never mind that most everyone here was expecting Edmond. I'm just his replacement." He raised his index finger for emphasis. "Not that I don't consider it an honor to speak alongside the other two presenters." He paused and looked around the room. "They didn't draw a sellout crowd, but I do recognize several headliners in the audience and a good number of my students."

After a few ear-screeching tests of the sound system—and as many apologies—the moderator stepped up to the microphone and introduced Bo. While Bo was all too familiar with his own bio, he appreciated being reminded of his credentials and accomplishments this morning. He could use the confidence boost.

After a polite round of applause from the audience, he stepped onto the stage and stood behind the lectern. The moderator had set a time limit for each presentation. Bo forwent any preliminary comments and plunged into the material he had prepared.

"The theme of the gathering this year is 'Investing in the Modern World.' It has been my observation that the fourth quarter is often the most favorable for investors, with its escalated year-end commerce and holiday optimism.

"Mutual funds often have a fiscal year end of October 30. In certain years, institutional traders introduce increased selling pressure into the stock market, which aims to offset losses and gains and book results for tax purposes. That is why the period of late August through late October is often *unfavorable* for stock prices.

"This may set up a positive move for stocks in November when the same institutions take the *buy* side of the trade and begin to add positions to portfolios. This adds a degree of buying pressure to the market, a pattern that can continue into the later part of December when what is referred to as the 'Santa Claus rally' finishes the year."

Bo paused to catch his breath and saw several of the attendees taking notes. He smiled to himself and continued, "These institutions often hesitate to sell positions for the remainder of the calendar year since it could force their investors to pay taxes when the corporate and individual tax deadlines arrive in March and April. The trend can sometimes continue into the first part of the next quarter, reaching a near-term high-water mark. At that point, institutions may sell positions en masse when the primary schedule for corporate earnings seasons winds up in February.

"As the year ends, renewed enthusiasm surrounds the investment markets. The older generations of investors seem to consent to the upward trends at a pace that is many steps behind the younger generations."

A female attendee near the front of the room, who appeared to be in her early twenties, raised her hand. Instead of waiting for Bo to recognize her, she spoke up directly. It was as if her asking the question was as important as the question itself.

"Mr. Parrott, I hear what you're saying, but isn't it different now than when you first started your career? I mean, technology and artificial intelligence have changed everything."

The question seemed innocent enough, but the look in her eyes struck a note of caution for Bo. Something about her gaze revealed understated erudition in this otherwise simplistic inquiry. Bo looked a little closer to see her name badge. His stomach knotted as he recognized the name of a competing investment advisory practice. He wondered if the questionable business ethics of the firm's manager had rubbed off on this young advisor.

With that in mind, more could be at stake here. A misstep on Bo's part could result in a victory for his opponent who, evidently, had chosen to use a younger cohort to take down a veteran broker whose practices she would publicly depict as antiquated and ineffective. He needed to proceed wisely, but what did *wisely* look like?

Bo glanced down at Selby in the front row. She mouthed the words, "Be yourself."

Bo realized at that moment that he could be nothing less. Unlike the other two lecturers, he wasn't an internationally acclaimed speaker. He was *more* than that. He was the person his clients trusted to manage assets that, for many of them, had taken a lifetime to accrue. He was both a teacher and a student of the stock market. He was a mentor and mentee. He had just received the confidence boost he needed earlier and was now ready to answer the question.

"To answer your question, yes, many things have changed. Technology has changed, politics have changed, even my hairline has changed!"

Bo paused as chuckles rippled through the audience. "But to effectively deal with change, a foundation constructed from time-tested and proven methods is essential.

"It's a lot like laying a solid foundation when building a house. All foundations look similar and are made of similar materials. However, the *design* of the house constructed is at the builder's discretion. The finance industry is an ongoing educational experience for all of us. I've been in the business for over forty years, and I'm still learning."

Bo looked at the young lady. "I hope that answers your question."

Bo detected the hint of a smile. Her response lacked the negative energy that had accompanied her question as she quietly said, "Yes, thank you."

With that out of the way, Bo could once again focus on his presentation. However, he made a mental note to follow up with this young lady afterward.

He took a swallow of water from a cup located beside the lectern and then proceeded. "A focal component of investing in the modern world involves technological advancements. Most of these have proven valuable and make our jobs easier. For example, we can now place trades at lightning speed and have various forms of client communication at our fingertips. However, whenever innovations exist for the betterment of society, there will always be those who employ them for their own dishonest gain.

"For example, information technology specialists frequently speak of foreign military cybercrimes and sabotage, acts that were unheard of years ago. It's now commonplace for major companies to report incidents of hacking. These assaults weaken beleaguered security systems already overwhelmed with compromised customer and employee records. Technology companies that offer services in these areas keep busy, and their profit and loss sheets reflect strong revenue numbers.

"Kinetic warfare seems almost passé as *virtual* conflict now rages in the public and private sectors. It's not hard to imagine the existence of programming and machinery that could damage vulnerable areas of the political and economic landscape."

Bo put his hands on either side of the lectern and leaned forward. "If *that* can happen, then couldn't global powers also launch campaigns to disrupt investment markets?" He leaned back once again. "I conclude that they could. Those of us who work in this industry have received enough anti-money-laundering and cybersecurity training to know that it's possible.

"So, we can all agree that technology plays a major role in modern investing. But a force as ancient as money itself continues to wield a mighty sword over the market, and that is human behavior. I've found it fascinating to observe investors' reactions at key inflection points in the market cycle. Some are predictable, and some defy reason. Then again, when fear and greed are involved—as they often are—responses aren't rooted in logic but are fueled by emotion."

Bo checked his watch. He didn't want to exceed his time allocation. "We may never fully understand what causes people to react the way they do. But it does make for an intriguing life-long study. Regarding how it affects the stock market?" Bo looked up toward the ceiling and shook his head. "Well, that may require more than one lifetime! Thank you for the opportunity and the honor to participate here today."

The audience laughed heartily and applauded even more so. Bo's heart warmed as he spotted Selby beaming with pride from her seat in the front row. For a brief second, it was as if time stood still. This snapshot of her would be one of many that would play through his memory one day.

Bo took his seat and listened as the other two speakers painted a picture of what was ahead that he deemed unrealistically optimistic. But he had to give them props for the energy and charisma with which they delivered their presentations.

Bo surmised, *I guess if you're going to be wrong, you may as well do it with a bit of flair.*

When the symposium ended, Bo excused his way through the crowd, shaking several hands extended to him. His face lit up when he saw Dimitri and Yulia. He shook their hands in turn. "I'm so glad you could make it."

Yulia glanced at her husband, smiled, and responded, "We enjoyed your presentation as always. We are grateful to learn how American economics works."

Dimitri leaned in, lowered his voice, and said in a thick accent, "It's easier than learning how the Russians do it!"

Bo threw his head back and laughed. "I'm not sure the Americans make it any easier. I've been working in this industry for over forty years, and sometimes I still feel like I don't know what I'm doing!"

"You are being too humble, Mr. Parrott," Yulia said. After glancing down at her watch, she put her hand on Dimitri's shoulder and then looked at Bo once again. "We don't want to keep you. I am sure you have many people who wish to speak with you."

Bo nodded politely. "Perhaps, but there's just one that I need to find before she leaves the building. It's good to see you."

Bo didn't want to rush his interaction with the Romanovs, but he did want to catch up with the young lady who had asked the questions. This time, he had one for *her.* She had already made it as far as the outside lobby doors when he caught up to her.

"Miss?"

She turned around and, after seeing that it was Bo, her gaze fell to the floor. Her display of embarrassment reminded Bo of a puppy who'd been caught chewing an expensive shoe.

"Mr. Parrott, I'm really sorry."

"I'm not here for an apology," Bo said gently, briefly putting his hand on her shoulder. "But I do have a question: Did Jacob Wiley send you? He's your boss, right?"

"*Was* my boss," she said as a tear escaped her eye. "He was watching a live-stream version of your presentation. When I couldn't"—she paused to use her fingers as quotation marks—"*take you down*, as he put it, he fired me over a text message."

Bo shook his head. "When I saw the company logo on your name badge, I had a feeling Jacob had put you up to it."

"Your presentation was phenomenal. It was humbling to find out just how much I didn't know. You taught me a lot in a short time."

"Actually, *you* taught Mr. Parrott something today."

Bo turned around to see Selby behind him. He didn't know how long she had been standing there, but evidently, she'd overheard most of the conversation. She extended her hand to the young lady. "I'm Selby, Mr. Parrott's wife."

"I'm Emily Dodson," she said as she shook Selby's hand. "It's nice to meet you. I was just apologizing—"

"No apology necessary!" Selby exclaimed, still holding Emily's hand. "You taught Bo Parrott something he didn't know when he stepped onto that stage today." Selby cast a glance in Bo's direction and winked.

"What could I have possibly taught him?"

Selby's face relaxed into a smile. "That the best response is an authentic one. None of us can be anything other than who we are. Maybe, in your case, getting fired wasn't such a bad thing after all. I've known Jacob Wiley for years. I've only known you for a few minutes. But I can already tell one thing: You're nothing like him."

Bo noticed a gentleman in a suit approaching him. He motioned down the hall as he said, "Mr. Parrott, lunch is being served in the cafeteria."

"Do you know what they're serving?" Bo asked.

"Yes, it's a seafood buffet."

As the man walked away, Selby looked over at Bo and scrunched up her nose.

Bo laughed. "Selby hates fish. I don't think I've ever met anyone who hates it more."

Selby nodded. "He's right. I can't even *be around* seafood without feeling, well, seasick! However, I love pizza, and there's a great Italian restaurant on the corner. How about it, Emily? Can we treat you to lunch?"

Emily laughed while wiping another tear off her face. "Since I'm now gainfully unemployed, I'll take you up on it!"

As they exited the building, Bo felt his phone vibrate in his pocket. He recognized the name on the caller ID as one of the headliner investors he had seen in the audience earlier today.

"Hello? This is Bo Parrott."

"Mr. Parrott? I'm Paul Cranston from Levi and Cranston."

"Yes, Paul, what can I do for you?"

"I just wanted to say that you did a fine job on your presentation today."

"Thank you, I appreciate you taking the time—"

"But that's not what impressed me. It was how you handled that young lady's inquiry. I have a few questions about my current portfolio, and since you demonstrated that you know how to think on your feet, I'd value your input. I'll have my assistant call your office to set up a time."

"Thank you, Paul. I'll be happy to try and answer any questions that you have. I look forward to meeting with you."

Bo slid his phone back inside his jacket pocket and smiled. *Take that, Jacob Wiley.*

CHAPTER TWENTY

While Dimitri dialed Lutz's number on his cell phone, Yulia looked out the car window to where Bo, Selby, and Emily were chatting just outside the entrance to the building where the seminar had taken place. A faint smile crossed her lips as she watched Selby put her arm around Emily.

Sitting directly behind Emily today at the forum, Yulia couldn't help but overhear her phone conversation, even though she could tell that Emily was making every effort not to be heard. Evidently, the man on the other end didn't share her concern.

It also didn't escape Yulia's notice that Bo and his wife were extending kindness to someone who had just tried to discredit him publicly. In Yulia's world, she rarely saw that virtue displayed. As she watched the three of them walk together across the parking lot, it was as if a heartbeat returned to a part of her that had long since died. With her face still close to the window, her breath fogged up a small section as she softly whispered, "Mercy still exists."

This realization—or perhaps it was just a longing—dissipated as quickly as the fog when she heard Lutz's voice on speaker.

"So, he suspects that a global plan is in the works?"

"Without coming out and saying it, yes," Dimitri responded. "So, whatever needs to happen to short the global market should be set in place . . . and soon. I will text my notes to you."

"After you do, destroy your phone. You have other burner phones, yes?"

"We do."

Yulia leaned in closer to the phone. "Lutz, I'm sure you heard about Edmond Brockett's death. We knew he had cancer, but we thought we would have time—" She looked over at Dimitri, who was shaking his head. Still making eye contact with Dimitri, she continued, "We thought we had more time to perhaps hear one of *his* lectures." Dimitri nodded in approval. "We know that *he, too,* was very knowledgeable about the stock market and the global economy."

"*Was* being the operative word," Lutz said coldly.

Yulia could feel anger rising in her. Dimitri must have sensed it because he shot her a cautionary look and, once again, shook his head. So, she regrouped. "I'm sure you heard *how* he died. It was tragic."

She and Dimitri could hear Lutz laugh. "I can't necessarily say that it was *tragic.* Although it's not how our agent, Mark, would have done it. I ordered a clean shot where it would look like suicide. You know, an elderly man with a terminal illness who wanted to end his suffering. But when Mark arrived on the scene, Edmond was already dead."

"What do you mean?" Yulia asked, trying to sound indifferent.

"Either it was an accident, or I wasn't the only one who wanted Edmond Brockett dead. At this point, the less I know, the better. All I care about are the results."

Yulia and Dimitri exchanged glances. It was Dimitri who spoke next. "Results are, indeed, what matter most. I am sure you'll pass along to Simon the intel I'm sending you?"

"I will. Meanwhile, you and Yulia continue to find out what Bo Parrott knows."

After the call ended, Yulia looked at Dimitri. With her voice shaking with rage, she asked him, "Do you want to call Simon, or shall I?"

CHAPTER TWENTY-ONE

Bo and Selby's lunch date with Emily turned out to be more than just a way for Selby to avoid the seafood buffet. As they split a pizza three ways, the conversation turned toward Emily's expertise and experience in the finance industry. Bo discovered that Emily was licensed in several areas and could make a valuable addition to his team. He didn't make her an official offer but told her he'd crunch the numbers to see if it would prove beneficial.

Bo did notice that, while Italian food was Selby's favorite, she barely finished the one small pizza slice she'd selected for herself. She could typically devour an entire medium-sized pepperoni and mushroom with the fervor of someone in a pie-eating contest. When he asked her about it, she dismissed it as having eaten a late breakfast.

With the seminar behind him and a possible new employee in the works, Bo settled back in his office for the remainder of the afternoon. Client phone calls were coming in one after another. Several of his top investors had seen blue chip industry names move up precipitously and felt like they were missing out. With such positive sentiment, they wanted to proceed more aggressively in the market. However, Bo wondered if he should talk them out of it. He feared it was a case of *if it's too good to be true, it probably is.*

Though yearly investment returns appeared higher than average, they did not seem high *enough* for classical portfolio allocations—that included balanced positions—to provide a buffer if markets became less favorable. Seemingly dauntless, these clients still insisted on throwing caution to the wind to ratchet the risk level without regard for time-honored risk management principles.

One of the clients who called and expressed eagerness to invest was Jim Portland, an orthopedic surgeon who ran a successful and busy local practice.

"Hi Bo, it's Jim Portland. Will you be in your office in, say, twenty minutes? I'd like to drop off a check." Like the other clients Bo had spoken with that afternoon, Jim's voice rang with confident optimism. But optimism isn't always a good thing when it comes to investing in the market.

For starters, where was all the money coming from? The supply seemed to exceed even the reasonable explanations offered by the Fed watchers—those who earned a living by carefully weighing the actions and communications of the Federal Reserve as it loosened or tightened liquidity.

Bo shook his head as he thought about how fear and greed represent two timeless catalysts that expose the extremes in people. Innumerable opportunities exist for investors who can maintain a clear state of mind in the heat of the moment and identify these two factors. Those same investors who also hold little regard for human welfare can make a fortune.

Bo heard a rapid and almost impatient-sounding knock on his office door. Having worked with Jim for several years, Bo knew to keep the conversation on topic and only address the questions Jim asked. Jim's tight schedule allowed for little more.

"How do I make the check payable?" Jim asked.

"Make it payable to the brokerage firm," Bo replied.

Without looking up while he wrote the check, he asked, "How will this be invested?"

"We'll add it to the current portfolio."

Jim had reluctantly consented to Bo's urging to reallocate to a defensive portfolio. It included a gold exchange-traded fund, funds in hedged equities and commodities, a long/short fund to allow position appreciation in a downward market move, and a large percentage allocation to short-term treasuries.

"Do you think that's the way to proceed?" Jim asked, appearing crestfallen and confused.

Without hesitation, Bo replied, "Yes. The smart money is selling. We need to play defense until it is time to play offense. If the normal market pattern persists, there has yet to be a true capitulation for equities, indicating a near-term reversal of the trend. Then, of course, we will want to become more aggressive. But now is not that time."

Jim agreed. "Okay. You haven't let me down yet." He ripped the check from the checkbook and handed it across the desk to Bo.

Bo felt relieved that Jim had listened to him. The same would not be true for all his clients. A dilemma arose when the charts depicted all the trappings of a bull market, yet an inflated bear market was actually in play.

As Jim headed out the front entrance, Spencer stuck his head inside Bo's office. "How did your meeting with Dr. Portland go?" he asked and then winked. "Besides brief, that is."

Bo smiled. "It went well. At this point in the economic cycle, people tend to have a surplus of money, and smart money converts to dumb money. Highly successful investors who are proficient in their area of expertise sense the need to diversify."

Spencer stepped inside and sat down in a chair across from Bo's desk. "That can be a good thing, right?"

"Not necessarily. They often make the mistake of choosing a new investment category that looks appealing but with which they are unfamiliar and inexperienced. They pay too much for the new assets, such as land or a business interest. Often, the intermediary who brokered the deal or managed the new capital investment is the only one who makes a profit. These investors, ultimately, may emerge unscathed, but it could be a while before the purchase price paid is recouped. Prices usually go lower in a reversion to the mean."

Spencer leaned forward in his chair. "So, what you're saying is that having a surplus of money pulsating through the financial system can make a broken market appear unbroken."

Bo nodded. "Stock prices remain higher than they should for longer than they should. Later, the stock market can correct—"

Spencer interrupted. "Or crash?"

Bo raised his eyebrows. "That's what I'm afraid is going to happen."

CHAPTER TWENTY-TWO

With so many unsettling headlines about the stock market, Bo flipped over to the sports section of the newspaper, hoping to find better news—and a momentary diversion. He took a bite of the apple that would serve as his breakfast for the day. The juice sprayed haphazardly onto the newspaper, resulting in a starburst of smudges. Ignoring them, Bo smiled as he read that, once again, his alma mater's basketball team was dominating their athletic conference.

"Now that's what I'm talking about!" Bo said aloud and with a little more volume than he had intended.

As he looked at the team photos, one in particular caught his attention. The photographer had used an auditorium on campus for the backdrop. Upon closer inspection, Bo recognized the building, and memories from his own college days came flooding back.

He pictured a younger version of himself, clothed in an oversized sweatshirt, jeans, and sneakers, making his way down the brick walkways of the old north side of campus. He could still smell the scent of fallen autumn leaves, sunbaked acorns, and smoke from a wood-burning fireplace nearby.

Bo was often accompanied by his friend Donald Rowan, and they engaged in small talk as they briskly walked to economics class.

The fast pace was necessary as the economics professor was known for locking the auditorium doors when it was time for class to begin. He had no tolerance for mediocrity, and that applied to punctuality as well. Students needed to arrive early or, at the very least, on time. Many were the disenfranchised who would gather outside, straining to hear him lecture on material essential to passing the course.

But what Bo remembered most about this professor was his skill as a true market technician with refined charting models. His personal net worth was exceptionally high, an anomaly for an academic. It seemed he derived his successes from his own exceptional stock trading rather than merely collecting biweekly payroll deposits for being a scholar and lecturer. The professor was a contrarian with a strong distaste for the establishment—despite having profited from it. Bo learned more traditional fundamental analysis and macroeconomics from the other instructors on campus.

Bo endured multiple classes under the stern eye of the professor during his tenure at the university business school. The professor also served as Bo's advisor his senior year, so he got a double dose. However, this resulted in Bo gaining keen insight into the character and dynamics of the stock market.

The professor enjoyed deriding the ignorance of uninformed and lazy investors. He never missed an opportunity to snipe at his critics, who made a living selling books and newsletters promoting competing theories. Bo suspected it was all part of the professor's attempt to develop a looming and persuasive persona to further galvanize the loyalty of his followers.

Still, there was no arguing with results. Since his undergraduate days, Bo had back-tested the professor's methodology and found it to be highly reliable. When clients posed challenging questions and looked to Bo for answers, he would recall the key tenets from the professor's lectures. His conclusions consistently aligned with those of the professor.

The alarm on his watch pulled Bo back to the present. He had a meeting scheduled with a client who would be arriving in a matter of minutes. For now, he had to abandon the feel of brick walkways beneath his feet, the woodsy scents of autumn. . . and those simpler days of his youth.

"What's Dr. Sturgeon saying?" Donald Rowan said as he took a seat in the chair across from Bo's desk. Since his college days, Donald had become the managing partner of a third-generation insurance agency in town. Bo admired his work ethic. He ran a successful practice but did so with a graceful stride, allowing him to have a life outside of work. He was well-liked by his clients and maintained an upstanding reputation in the community.

Bo couldn't resist. "He's still dead, you know."

They both laughed, aware that the professor's voice lived on in their heads, indelible in their memories.

"However, since you asked, he would say that if we apply the multiday chart within the context of the weekly and monthly charts, we can determine that the market will go down from here. I would elaborate on all the boring details, but since we're old friends, I'm giving you the shortened version."

"So, you're saying I should sell?"

"Yes," Bo replied. "Since it's an IRA, there won't be current tax implications. If you like, we can go to cash. You know how people say the market goes up seven out of ten years? This is one of those years when the market doesn't go up. And it may last longer than one year."

"Sure. Go ahead."

That's all Donald needed to say. Bo contacted Martin Beargrass at the trading desk to walk through the order execution.

After he met with Donald, Bo sat down in his desk chair and gazed out the window. *How many other clients will make the same decision? Moreover, how many clients must he contact to advocate making that decision?*

Bo remembered his college days once more and how briskly he would walk to economics class to avoid the time-honored tardy bell and those closed auditorium doors. He felt the same sense of urgency now.

There were open doors that would soon be closing. The bell that he answered to now was the one that announced the opening and closing of the stock market each day. He knew he must make the most of the time in between.

Going forward, in-person, one-hour client meetings wouldn't constitute the most efficient use of that time. He would need to schedule fifteen-minute phone calls to reach four clients in the same amount of time. He readied his list of client contacts to coordinate with his associate advisors.

It was time to quicken the pace.

CHAPTER TWENTY-THREE

Bo felt a strong urgency to reach out to his client base, but he also experienced a pang of guilt, knowing that doing so would require him to spend even more time at the office. This inner conflict had been a recurring theme throughout his long career in the finance industry. For decades, he had worked diligently to ensure his clients made investments that would yield lasting and profitable returns. However, the career itself often felt like a bad stock pick. While it had allowed him to earn a substantial salary, the losses in terms of time spent away from his family were immeasurable.

From a market perspective, this was not an ideal time for Bo to take a few days off. He decided, however, to do so anyway and spend quality time with Selby in one of their favorite vacation spots: the North Carolina mountains.

He yawned as he made his way out to the garage and pressed the button on the wall that lifted the door. The apparatus hummed to life, and the door slowly creaked open. When it did, the morning air scurried in like a stray animal seeking shelter, carrying with it the fragrance of spring. Bo stepped over to open the trunk of his car and breathed in the mixture of cut grass, daffodils, and his favorite flower—wisteria.

While Bo appreciated wisteria's intoxicating notes of tuberose and jasmine, he wasn't just drawn to the fragrance; the flower represented a type of carefree existence he envied. The delicate blossoms hung at ease and appeared content to grow almost anywhere, nestled among the foliage of the finest homes or gracing the wooded areas around dumpsters.

The trunk lid squeaked open as Bo tossed in his duffel bag and Selby's suitcase.

"Did you remember to pack the cooler?" Selby yelled from inside the house.

He hadn't remembered but decided to keep the peace. "I'm getting ready to grab it now."

Bo suppressed a laugh when Selby entered the garage a few seconds later. Her hair was in rollers, and she had dental bleaching strips on her teeth. She dried her hands on a dish towel and spoke with a discernible lisp. "Bo Parrott. You'd forget your head if it wasn't attached."

He smiled and said, "You do know it's hard to take you seriously right now?"

Selby's eyebrows snapped together, and she threw the dish towel in his direction. "If we're going to beat the Easter weekend traffic, we have to leave soon." She turned to head back into the house and called out, "Chop, chop!"

Bo always enjoyed it when he and Selby could get away for a few days to visit the North Carolina mountains. As usual, Selby preferred sitting behind the wheel rather than in the passenger's seat. This worked well for Bo as he could stay plugged into communication with clients and staff while Selby drove. He never knew what situation might arise back at the office while he was away, especially during market hours.

Once they were on the road, Bo spent the first hour or so catching up on emails and client phone calls. Afterward, he closed his laptop and looked over at Selby. Her hair now styled and her makeup applied, she looked nothing like she had earlier when she spoke with him in the garage. Not that he necessarily preferred the one look over the other.

There was something endearing about seeing her in curlers and with dental strips on her teeth.

He had noticed over the past few weeks that Selby seemed more tired than usual. On any given day, she typically could work circles around him. Now, the circles she displayed were under her eyes. Today, they were noticeably visible despite her attempt to conceal them with makeup. Bo wanted to ask if she had followed up with Dr. McGill regarding the possibility of her ordering additional diagnostic tests. Then again, if Selby felt she needed to contact her doctor, she'd address it soon enough.

"Selby," Bo said, "do you have any regrets? You know, anything you would have done differently? Raising the children? Our marriage? Anything in particular?"

Selby sighed. "First of all, you know how I hate these questions. Next time, give me the courtesy of a heads-up when there's going to be a *road trip quiz*." She paused for a moment and then said, "My answer would be, yes, of course. I think everyone has regrets. I would have done many things differently, but I still would have chosen the same path."

Bo nodded. "I agree. How about our relationship? I know I haven't done us any favors by the long hours I've spent at the office."

"I do feel like a work widow sometimes," Selby said as she quickly darted her eyes back and forth in his direction. "It's not just the hours you spend at the office or meeting with clients. When you're home, your thoughts are often elsewhere. That being said, I know you carry a lot on your shoulders."

Bo gazed out the window. The trees along the side of the road hung heavy with cascading wisteria vines creating a blur of lavender as he and Selby drove past them. "I'm sorry, Selby. My greatest fear is failing. I don't want to fail my clients, our children, and, most of all, you."

Bo could feel Selby slipping her hand into his. "Since you've opened the door to this reflective—and might I add *depressing*—line of questioning, what else are you afraid of?"

He let out a heavy sigh. "It's going to sound trivial coming from someone who's managed millions of dollars of client assets over the years."

Selby smiled. "I can handle trivial."

"Honestly? I don't like it when people get angry with me. I shouldn't let it bother me so much. After all, with the work I do, it's inevitable."

"Your work is only a part of who you are. You're also a Christian, and the Bible teaches that the fear of people is a snare. You need to let that truth travel from your head to your heart. Trust God. He won't fail you."

"You're right. As usual." For that moment, the weight lifted off him. He felt in sync with their drive as they ascended the mountain. With such a great expanse of nature, he felt like he could find his way into hiding where nothing could harm him. It was part of the allure of the mountains, and one of the reasons he carved out the time for a visit at least once a year.

While he temporarily retreated to this safe place in his imagination, another scripture gently tugged at his heart. It was from the book of Psalms where David proclaimed that *God* was his hiding place: God, who created those majestic mountains, was the ultimate refuge. The truth brought even more solace to his soul.

Bo's thoughts were interrupted by Selby exclaiming, "Look, there's one of those runoff areas on the other side of the road—you know, with the beveled mounds of sand? There's a truck there now. That must have been scary!"

Bo turned around in his seat to look over to the area Selby was describing. Wafts of smoke arose from the scene where, evidently, a truck driver had either blown a tire or distressed his brakes. It reminded Bo of how the steep slope and winding curves challenge even the most experienced drivers as they attempt to descend from the upper elevations. The highway signs remind everyone not to go too fast or too carelessly. It was sobering to witness a scene where that, indeed, had happened. Very sobering. The sight transitioned his thoughts back to the investment world.

He turned back around in his seat and looked over at Selby. "I know this is our vacation, but that truck reminded me of the stock market. Do you mind if I share my thoughts?"

Selby laughed. "I'm trapped in the car with you. Do I really have a choice?"

Bo smiled and pointed to the side of the road. "Just like those highway signs coming down the mountain are there for our safety, it's my job to recognize the warning signs in the investment market—and help investors avoid a crash. Right now, I'm concerned that the fast pace of monetary and fiscal stimulus may have overheated the economy to the point where a crash landing is inevitable." He shook his head. "I only hope investors won't have to experience that."

"Believe it or not, I actually understand what you just said."

Bo chuckled. "Good, because there's more! If the stock market movement repeats trends from prior weeks and months, it will likely mean a descent from a higher level than the one to come. It seems so much easier to travel down a mountain than to go up one, and it's the same with the market. The runaway truck ramps are like the central bank's efforts to slow it down. They provide some remedy but still pose a bumpy ride."

"When does the market go back up the mountain, so to speak?"

Bo looked out the window as he spoke. "When investors finally admit that a bottom has occurred. At that point, the market stops declining and begins going up again, which gives me hope. If I can step back from the overwhelming sense of disillusionment on the part of so many who have thrown in the towel on investing in stocks and bonds, I can imagine a level where investors may once again find value. It's all based on the quirkiness of human nature: What we *want* to do is often the opposite of what we *need* to do."

"I definitely understand that last part," Selby said as they arrived at an intersection just as the light was turning red.

The car came to a stop. Selby's brow furrowed as she turned to look at him. She hesitated at first, but then blurted out, "Bo, I don't think the iron supplements are helping. I need to follow up with Dr. McGill, but I'm afraid. I know it sounds silly. Putting it off only delays any help she can give me."

Bo felt a twinge of panic but remained calm for Selby's sake. He slowly nodded. "Okay, let's think about this. Why don't you pull off the road at that gas station up ahead? Call your doctor and make an appointment. I think it will help you to enjoy your weekend more."

Selby's eyes welled with tears, and she nodded. "You're right. That's what I'll do. And while we're at the gas station, why don't you top off the tank?"

Bo smiled. "Good idea."

When Selby pulled into the gas-station parking lot, Bo got out of the car and placed his credit card into the card reader at the pump. When he did, a cool breeze off the mountains brought with it a familiar smell.

Wisteria.

He looked around to see where it was coming from and then spotted it over by the dumpster. The location was typical for wisteria, but what wasn't typical was the amount that was growing there. Bo had never seen so many blooms all in one place. The vines all but draped over the dumpster, bringing beauty—and fragrance—to something that possessed neither.

As the gas pump began clicking off the gallons, Bo could see Selby inside the car, talking on her cell phone. He could smell the wisteria— that blend of tuberose and jasmine that defines a flower that stays for only a little while . . . and then fades away. He looked once again at Selby.

He wiped a tear from his eye before he replaced the gas hose and got back in the car.

CHAPTER TWENTY-FOUR

Selby's phone call to her doctor appeared to have lightened her mood. For the rest of the drive, she was back to her talkative, cheerful self. Bo made an extra effort not to discuss business and to steer the conversation away from serious topics.

No more road trip quizzes, he silently admonished himself.

Once they had arrived in Black Mountain, they took their time browsing through several local shops, where Selby bought an extra sweater for the trip. That evening, after eating dinner at a restaurant known for its breathtaking view of the Blue Ridge Mountain Range, Bo held the door open for Selby as she wheeled her suitcase into the hotel room they had reserved. As soon as the door clicked shut behind them, Selby—with childlike excitement—quickly set her suitcase on the luggage rack, unzipped it, and began rummaging through her clothes.

Bo's duffel bag slouched as he casually tossed it onto one of the two double beds in the room.

Briefly looking up at Bo, Selby pointed over to the bathroom. "While you get a shower, I'm going to change into my pj's. Afterward, we'll look through the brochures we picked up in the hotel lobby and make a plan for tomorrow."

Bo grinned. He had hoped to take a shower and go straight to bed, but Selby's enthusiasm was contagious. He now looked forward to planning their day, a day where they could set aside concerns about the stock market and doctors' appointments and simply enjoy the beauty of nature.

While Bo was in the bathroom, locating the hotel's amenities, including a clean towel, soap, and shampoo, he could hear Selby at the vanity washing her face and brushing her teeth.

He adjusted the water temperature in the shower to ensure it was as hot as he could stand, hoping it would ease at least *some* of the tension that seemed to have taken up permanent residence in his neck and shoulders.

Occupational hazard, he reminded himself.

After a few minutes, which went by all too quickly, he fumbled for the faucet handles to shut off the water. Grabbing the towel he had hung over the side of the shower stall, he noticed the thick layer of condensation that had formed on the glass door. For a moment, his mind went back to when, as a child, he would finger-write his name on the windowpanes of his parents' house when the summer heat and humidity outside clashed with the air conditioning inside. Tonight, the name on his mind was Selby's. He smiled, drew a heart with his finger, and then stepped out of the shower.

Wrapping the towel around his waist, he made his way over to the bed where he expected to see Selby sitting up, surrounded by a collection of travel brochures. But the brochures remained in a neat stack on the nightstand, and Selby was fast asleep on top of the covers.

Bo's breath caught in his throat. This wasn't like her at all.

He gently pulled down the covers and slid them over her until she looked comfortable. He stepped back and sighed.

Returning to the bathroom to collect his clothes, he glanced over at the heart he had drawn on the shower door. The sides had collapsed, forming a straight line of water droplets. The fact that they looked like a trail of tears was not lost on him.

He took his clothes and draped them over the single chair positioned in front of the desk. He changed into his pajamas, turned off the light, and went to bed.

CHAPTER TWENTY-FIVE

Lutz squinted as he peered through the window-blind slats at Kathryn crossing the gravel parking lot and getting into her limo. "Maybe she will fall from wearing those ridiculous high heels," he said with a smirk as he took a draw from his cigarette.

He watched the limo slow down as it drove past the cars still parked in the lot. He couldn't see what Kathryn was doing because of the tinted windows, but he suspected she was checking to see if anyone else had left the meeting.

"Do you wonder if we're plotting against you in your absence, Kathryn?"

He patiently watched until the limo was out of sight. He hoped that seeing the taillights fade was a sign of things to come: He wanted Kathryn's light to diminish and then be extinguished altogether. But first, he must convince the other members of The Circle. Not that he necessarily needed their permission; his position as leader all but gave him carte blanche on such matters. But it wasn't just his title. No one else had the stomach for it.

No one except for Simon, that is, and he appeared a little *too* detached from the emotional kickback that can follow an assassination. It's like a delicate necklace chain containing a knot. If not properly dealt with, the one carrying out the order—or the one who issued it—can easily break. After all, human life has been destroyed. For those who give in to their emotions, the burden can prove too heavy to bear.

In Lutz's opinion, a true world leader is someone who can focus on the results and not the sacrifices required to achieve them . . . and convince others of the same. This was what he needed to do with The Circle members. He took one more draw from his cigarette before stomping it out with his foot.

He quietly descended the stairs that led to the basement. He could see the other Circle members sitting at the table. He cleared his throat from the doorway and then said, "Kathryn's usefulness will end soon."

He watched as the eleven members exchanged glances of disbelief. Finally, a representative from the northernmost region directed his words toward Lutz. "But it has just started."

Lutz entered the room, but instead of taking a seat at the table, he slowly circled it as he spoke.

"At the appointed time, Kathryn will be essential to our plan by ordering her military commander to begin the attack. When war breaks out—and it will—it will be like an unpredictable wildfire that could take any path."

One of the members spoke up. "In other words, global chaos."

"Yes. Then we will attack, so to speak. We will pick the time when the market is most vulnerable. Do you remember what I said about letting the economic bubble build? Hmm? Anyone?"

A man from South Africa answered. "You said that if we let the bubble build, it would burst beautifully."

Lutz smiled. "Well, at least someone was listening. The hour is fast approaching when I will instruct you to sell your equity positions. If you really want to clean up, you can also instruct your brokers to short the stock market and go long on gold, oil, commodities, and volatility.

"And, by all means, dump your cryptocurrency. Our agents at every global central bank have confirmed that gold has been amassed as collateral for the global debt. Crypto is way too pesky to threaten our lock on this stock of gold. Now that major financial institutions, governments, and business leaders have invested in it, this is the time to pull the rug out from under them and show them that it was only a ruse."

A woman from central Asia raised her hand. "But what about Kathryn? Why must she die?"

Lutz jerked his head back in disbelief. "Why? Because her death will prove more useful than her life."

"How so?"

"It has to do with the manner in which she dies. Our assassin will make it appear to be a case of espionage. The big question will be, by what nation?" He stopped and turned around to look at each member before continuing. "This will draw all the significant world forces into the battle so that none can remain neutral.

"The global debt has mounted, and each nation must protect its interests. The borrower has, indeed, become the servant to the lender. We'll let them wear themselves out. Then, when they are desperate for a peaceful resolution, we will dictate the terms and build an enduring hegemony that can never be displaced. Are there any questions?"

No one spoke, as Lutz had expected. His words would take time to digest. But he would interpret the absence of any objection as unanimous consent.

"Very well then." He smiled as he gave one of the members a friendly slap on the back. "Let the games begin."

CHAPTER TWENTY-SIX

In the weeks following his and Selby's weekend trip to the mountains, Bo recognized the importance of Selby's consult with Dr. McGill. In response to her concerns, Dr. McGill had prescribed several additional supplements and recommended allowing a few weeks for them to work before considering any further tests. The results were encouraging; Selby's energy levels saw a significant boost throughout the summer months. Bo could tell things were returning to normal when she began hinting at another weekend excursion, this time to see the fall foliage. So, in October, they once again packed the car and headed for the North Carolina mountains.

"Are you sure you feel well enough to drive?" Bo asked as he shut the trunk.

Selby smiled. "Even if I didn't, I'd rather drive than ride in the passenger's seat while you take phone calls. I've got a better chance of surviving anemia than your driving! Now give me the key!"

Bo grinned as he tossed the fob over to Selby, who ducked instinctively.

She giggled as she leaned over to pick it up. "You know I can't catch!"

As she stood back up, she immediately steadied herself by leaning on the car. "Whoa. I just got a little dizzy," she said as she pressed her fingertips to her forehead.

Bo's eyes narrowed as he stepped over and put his hand on her shoulder. "Are you okay?"

Selby nodded. "I'm fine. I probably just stood up too fast. Next time, how about just *handing* me the keys?"

Bo chuckled. "Deal. But are you sure you're okay to drive?"

"Positive. Now let's hit the road."

Frequent stops punctuated their drive into the highlands as Selby kept insisting on getting out of the car and taking pictures of the leaves. Bo had to admit that the colors appeared more vibrant than in prior years, which was evidently due to either less rain or more rain. He had heard both as plausible explanations.

Between his chitchat with Selby and conversations with long-winded clients along the way, Bo was "talked out" by the time he and Selby slipped under the covers at the Airbnb they had rented. The day had been full, as was his stomach after a hearty dinner of a locally prepared barbeque brisket complete with all the fixings. The quiet and calm of the mountains provided the perfect backdrop for a much-needed night's rest.

Bo had just drifted off to sleep when he heard Selby exclaim that there was an alligator loose in the area. He then found himself in a house where the owners had converted the garage into a den. As he stood by the steps leading from the den up to a door that gave access to the rest of the house, he saw an alligator partly hidden in the floor. When the alligator saw Bo, it angrily rose out of the floor holding a large lizard in its jaws. The alligator then retreated and didn't appear to be an imminent threat.

Next, Bo saw three dogs playing in the same room. One resembled a dog that Bo, Selby, and their two daughters had had for many years. He was cute and compact, with black markings. He seemed to recognize Bo. The other two dogs looked like siblings. They were larger than the black dog, with handsome, well-groomed white coats. Bo didn't recognize these dogs and, evidently, they didn't recognize him as they didn't respond to him like the black one did. Besides looking different, they also didn't seem to have the same lively personality or vivacity as Bo's dog.

The three dogs innocently romped but soon wandered too close to the alligator's location, and the alligator attacked. Bo realized it was his job to help the dogs, even if it meant putting himself in harm's way. Somehow, he rescued them without injury to himself or the dogs.

Then Bo saw three children playing outside. He recognized the blonde-haired one as his daughter Amelia when she was a child. The other two, possibly twins, were older and taller, with dark hair. Like the two white dogs, Bo didn't know the identity of the other two girls. They didn't appear to know who he was either, as they didn't respond to him in the same way his daughter did.

Suddenly, the alligator emerged from its hiding place and lunged at the girls. To help them, Bo had to respond quickly and, once again, put his own life at risk. After he had rescued them, he moved them inside to the den where he had a workstation. While they played, he tried to complete his routine client calls but became frustrated when, for some reason, no one could hear him.

Despite not being able to get any work done, Bo assessed that, for the moment, everything else was okay. But, because of the alligator attack, he called the girls over to his workstation and admonished them to listen to him regarding their safety. Amelia seemed to heed his words. Still, the other girls rolled their eyes, appeared distracted, and otherwise did not take Bo seriously.

Then, once again, the alligator appeared out of nowhere and moved swiftly and aggressively in pursuit of Bo and the three children. This assault was even more vicious and life-threatening than the prior ones.

Bo hurried to get them out of the room. With this intensified assault, the two girls agreed to listen to Bo, and he helped them escape the alligator's reach. They ran out of the den and through the door that led to the rest of the house. When all three children were in the house, Bo slammed the door shut. The alligator was now on the other side of the locked door, and everyone—including Bo—was safe.

Once inside, he could faintly hear Selby calling him from somewhere inside the house. He followed the sound down the hallway. When he stepped into the bedroom, her voice sounded louder, and he could hear her words more distinctly. "Bo? Can you hear me?"

"Bo? Wake up! You're having a nightmare."

Bo sat up in bed. He looked around and realized he was in the Airbnb with Selby. It took a few seconds for the cobwebs to clear. He rubbed his eyes and picked up his glasses from the nightstand.

"You wouldn't believe the dream I just had." He sat up and draped his legs over the side of the bed. "I really need to share this with you. Since we're both awake—"

Selby interrupted. "Hold that thought. I'll make us each a cup of tea, and we can talk about it."

She got out of bed and slipped on a bathrobe she had laid across the foot of the bed. As she tied the belt, she looked over at him. "Well, I don't know what the dream was about, but you acted—and sounded—like you were wrestling an alligator."

Bo's eyes grew wide. "That's *exactly* what I was doing."

CHAPTER TWENTY-SEVEN

The ticking of the wall clock in the kitchen filled the silence as Bo watched Selby process the details of the dream he'd just shared. As they sat on barstools at the counter, Bo anxiously awaited her feedback. He sensed that the dream wasn't just the by-product of a long day or a late dinner. It meant something.

After Selby dipped her tea bag into the water for what he considered to be an unnecessary number of times, he put his hand on hers and said, "Please say something!"

"Even though the tea is decaf, I'm pretending that it has caffeine. Give me just a minute to collect my thoughts. After all, it is"—she craned her neck to look over at the clock—"two fifteen in the morning."

"Fair enough," Bo sighed.

After taking a sip, Selby turned in her seat to face him. When she did, Bo noticed that the circles under her eyes looked darker and more deep-set. Then again, he had awakened her in the middle of the night, and she was sitting underneath a pair of ceiling fluorescent bulbs. For now, he would chalk it up to a lack of sleep and harsh lighting.

"I think the dream has to do with the stock market and the work you do. I wouldn't be surprised if you find the interpretation in those charts you study all the time. It reminds me of another dream you had a few years ago. I think it was about a bear. Do you remember?"

Bo nodded. "I do remember. It was 2018. I dreamed I was riding a bicycle through a local neighborhood when, out of nowhere, a tall white bear ran out and charged at me."

"That's right. I remember now because it was unusual for a polar bear to be in North Carolina!"

"Exactly. But the bear was gaunt and menacing, not like your typical polar bear. It attacked and destroyed the bicycle, but I escaped unharmed."

"Remind me of what happened in the market after that."

Bo set his cup down after having taken a few sips. "Well, weeks later, the Federal Reserve announced a plan to tighten monetary policy. The 2018 market began with declines. When this happens—and the market stays at a higher level through September—it can set the stage for a volatile fourth quarter. With minimal unrealized carried gains to hold them back, institutions and programmed trading triggered selling. As a result, the fourth quarter saw a sharp decline. It was the worst Christmas Eve shortened market day I had seen in a long time. Indeed, a *small bear market* had occurred."

"In other words, that dream was inspired. Is it so far-fetched to think that God gave you that dream—and possibly the one tonight—to direct you with the market?"

"It's not far-fetched. However, I spend hours each week conducting investment market research. Perhaps I've lingered a little too long over the charting programs that I use, and those images are recast in my mind while my thoughts turn over at night."

"Maybe it's both."

"What do you mean?"

"What if God takes you doing *your* part with market research and charting, and weaves it together with His part—the part that only *He* can do—and the result is dreams that help you to better serve your clients?"

Selby leaned forward and folded her hands on the countertop. "A mistake we make as Christians is to compartmentalize God. We know He cares about our souls and our eternal salvation. But He also cares about our everyday lives." She smiled. "It wouldn't be the first time He's given someone a dream. There are numerous examples in scripture. Maybe we wrongly think He doesn't do it anymore. Or, that He wouldn't do it for *us*."

"I agree . . . and I'm glad you understand." He leaned over and kissed her on the cheek. He stood, picked up his cup, and walked over to rinse it out in the kitchen sink. With his back turned, he said, "I'm going to stay up a few more minutes so I can put the details of this alligator dream into a Word document. Then I'll come to bed."

He heard Selby's barstool scrape across the floor and then felt her arms wrap around his waist. She rested her head on his back. Her body heat was comforting.

"I'm proud of you, Bo Parrott. Don't you ever forget that."

Bo turned around and embraced her. Was it his imagination, or did she feel like she'd lost weight? He held her even more tightly and then kissed her on the top of her head. "You get some sleep."

"I'll try," she said, looking over her shoulder at him as she made her way back to the bedroom, "if you'll try to avoid any more wildlife wrestling matches, at least for tonight."

Bo laughed. "I'll give it my best."

CHAPTER TWENTY-EIGHT

Bo's dream stayed at the forefront of his mind for the better part of the night, making it nearly impossible for him to get back to sleep. If the dream was, indeed, predicting a significant shift in the market, this change could occur swiftly. It would be Bo's job to stay ahead of it. He was anxious to get started on his research but planned to wait until he and Selby had returned home. He didn't want his work to interrupt their short getaway any more than it already had.

That plan, as well as his and Selby's tour of a nearby vineyard, got derailed that Saturday morning by heavy showers that refused to subside. Even though Selby was the one who had arranged the outing, she didn't appear all that upset when it was canceled. She reminded Bo that she liked nothing better than a cold, rainy day where she could sit on the couch and devour a novel. With a fire crackling in the fireplace and the colorful autumn scenery visible from the row of windows lining one side of the den in the Airbnb, she assured him that she was content to stay inside. Better yet, she gave him permission to do his market research or, as she put it, "go alligator hunting."

Bo decided to conduct that research at the kitchen counter. There was an electrical outlet nearby and, after trying several locations in the house, the internet signal appeared to be the strongest there. After settling onto one of the barstools, he performed a Google search on alligators. Along with other interesting facts, he learned they were more savage than he'd realized. They will eat each other.

"Hmm," Bo said quietly as he scrolled through the online article. It reminded him of how competitors in the same arena will stoop to similar animalistic instincts. Jacob Wiley came to mind. Still looking at his computer screen, he called out, "Selby, did you know that alligators—"

"No, and I don't want to know," Selby said, her voice sounding from the adjoining den where Bo detected the faint rustle of pages turning in a book. Evidently, she did not want to be disturbed.

"Fine, I'll just go on this safari solo," Bo mumbled as he typed in a few commands that populated his computer screen with stock market charts.

He clicked from screen to screen to review his latest findings. He stopped at one technical analysis where the charts displayed the price line of the stock market tracking upward in a diagonal pattern. The chart below the price line measured internal strength or weakness, a stochastic relative strength indicator.

"Wait a minute," Bo said as he looked more closely. He could see where the latter had been dipping for months in a downward diagonal while the price chart had been extending upward. Together, the two resembled an alligator jaw that was open wide, indicating that a significant market correction was imminent.

Bo's own jaw dropped. "You've got to be kidding me!"

Bo always made it a point to be a rational person. But there are moments of inspiration that transcend logic and reason. This was one of them.

"Selby, you've got to come see this!"

He could hear Selby sigh as she set her book on the coffee table. "I don't want to see scary pictures of alligators."

"I can't make any promises," Bo said, staring in disbelief at the chart.

"Okay, what do you need to show me? I need to start lunch anyway. And as much as I'd rather not look at pictures of an animal that would like for me to be its food while I'm preparing ours, I guess I can make an exception this time."

Bo motioned toward his computer screen. Selby leaned in for a closer look. "Wow, those chart lines really do look like an alligator's mouth. I take it that's not a good sign?"

"Not at all. It could indicate a substantial market downturn."

Selby retrieved what looked like an entire produce section of garden vegetables from the refrigerator. She turned to face Bo and used a kitchen knife to point to a pile of greens that, to Bo, resembled a collection of yard clippings. "Not to change the subject, but these darker leaves, like spinach? They contain the most iron."

"Are you trying to turn me into Popeye?" Bo winked.

Selby raised an eyebrow. "No, I'm trying to turn *myself* into Popeye! Those nutrients aren't going to get into my bloodstream by themselves."

While Selby prepared a salad for their lunch, Bo continued looking for clues online, enjoying the occasional waft of sliced cucumber and onion that drifted in his direction. The ingredients smelled fresh, like they'd just been harvested. Summer was Bo's favorite season, and the aroma made him feel like he and Selby were outside on a picnic in the middle of June, not stuck inside a cabin in the middle of October. When she set it on the counter in front of him, he couldn't help but be impressed.

"That smells delicious! And it's"—he paused for a moment and then sheepishly looked up at her—"pretty? Can you say that salad is pretty? It's just the way you have everything arranged."

Selby pursed her lips as if trying to stifle a laugh. "Sweetheart, in the culinary world, I think they call it *presentation*."

Bo grinned. "Maybe *pretty* wasn't the right word."

"It is . . . if you're talking about the chef!" Selby gave him a quick kiss on the cheek and then sat beside him at the counter. After dousing her own salad with dressing, she passed the bottle over to Bo.

"But what about the dream itself? What do you think those specific alligator attacks could mean?"

"That's what literally kept me tossing and turning last night. Now that I know what the alligator represented, I think I understand what the rest of it might imply. Do you want to hear my interpretation?"

"Of course I want to hear it," Selby responded through a mouthful of salad. "Will I understand it? Probably not. But I'd still like to hear it!"

Bo turned in his seat to face her. "Okay, scene one: The alligator came out of hiding and then retreated as if it had decided to wait for a better moment to strike. Scene two could represent the early stage of that strike, or a market decline, where the alligator targeted smaller prey."

Selby wiped her mouth with her napkin. "The dogs would be the smaller prey?"

"Correct. Scene three could indicate an even more destructive phase as the alligator pursued a larger target: the children."

Bo picked up the dressing bottle and shook a small amount on his salad. "The next part of the dream was where I couldn't get any work done. Even though I had been able to reach several people by phone, I couldn't get them to hear me. In real life, it can be challenging to convince clients of the need to implement defensive allocations to preserve their accounts when a market downturn is on the horizon. I think this could be related to the children's reluctance to follow my safety instructions.

"Scene four could indicate a bear market, allegorical of an all-out attack on even larger prey—the adults *and* the children—intent on inflicting maximum destruction."

"Believe it or not, I understood all of that," Selby said. "But you left out the part about the dead lizard."

"I'm getting to it. I've been thinking about how only the dead lizard ultimately succumbed to the alligator's attack. Perhaps that's symbolic of weaker market participants who don't understand current investment circumstances. A declining market can paralyze them."

Selby wiped her mouth with her napkin and then said, "I'm just curious, why didn't the alligator *eat* the lizard? I thought that cats were the ones that played with their prey."

"Good question. The alligator could have been savoring it to eat it over time. That would allow the kill to be tenderized and softened for better digestion. It's amazing what you can learn from a Google search!"

Selby's salad bowl made a scraping sound as she pushed it away from her. "I think I just lost my appetite."

Bo crinkled his nose. "They also eat each other."

Selby recoiled. "That's so gross! Now *I'm* going to be having nightmares tonight."

Bo chuckled and raised his hands as if surrendering. "Okay, enough alligator trivia!"

Selby pointed at him and sternly said, "You could have left that part out. But I am curious: What does *time-released alligator digestion* have to do with the stock market?"

"I'm glad you asked. The stock market is similar, with measured losses and destruction of value. For the traditional investor, that occurs in segments, much like the first alligator attacks. It sets the system up for a more significant decline. It's as if the overextension of the stock market to the *upside* only creates a more substantial profit for market forces to take advantage of unsuspecting traditional investors on the *downside*."

"Remind me what market forces are," Selby said as she reached for a cucumber slice from her salad and popped it in her mouth.

"They are the people who make things happen in the market—by shorting it, for example. This is where conspiracy theories can be, well, more than just theories. It wouldn't be difficult to imagine a nefarious component of the global economic culture implementing a dynamic that went beyond typical or natural occurrences in the investment market cycle."

Bo picked up a pepper mill from the counter and crunched out a generous amount over his salad. "It's similar to how rumors swirled around the stock market crash of October 1929 and the Great Depression that followed."

"So, market forces are the movers and shakers that aren't just your rank-and-file investors."

"That's right," Bo said as he picked up his knife and fork and began slicing through a large section of lettuce in his salad bowl.

"All of this is really interesting, but here is the million-dollar question, Mr. Stockbroker." Selby leaned back in her seat and folded her arms. "What does it mean for your clients and your staff?"

Bo's countenance fell, and he slowly placed his fork and knife back on each side of his bowl. Selby's question had packed more of a punch than she realized.

"For my clients? It means they will have to trust me when I tell them that, in the middle of an upswing where they are making money, they need to pull out of the market. For my staff? It means I've got to ready them to tackle a huge client outreach project." He paused. "For me? It means spending more time at the office and less with you."

Selby put her hand on his shoulder. "We accepted a long time ago that your work is not just a career; it's a calling. You spending more time at the office certainly isn't anything new! Look on the bright side: Everyone in the dream who was targeted in the attack—sans one unfortunate lizard—made it out alive."

Bo took a deep breath. "Believe it or not, that's what's worrying me."

Selby jerked her head back. "I don't understand."

"Again, it's just a dream and may not mean anything, but you were the one who warned me about an alligator on the loose. But you're not in the dream after that." Bo swallowed hard. "Selby, I know you're not well."

"I'm fine, it's just that the vitamin supplements—"

"What are you not telling me?" Bo persisted. "You don't have to protect me."

Selby squared her shoulders. "Yes, I do. *Somebody* has to. Bo, you work tirelessly managing your clients' money. You basically serve as a human shield to protect them from the brutality of the stock market. But who protects you? Who filters what comes into *your* life?"

Bo shook his head and tenderly tucked a strand of Selby's hair behind her ear. "There are times when we shouldn't be protected. I didn't want to have that dream about the alligator, but I needed to know it was out there. I found the alligator symbolism in the stock market and, yes, a downturn could cause my clients' accounts to lose value." Bo's voice shook. "But, second only to my faith, you are what I value more than anything in this world. If there's another alligator, so to speak, and it's assaulting your health, I need to know."

Selby paused for a moment as her gaze fell to the floor. Bo could tell that she was collecting her thoughts, trying to find the best way to say whatever it was she needed to say. She then cleared her throat, looked at him, and said, "In my defense, I just found out about this particular"—she used her fingers to form quotation marks—"*alligator.* It's attacking my red blood cells." She took a deep breath. "I don't just have a low hemoglobin count. I have leukemia."

Bo could feel the room spinning. *This can't be happening!*

"I didn't want to tell you until after we returned home tomorrow. This weekend was supposed to be a time for you to relax and not worry about anything. But, before you panic," Selby said as she took his hands into hers, "it's treatable. I'll fill you in on all the details, but there's no imminent crisis . . . or market crash, so to speak. Okay?"

Bo didn't know what to say at this point. Just hearing the word *leukemia* was a punch to the gut, and he felt guilty that Selby thought she had to protect him from it. Sadness prevailed in a way he couldn't even address right now. Not knowing what else to do, he pulled Selby into a hug. And he cried.

After a few moments, he wiped his face on his sleeve and motioned toward the fireplace. "How about I get that stoked while you pour us a glass of wine? We can sit in the den and talk." His laptop made a clicking noise as he closed it. "I think we need to put some space between us and all the scary alligator images."

Selby smiled reassuringly as she cupped Bo's face in her hands. "You do know that not all alligators win in the end, right? We have the ability to put them under our feet. Come to think of it, we put them *on* our feet!"

Like a pressure-release valve, a laugh escaped Bo's mouth as he said, "They become belts and handbags, too!"

Before he knew it, Bo and Selby had tears streaming down their cheeks, this time from laughing uncontrollably. Selby reached for a napkin from the counter to wipe her eyes and then looked intently at Bo. "We're going to make it through this next season."

Bo nodded and smiled. He knew they would.

They had to.

CHAPTER TWENTY-NINE

As Bo packed the car that Sunday morning in preparation for his and Selby's drive back home, he noticed that a dusting of snow had fallen overnight. It reminded him of how winter tended to arrive earlier in the higher elevations. He couldn't wait to show Selby. It was the one thing she disliked about living in Eastern North Carolina: The area rarely, if ever, saw any significant winter precipitation.

Bo's conversation with her the afternoon before had been difficult, but he felt better now that everything about her condition was out in the open. Afterward, the rain that had kept them inside subsided, and they found a cozy restaurant where they enjoyed a candlelit dinner. They had wanted to squeeze in as much of a normal evening as possible, but the events of the day had taken their toll. They called it a night shortly after arriving back at the Airbnb.

Even though Bo's body had been tired, his brain wouldn't shut down. His thoughts bounced back and forth between considering the next steps for Selby's treatments and those he would need to take with his advisory team regarding what he saw coming in the market. Neither could be avoided or delayed. On every front, it appeared that, like it or not, winter was approaching.

Unlike Selby, Bo wasn't a fan of snow, cold temperatures, short days, or winter in general. Yet he knew that winter was both inevitable and necessary. Nothing in nature bloomed or produced fruit indefinitely; a time of rest was required. To assume that investors could continue to make money in the market without a downturn wasn't just unreasonable, it was a mathematical impossibility. But try telling that to investors who are making money. Unfortunately, that was the task Bo had ahead of him.

***

The following morning, Bo arrived at work early to finalize his presentation for his advisory team. He set up his laptop in the conference room and composed an email notifying them of the meeting time. Those who couldn't attend in person would need to join online.

Spencer was the first one to show up for the meeting. After setting a travel mug of coffee on the conference room table, he unzipped a blue book bag bearing the company emblem and slid his laptop out. He looked over at Bo as he clicked the prompts to boot it. "How was your mountain vacation?"

Not looking up from his laptop screen, Bo replied, "It's not a vacation if it's only for the weekend, and you spend a chunk of your time driving."

"True." Spencer took a sip of his coffee and then paused. "Bo, you look tired. Is everything okay?"

Bo forced a smile. "No, but it will be. Eventually."

Bo sensed that Spencer wanted to probe further, but several other team members had begun arriving and taking their places. After they each had found a seat, Bo took a deep breath and said a silent prayer. He leaned forward and folded his hands on the table.

"I called this meeting to share with you a trend I see coming in the market. I've been looking for a downturn—the beginning of a bear market—since 2018. Some of you may recall that I had a dream in 2018 about a bear attacking a bicycle, which I interpreted as an indication of an imminent bear market. My charting and research had supported as much.

"While a bear market did occur, it was less severe than I had anticipated; it turned out to be a relatively mild downturn, or a small bear market. The Federal Reserve employed monetary intervention, better known as quantitative easing, to ward it off. However, this flow of money in the system has only served to mask how the investment markets and global economy should look at this point. It could be said that we've averted a possible collapse or economic depression. My concern is that we've only delayed the inevitable."

Bo stopped and looked around the room at each team member. He knew the weight his words carried, and he took no pleasure in saying them.

"I'm convinced that we are entering a winter season of financial history. It may have started during the Great Financial Crisis of 2008 when central banks around the world created massive liquidity to avoid the difficulties experienced following the stock market crash of 1929. Back then, those same institutions employed monetary *tightening* measures that halted the flow of money, and interest rates rose. This only served to worsen an already dire situation.

"So, the US Treasury Department implemented stimulative measures following the 2008 market disruptions to keep the global financial systems from failing. But herein lies the problem: *We borrowed* the money for the stimulus. The bill is enormous and only getting bigger.

"I believe that, just as with the seasons of nature, winter follows autumn in economic terms. Trying to simulate springtime characteristics during a winter season simply will not work. Winter must come, and delaying its arrival could prove dangerous. The Santa Claus rally is right on time to begin at Christmas this year. It concludes promptly at the end of the first week of January. After that, we could be looking at the beginning of a bear market."

Bo paused for a moment to read the room. A few team members were taking notes on their laptops. Others just stared ahead with blank expressions. Spencer raised his hand. "You've been concerned about this for a while. For the most part, we've been getting clients out of the market. Have you seen something different in your research that has heightened your concern?"

"It's more like something I *didn't* see—until this past weekend, that is. I had a dream Friday night about a series of alligator attacks, each getting worse with every attempt. Yet, in the end, no one was hurt. When I began researching to see if I could give the dream credence—or just chalk it up to a late dinner—I ran across a chart where the patterns literally looked like an alligator with its mouth open.

"Then, when Selby and I were driving back home yesterday, I remembered a theory I learned in one of my college economics classes. It's called the Elliott Wave Theory, and it's where a five-wave pattern movement can occur in the market. It ties it all together. I'll show you how it works."

Bo rolled his chair to one side as he stood and took a dry eraser from the whiteboard behind him. After wiping the board clean of prior math equations and notations, he picked up a black marker. It squeaked against the board as he began illustrating.

"It looks like a lightning bolt. If the move is upward, the first leg extends from the lower left corner to the upper right corner. Then, a movement occurs toward the lower right corner, but that movement is often not as large as the first one. Then the largest move, the third wave, moves upward from left to right."

He pivoted to face the conference room table. "Is everyone with me so far?" Most of the attendees nodded, and a few said yes.

Turning back toward the whiteboard, he continued drawing. "The fourth wave follows with a downward shift of direction. Finally, the fifth and final wave finishes moving from left to right. When that ends, the trend is over."

Once again, he looked toward his team members. "I've seen this market pattern numerous times in the last four decades. However, this time—" Without turning around, he stretched out his arm and drew a line downward and said, "I see where an extended downward move is developing."

Focusing back on the board, Bo continued, "Strangely, as I applied the Elliott Wave overlay to my charting, each leg of the market movement seems to mirror the alligator dream I had." He used the marker to point to different places on the board as he spoke. "The first scene involves danger with a group of dogs rescued from the alligator attack. Then, there is a reprieve, followed by an upward retracement move of the major indexes. Next, a new downside interlude arises, accompanied by even greater risk. Finally, a moment of calm ensues as indexes again rally upward for a partial retracement.

"In this narrative, despite the alligator's aggressive attempt to inflict maximum damage, the crisis is narrowly averted. This could correspond with the fifth wave down in the Elliott Wave pattern and a lower Fibonacci retracement of 23.6 percent, 38.2 percent, 61.8 percent, and 78.6 percent. Ultimately, this could lead to a blow-off bottom as the markets trend lower to exhaust the downward momentum."

The marker made a clicking sound as Bo returned it to the metal shelf beneath the whiteboard. His brow furrowed as he said, "Meanwhile, each of these progressions foreshadows the mounting decline of the stock market and a substantial risk to investors."

Bo took his seat once again at the head of the table. The worst was over, for now anyway. He had delivered the news. It reminded him of when Selby told him about her leukemia diagnosis and when he learned of Edmond Brockett's death. He couldn't control those any more than he could control the direction of the stock market. But going forward, he could assist with the remedy or, at the very least, maximize damage control.

"So, what's next?" The question came from Martin Beargrass, who was attending the meeting virtually.

Bo glanced down at his computer screen before addressing the room. "Good question. We'll need to intensify our systematic client outreach program immediately. Let me be clear that this action is needed not because I had a dream, but because this dream confirmed my research."

Again, Martin spoke. "Your dreams have proven true before, Bo. And if it's God giving them to you, we'll take it. We need all the help we can get!"

Everyone in the room laughed, including Bo. He felt thankful for Martin's well-timed humor that helped ease the tension in the room. Bad news had a way of sapping people's strength, and Bo needed his team members to be strong and energized to complete the next leg of the project, one that would require them to work long hours and deal with a gamut of client personalities and responses.

"In anticipation of times like this, we have segmented the client base. You each have assigned client contacts. As soon as this meeting is over, you'll need to begin contacting those clients and discussing allocation changes to their investment portfolios.

"With a project of this magnitude, we will need additional hands on deck. That's why I've decided to hire someone to help, at least for the short term. The new addition to our team is Emily Dodson, a young lady who attended the Carolina Economic Forum. She possesses impressive credentials, extensive experience, and, most importantly, proven character. Long story short, she was fired by Jacob Wiley because she dared to display a strong work ethic and a moral compass. I believe she will be a timely and positive addition to our team. It took a few months to settle her contract terms with her former firm and establish a work agreement here.

"Moving forward, if we're right about the market—and I believe we are—our clients will view us as heroes and tell their friends and peers about our timely intervention. We may even get a few new referrals."

Without raising his hand, Spencer shuffled in his seat and asked, "What if we're wrong?"

The room grew uncomfortably quiet. Bo paused and looked at his young protégé. If he had ever had doubts as to whether Spencer was the right choice for his successor, they all dissipated in that moment. Being an effective financial advisor meant being willing to question even your best judgment. It's not about *getting it right* as much as it is about *doing what's right* for your clients.

Bo gave Spencer a nod of approval and then responded to the team. "The question no one wants to ask, but most needs to be addressed. The answer? If we're wrong, our clients will miss opportunities, and their accounts will underperform. Perhaps we *are* overreacting and should let the market take its course. Less intervention certainly would be an easier approach."

Bo made sure to look each team member in the eyes. "But that is a risk I am unwilling to take. Now, let's get to work!"

CHAPTER THIRTY

Simon quietly brooded in his study, a richly decorated room that some would find enviable, while others would recoil at its lavish adornments that propagated an aura of self-importance. But mixed reviews were nothing new to Simon. He rather enjoyed observing the division he was so adept at creating, even in small matters.

His top-floor flat overlooked the heart of the City of London, a key global financial center. This morning, the fog had lifted, and the sun illuminated the skyscrapers of Canary Wharf. Simon interpreted this as a favorable sign and allowed himself to savor the moment. He'd been following world markets closely, waiting for the crescendo to build. He felt hopeful he wouldn't have to wait much longer.

At the sound of his cell phone ringing, he picked it up from his gilded desk. When he recognized the number as belonging to his hedge-fund manager, he smiled. Leaning back in his chair, he answered. "I trust you're delivering favorable news?"

"Everything is ready, and everyone is in place," the caller responded.

"Excellent! Did we get the best possible price on the index put options I identified? A lot of money can be made on a precipitously dropping market if the timing is right and the options market is priced to perfection."

"Affirmative."

Simon had thoroughly trained his broker team in the best market trading techniques. In particular, they were proficient at Japanese candlestick charting, a discipline that predated automated trading for the stock market. The centuries-old methodology tracked trading prices in various global markets, spanning commodities, precious jewelry, and fine art.

Simon knew that when the stock-charting-diagram wick formed at the top of the white candle on the computer monitor, it represented the entry point to place the trade. In other words, the market was at its zenith. Emotions were running high, and so was investor optimism. The dumb money was all in. In fact, many of those investors had borrowed two or three times the amount to lever up the trade and maximize their potential profit.

And this time, like other times in history, the profit would ultimately belong to Simon.

However, he didn't measure his profits merely in terms of dollars and cents. He also bought and sold world leaders with his allure and irresistible offers for unmitigated patronage. The price of entry for his clients was total allegiance and a strong representation of his various global interests. He was currently playing for his biggest prize yet.

What could be better than to establish enduring authority as I recreate the money systems and flush out the old political orders? he thought, feeling quite satisfied with himself. *I'll ruin anyone who stands in my way as I make a fortune . . . again.*

"Did you tip the market maker as I instructed?" Simon asked.

"Yes, sir," came the reply.

One of Simon's favorite strategies involved placing large orders where his brokers would offer to pay a premium slightly above the ask price of a security. This approach allowed them to fill all lots quickly, rather than executing one block at a time. Market makers, who manage the bid-ask spread for trades, could then fill the order at a price above the initial ask.

Market makers are individuals or firms that facilitate the trading of securities by managing the spread between the bid and ask prices. Typically, they fulfill part of a purchase order first, then increase the price for the next part of the order. By doing this repeatedly, they can sell the security at a price higher than the previous purchase price, effectively driving up the price. Simon's strategy is just one of many tactics employed by successful investors to maintain a competitive edge in the market.

Simon offered a slightly higher initial price to fill the entire order at one price . . . *his* price. He informed his brokerage team that, while "to insure prompt service" wasn't the true meaning of the word "tips," it often played out that way.

"When it's time to sell, I pay a little higher price than the bid price to, likewise, avoid the game and dictate the market. It's called the gratuity. I do the same thing at the very best restaurants, which is why I never need reservations, and I never have to wait."

"It's quite brilliant," the caller responded.

"It's actually quite simple," Simon said matter-of-factly.

After ending the call, Simon checked the time on his watch—an important appointment was just an hour away. Swiveling in his chair, he took in the sweeping view of the city from his office window. He scoffed as he thought of Lutz, who so arrogantly believed he was in control of what was about to happen next.

"Let the *real* games begin," Simon hissed as a broad, sadistic smile spread across his face.

CHAPTER THIRTY-ONE

"Have you lost your mind?" Polly Dunnigan blurted out the question over the phone. Her words were scalding, but then again, they represented what most investors would have said after having made money for such an extended period in an upward-moving market.

Not all of Bo's clients came with an A sanitation rating, and such was the case with Polly. Her full name was Polly Sullivan Dunnigan, a wealthy heiress of the infamous Sullivan Family Enterprises. Investors and friends alike took pride in scoring an audience with her. So much so that they overlooked the *source* of her family's wealth, specifically the questionable business dealings of her great-grandfather, Hector Sullivan.

Local lore had not painted a favorable picture of Polly's family history. Yet, it wasn't rumor or reputation that counted in the context of Bo managing her accounts. Instead, it was background research based on thorough due diligence. And, once again, Polly's money had earned the green light from compliance as funds in good order.

Bo had always been aware of how he and Polly hailed from different worlds. Bo had long established a reputation in the community for being honest and forthright, while Polly appeared to enjoy playing a round or two of dodgeball with the law. Nevertheless, she had proven to be a solid client and a valuable source of referrals. Bo often wondered why she had selected him as her broker. Perhaps the time-tested adage also applied to stockbrokers and their clients: Opposites attract.

Responding in a calm demeanor he'd had plenty of practice using recently, Bo replied, "Polly, I admit it looks like a departure from conventional wisdom, but that's how the market works before a downturn. Doing the right thing is going to feel, well, *wrong*. Counterintuitive at best. Why would I risk upsetting one of my best clients if I wasn't certain about this strategy?"

But Polly sounded inconsolable. "Bo, I like you, but I've run your theory by another stockbroker, Jacob Wiley. He doesn't understand why you're advocating straying from a portfolio model that was developed with such meticulous care. He assures me that, if I stay in the market, he can increase my earnings exponentially."

Of course Jacob would say that. He'd say anything to get a new client, especially one he took from me.

"I've known Jacob for a long time," Bo responded. "He will opine on the market based on beliefs and methods that mostly come through popular media." *That's the nicest way I can put it,* Bo thought. "I'm basing my recommendations on hours and hours of market research. I don't take the job of being your investment advisor lightly. I want to help you steward your money in a way that will best help you in the long term, even if it makes me unpopular in the short term."

Bo could hear Polly sigh. "I don't doubt your sincerity. I just think that, going forward, your approach may be too conservative for me. I'm a risk-taker, and, as much as I hate to do it, I'm going to move all my accounts to Jacob's firm."

He could feel his stomach twist, but he kept his composure. "I'm sorry to hear that, Polly. I consider you a friend, and even if you do move your account, that won't change. I wish you the best."

Her tone softened. "It's nothing personal. I appreciate all that you've done for me. I just think it's time for a change."

Bo knew it would be a waste of his time to try to change Polly's mind. The best thing he could do was not to burn any bridges and maintain a favorable standing with her.

"You have every right to do that. Just know that if you ever need to talk, you know how to reach me."

Polly giggled. "Well, you know I have to keep you up on all the family gossip!"

Bo felt a twinge of sadness. It was one thing to forfeit a client, and to Jacob Wiley, no less. It was another to lose a friendship. He hoped that Polly would stay in touch with him. He let out a heavy sigh as the conversation ended. He was so distracted that he didn't hear Spencer step into his office.

"Do you have a minute?" Spencer asked.

"Of course," Bo responded.

"If you don't mind my saying so, you look like you just lost your best friend."

Bo raised his eyebrows. "How about my best client? Or, at least, *one* of them." He picked up the piece of paper he had used to jot down a few notes while he and Polly talked. He crumpled it up and tossed it in the wastebasket beside his desk. "Polly Dunnigan is moving her accounts . . . to Jacob Wiley's firm."

Spencer's eyes grew wide. "I bet you didn't see that one coming."

"No, but I should have," Bo responded as he put his hands over his face.

Spencer added, "I know it sounds cliché, but you can't win them all."

Bo slapped his hands down on his desk. "You're right. Jacob may have won this battle, but we will win the war."

Bo leaned back in his chair and looked off into the distance as he remembered a comment Polly had just made. He said, more to himself than to his young protégé, "Even if we don't, and we lose more clients than we keep, we still have something that can't be taken from us."

He looked over at Spencer and smiled. As he inched toward eventual retirement, Bo wanted to ensure that Spencer, one of his intended key successors, was on firm footing, not only with his knowledge of the industry, but also with his ethics.

"We not only make it a point to do things right; we make it a point to do the right thing."

Spencer nodded. "I'd say that's a win in and of itself."

"I agree. So, what did you need to see me about?"

"There was a client on my call list that should have been on yours, since he's a close friend of yours. Casey Balan, the journalist guy you have lunch with once a month."

"Good ol' Casey. How did he respond to our recommendation of coming out of the market? He and I don't always see eye to eye on such matters."

Spencer laughed. "Yes, he said as much. Believe it or not, he *agreed* with your recommendation. In fact, he wanted to write an editorial in the local newspaper touting your insightful, not to mention timely, approach to what's coming in the stock market."

Bo groaned and shook his head. "That's the last thing I need!"

"He said you'd say that. So, he took the liberty of landing you a spot on a local radio talk show. That way, as he put it, it would be your words and not his. Even though he quipped that he was much better with words than you. You know, being a writer and all."

Bo laughed. "That's classic Casey!" He couldn't help but think that if Casey himself had asked him, he would have found a perfectly valid excuse to decline—most likely citing his busy schedule. "He really one-upped me on this one! Did he say which radio show?"

"The Financial Roundup with Dallas Tyler. Have you heard of it?"

"Oh, yes. Dallas is a former competitor. When he retired a few years ago, he started a radio show where listeners call in and ask questions, such as how to get out of debt, that sort of thing. I guess it keeps him sharp on financial matters without the responsibility of running a practice. More than likely, it also serves to feed his ego a bit. He always liked to hear himself talk."

"Then it sounds like the perfect retirement gig for him. The guest he had scheduled for the interview canceled at the last minute. The guest was Casey's duplicate bridge partner, which is how Casey found out about the opening. He then contacted Dallas and told him you'd fill in. But here's the kicker: He's interviewing you at eight this evening. That gives you about five hours to prepare."

Bo's jaw dropped. "You've got to be kidding me. TONIGHT?"

Spencer shrugged his shoulders. "What was I supposed to say? It's not like you need to go home and change your clothes. It's *radio*; nobody is going to see you. You just have to sound articulate and answer a few questions. The interview itself lasts only twenty minutes."

"Good enough," Bo said with a sigh. "Depending on how the interview goes, I'll reach out to Casey tomorrow to thank him . . . or let him know that he's paying for lunch the next time we get together!"

After Spencer left the office, Bo considered what had transpired that day, specifically Polly's reaction to the reallocation recommendations, and then Casey's. Polly always liked to dance a little too close to the fire for Bo's liking, but she trusted Bo's approach to financial management. When push came to shove, she opted to take her accounts elsewhere. Casey, on the other hand, had always been quick to point out his and Bo's differences. Yet, he ultimately demonstrated loyalty and support when Bo needed it most. Perhaps people and their personalities couldn't be reduced to a single adage. Maybe we're all more complicated—and less predictable— than that.

"I guess it's what makes us human," Bo concluded, as he clicked his phone setting to Do Not Disturb and began preparing material for Dallas's radio show.

CHAPTER THIRTY-TWO

"Good evening, folks, and welcome to the Financial Roundup, with your host, yours truly, Dallas Tyler. As you know, I feature a local investment advisor once a month to offer their perspective on current events. This month's guest is Bo Parrott, a partner with the Crawford Webb and Parrott investment firm. He also teaches a course in financial history at the college. Most importantly, he is a hometown Wilson boy. Welcome, Bo."

Bo started to speak but stopped to clear his throat. He wasn't expecting to feel nervous, but he could feel his palms sweating. "Thank you for having me on your program."

Bo sat at a small wooden table across from Dallas, where a sound technician had tested his microphone moments earlier. A digital clock on the wall ticked down the remaining minutes of the interview. Bo took note that, aside from putting on a few pounds, Dallas looked like he was doing well. Even though he was approaching his late sixties, he still had a headful of salt-and-pepper hair. The bright blue eyes that stood out behind his wire-rimmed glasses didn't appear puffy and strained as they once had. Overall, Bo concluded that retirement agreed with him.

"So, Bo, let's talk about the economy. Do you believe we are heading into a recession?" Dallas's eyes narrowed as if he were anxious to hear Bo's response.

"Last autumn, I began using the word *recession* to describe the state of the economy. Since it carries negative connotations, I'm careful only to use it in the context of how clients prepare for an economic slowdown from an investment standpoint. When it comes to investment advisory work, the word becomes a discussion point when clients are considering debt management and credit exposure."

Dallas nodded and pouted his lips as if he was processing what Bo had just said. He appeared satisfied with that answer. In fact, Bo might go so far as to say that he seemed impressed.

"Now, what about a depression? Do you think that could happen again in our lifetime?"

Bo chuckled. "It may not win me any friends, but, yes, I do."

"Why do you say that?" Dallas asked as he took a sip from a coffee mug he had sitting nearby.

"Well, you know from your career as a financial advisor that no one wants to hear that difficult times could be ahead. But with such overextension of debt at the national level, and an unprecedented amount of liquidity artificially injected into the financial system, I can't help but think that an economic depression is at least possible, if not probable. Global economies are also similarly strained. Ultimately, this all translates to a contraction of the money supply."

"How do you think that would be imposed? And by whom?"

At this point, Bo felt like Dallas wasn't conducting an interview as much as he was seeking answers for himself. The possibility also existed that he wanted to address a controversial topic to boost ratings. Maybe it was both.

"Some of that would be imposed on the economy through a monetary policy shift at the behest of the Federal Reserve. Some of it would be the work of the US Treasury, implementing fiscal measures to try to rein things in. The time cycle has been set up for it since the last economic trough."

Dallas's chair creaked as he adjusted his posture. "Are you saying you think that we are headed for something more serious than a recession, like an actual depression?"

Bo knew to stick with the facts and not merely give his opinion. Making his guests look inept was another way Dallas could boost those ratings.

"Well, let's look at recent history," Bo said matter-of-factly. "During the 2008 Great Financial Crisis, individual households were overextended, and businesses were highly leveraged. Yet, because of prolific loan nonperformance, it was the banks and financial institutions all around the world who were left holding the bag. Under great duress in the American economy, the *fire chiefs*, as it were, of the nation's central bank and Treasury Department, came out in full force with unprecedented measures for intervention and relief."

"So, this massive debt load of the populace shifted to the banks, right?"

"Yes, and the enormous debt load of the banks went to—"

Dallas's eyebrows knitted, and he completed Bo's sentence. "The government," he said.

Bo wondered if, for the first time, these puzzle pieces of history were falling into place for Dallas. "That's right. That heavy debt remains on the government's balance sheets, and it's causing the system to buckle under the weight. While stress fractures—so to speak—may be appearing, the overall damage is not readily apparent now."

"Can you elaborate on that?"

"Think of it like engineering. An experienced engineer can detect when a bridge is becoming stressed, damage that may not be noticeable to the untrained eye. They know what to look for and can detect compromise within the structure before the problems actually occur.

"By contrast, the agencies and government officials who are tasked with overseeing the financial system and the economy have ignored or explained away blatantly obvious signs of wear and tear. Abrasions appeared years ago, but, despite various administrations, the political machine lacked the resolve to tackle the matter. Perhaps it was due to the constant flux of leadership or the emphasis on other priorities to achieve political goals. But, at some point, the bill comes due. And debt service is a huge problem."

"All of this makes sense. But, for now, the market is doing well. Are you actually taking your clients out of a situation that's making money for them—*and* you?"

Bo displayed a half smile. Up until this point, Dallas's questions had sounded harmless enough. But this one made Bo question his intent; maybe this really was all about ratings. On the other hand, if Dallas was sincere and Bo came out swinging, it would make Bo appear to be the villain. Bo reminded himself that he had just lost one battle, and he certainly didn't want to fight—and potentially lose—another one, especially not on the air.

He decided to give Dallas the benefit of the doubt. "That's the tricky part, Dallas. I think it comes down to *why I am in the business to begin with.* If it's just to make money, other careers pay way better and with a lot less stress."

Dallas chuckled and said, "I was in the business for over twenty-five years. I couldn't agree more."

Bo had made the right call. He allowed himself to relax a little. "In some ways, it's like parenting. Our children trust us to lead them in the right way, even if they don't fully understand our judgment calls every time. Sometimes we get it wrong. But I'd rather risk my clients forfeiting a little in the short run than to risk losing, well, everything later on."

Dallas adjusted his glasses as he spoke. "Doing the right thing doesn't always make us popular. Have you lost any clients over this?"

Bo nodded. "I lost one today."

Dallas pouted his lips once more, as if he was thinking about what he was going to say next. Bo wasn't sure what to expect.

He raised an eyebrow and said, "So, one less client means you might have an opening in your schedule. Would you have time to meet with a retired advisor who might have a few more questions about his own accounts?"

Bo's heart warmed. He smiled and reached across the table to shake Dallas's hand. "I'll *make* the time."

On his way home that evening, Bo rang Casey's cell phone number. After four rings, it went to voicemail.

"Hey, Casey, it's Bo. I just wanted to thank you for arranging the interview with Dallas Tyler. Please call me back when you have a chance. Meanwhile, just know that the next time we meet for lunch, I'm picking up the tab." Bo paused and smiled. "And the time after that, if you'll let me. Talk to you soon."

A few seconds later, Bo heard his phone vibrate. "That was fast," he said out loud. "I guess when free food is involved, Casey doesn't waste any time."

Without checking the caller ID, Bo answered, "Casey, thanks for getting back with me so quickly."

"Bo," the voice on the other end said, "this is Jack Prescott. I just heard your interview on Dallas Tyler's radio show."

Bo swallowed hard. "Senator Prescott. I apologize, I thought you were someone else calling. Since I haven't heard any feedback as to how I sounded on the air, I hope you're not moving your accounts!"

"Quite the opposite," Jack continued, his tone somber. "I've made note of your timely intervention regarding the reallocation of investments in my portfolio, as well as your explanation of the rationale justifying the change. The way you just articulated what you see happening in the market was quite impressive."

Bo felt relieved. "Well, thank you. That means a lot coming from you."

"I wanted to ask if you could be available for a conference call tomorrow morning around nine Eastern Standard Time. You'll need to take the call online, no cell phones."

"Of course," Bo responded, his heart racing. "Do I need to prepare anything in advance?"

"After hearing you speak on Dallas's show tonight? No. Just prepare for the call to take a while. I'll have my assistant set that up."

"I'll clear my schedule," Bo said as he steered his car into his driveway.

After Jack ended the call, Bo paused for a moment and just stared ahead.

What was that all about?

Any conversation with the senator felt like a conversation with royalty. Bo knew it wasn't, but it sure felt that way. Jack Prescott had the power to pull political levers; he knew what it took to get the job done. But he wasn't unscrupulous. His contemporaries dubbed him one of the "white hats" in Washington, which Bo considered to be a good thing. He hated to think of all that wit and moxie misdirected toward destructive ends.

Like many of Bo's clients, the senator also fell into a category called *accredited investors,* which included single individual taxpayers earning more than $200,000 in income per year or married individuals earning more than $300,000 per year. An individual, combined with their spouse, would need to demonstrate a net worth of more than $1 million, excluding their primary residence. The senator met and even exceeded the criterion. Knowing that he—and his father before him—had earned their money through honest, hard work made Bo revere Jack Prescott even more.

As Bo was dozing off later that night, it occurred to him that those joining the call the next day would most likely hold positions of influence and power. Therefore, he planned to get up early and scour through his research notes. He wanted to have a list of changes he would recommend when the economy reached a point where drastic reform was required.

In his opinion, it already had.

CHAPTER THIRTY-THREE

Yulia and Dimitri had spent the past several months attending Bo's classes at the community college. Their goal was to learn how the American economic system functioned on a global scale and then report their findings to Lutz.

In their quest, they weren't just looking for basic information; they could have easily obtained that through an internet search. Instead, they sought to gain a more in-depth understanding of the stock market from someone who had invested years in studying it and, more importantly, had unique insight into what could happen next. Bo Parrott fit that profile perfectly and had made their time in the United States worthwhile.

Yulia felt confident that, if Lutz had had any doubts regarding Bo's qualifications, he wouldn't after he heard tonight's radio interview. When she caught the last-minute announcement from the college regarding Bo's presentation on the Dallas Tyler show, she immediately alerted him.

As Dimitri dialed Lutz's number, Yulia's heart raced. She'd recently begun to fight an internal battle, one that had her suspended between two very different worlds. The first she knew all too well; she had sworn allegiance to it years ago. The second was less familiar but had recently unleashed a powerful undertow on her emotions. All in all, it was her head and her heart that were at odds.

Yulia watched as Dimitri impatiently drummed his fingers as he waited for Lutz to answer. When he finally did, Dimitri forfeited any greeting and immediately inquired, "Were you able to access the radio broadcast?"

"Yes," Lutz responded. "We now have sufficient data as well as a clear recording of Mr. Parrott's voice that we can duplicate using artificial intelligence. I will contact Kathryn and tell her to issue the orders. Your time in America has been productive after all. When will you return to Europe?"

"Soon. Our work is finished here," Dimitri said. Then he ended the call.

From where they sat on the bed in their hotel room, Yulia turned to face him. "I want to talk to you about something, and please do not become angry."

"Of course, my love. What is it?"

She swallowed hard, aware that Dimitri would be surprised by what she was about to reveal. He would likely object and might even scold her for entertaining such an idea. Though she was nervous, there was one thing she wasn't any longer, and that was unsure. She straightened her posture and looked him in the eye. "My heart has won."

"What do you mean?"

Yulia put up her hand. "Just hear me out. When we arrived in America, I was fully committed to our assignment. My loyalty ultimately wasn't to Lutz. It was, as it always has been, to help Kathryn rise to power. And, as premier, Kathryn is often obligated to act in ways that go against how we raised her."

"We raised her to be a leader, not a saint," Dimitri said with a slight smile.

"True, but in the process, I've gone against my own conscience . . . too many times," Yulia said as she looked off into the distance. "I think my sense of right and wrong became blurred along the way. Until now."

"What are you trying to say?"

Tears slid down her cheeks as she looked intently into Dimitri's eyes. "We have lived in a world where mercy is treated as weakness and kindness is regarded as a frivolity. Yet, when I saw Bo Parrott and his wife extend compassion to that young woman after the seminar, it awakened something deep inside of me." She shook her head. "I'm not ready to go back to Europe just yet. I would like to stay in the States for longer. I need time to do some long-overdue soul searching."

Dimitri took Yulia's hand once more. "That is fine. We can extend our visas. Why did you think I would become angry? This is reasonable."

"I'm not finished," Yulia said, adjusting her posture once again. "Bo Parrott has done nothing to cause his years of study and research to be used for political gain, even if that political gain is Kathryn's." She threw her hands in the air. "The information he has provided could potentially start a war, Dimitri!"

"Yulia, calm down." Dimitri reached for Yulia's hand, but she pulled it away.

"It's wrong, and if you don't tell him what's going on, I will."

Dimitri jerked his head back in surprise. "You can't be serious. What purpose would it serve? Besides, Lutz's plan is already underway."

"It would ease my conscience, that's what purpose it would serve. I cannot continue to live like this."

Dimitri's eyes narrowed. "If Lutz finds out, you may not live at all."

"Then so be it!" Yulia said. "I am as good as dead anyway with the guilt I shoulder day in and day out. Don't you feel it, too?"

Yulia watched as Dimitri's expression grew somber, the weight of her question evident in his eyes. "There was a time when I felt so deeply. But now? I hardly feel anything at all."

"America has given me a taste of something I have never experienced before, and it would be worth any price to keep it."

Dimitri took both of her hands into his and let out a heavy sigh. "I think what you have tasted is called *freedom*."

Yulia smiled as she began sobbing. "Yes, that's exactly what it is."

Dimitri lowered his head as if collecting his thoughts. When he looked up at Yulia again, his own eyes were filled with tears. "We will talk to Bo Parrott together."

CHAPTER THIRTY-FOUR

The following morning, Bo pulled into the parking lot at work before sunrise, but only after Selby had armed him with an ample supply of freshly perked coffee. She had served it, of course, in the coffee cup she had given him years ago as a gift. Bo concluded that she was even more excited about this opportunity than he was.

Once he had arrived at his office, he began scrolling through screen after screen of research and charts, jotting down key points to reference. He had asked Spencer to take any calls that he felt like he could handle and hold the rest until Bo got off the conference call.

Before he knew it, it was nine o'clock. Right on time, he heard his computer chime, and his screen populated with over a dozen video call participants. Only a few had activated the visual function, which confirmed his earlier assumption that high-profile individuals were in attendance.

"Good morning, Bo," Jack Prescott's voice boomed. "I have informed my colleagues about your impressive interview with Dallas Tyler, as well as the expert advice you've offered me over the last several years. They are interested in hearing your ideas for addressing the shortcomings of our current financial system."

Bo could feel his breath quicken. The moment felt surreal. When he sat for the Certified Financial Planner exam years ago, he hoped his education would provide him with insight into sound financial stewardship. But that was only the first step. Achieving mastery had required years of hard work and effort, far exceeding any formal training. For the presentation at hand, he would need to draw from the findings of all those long hours of financial research. Today, more than any other, he wanted to put what he had learned into practice, hopefully for the greater good.

"Good morning, everyone," Bo said. "I'm certain you all have busy schedules, so I'll dive right in. Please interrupt me if you have questions or comments.

"My first observation is that a debt-based money system is at the root of our problems. Our currency exists when debt is created. The US Treasury borrows money, and the central bank purchases the debt—specifically, government bonds—on the open market. Typically, national banks initially buy these government bonds from the Treasury, meaning that major national banks are essentially lending money to the government."

Bo paused to allow for any comments or questions. When silence followed, he continued. "The Federal Reserve Bank, which serves as our central bank, buys the bonds from these national banks. At that point, the Federal Reserve credits the national bank for the bonds it has purchased. This process creates money that the national bank can then loan out at a ratio of 10 to 1, thereby increasing the overall money supply.

"Why can't the government issue the money without charging interest? I admit it does sound a bit radical."

Bo looked at the screen and listened to the audio to see if there was consternation on the part of the listeners. Not seeing or hearing anything, he continued. "The Constitution is mostly silent regarding money creation at the national level. Throughout our nation's history, different forms of fiat currency have existed. The first was called Colonial scrip, which predated the American Revolutionary War. It worked well based on its acceptance across the colonies.

"Colonial scrip was later replaced by the Continental dollar, which, during the war, was devalued and considered a failure. This was partly due to England's counterfeiting efforts to flood the system with money. England didn't want the colonies to succeed with a currency apart from one established within a trade system backed by gold. England had more gold stock than the colonies, so they could manipulate the gold market more easily than they could control paper currency."

Bo paused to catch his breath and take a sip of water. "In the 1800s, President Andrew Jackson issued currency from the Treasury. Under his leadership, this money was issued without interest, which helped to eliminate the national debt. This decision led to a significant conflict with the central bank. Decades later, President Abraham Lincoln successfully introduced greenbacks, a type of currency issued by the US Treasury that, like Jackson's money, did not involve debt-based interest accumulation.

"If the US Treasury Department were to issue currency today in the form of US government dollar bills, these could replace the dollar bills currently issued by the Federal Reserve. Unlike Federal Reserve notes, US government dollar bills would not be based on debt or issued with interest. If the US government can support the dollars issued by the Federal Reserve, along with the associated debt, then it can also support a US-government-issued currency that does not involve accruing debt.

"Numerous national political and business leaders have advocated this concept over time, including Benjamin Franklin, Thomas Jefferson, and James Madison. Inventor and thought leader Thomas Edison also supported it."

"What else would you do?" asked one of the conference call participants.

Bo noted that the man's voice sounded familiar, but he couldn't readily identify it.

"If we could implement what I have proposed so far, it would go a long way toward addressing our financial problems. The newly issued currency could be used to pay off the national debt. We could maintain bank reserves without causing any disruptions to the economy. Additionally, there would be less pressure to raise taxes and fewer restrictions on free commerce if we weren't burdened by a growing national debt."

"But what other suggestions do you have?" the voice asked.

Bo's heart was beating so hard in his chest that he wondered if it was audible. He took a deep breath and said, "Over time, I would decrease the fractional reserve lending practices of financial institutions to achieve more of a one-for-one ratio of dollars to debt. This adjustment would ensure that the growth of the money supply aligns more closely with the measured growth of gross domestic product and the population. As a result, we would experience reduced volatility in the business cycle, leading to fewer fluctuations between booms and busts and less economic impact from inflation and recession.

"However, it's unlikely that this will ever happen, as it would significantly undermine the influential lobbying groups and banking associations."

"Go on," the voice said.

"I believe Congress should repeal the National Banking Act of 1864. At the height of the American Civil War, the banking sector made significant efforts—and succeeded—in shifting the US government's power to create and regulate money back to the banks.

"I think legislators should also repeal the Federal Reserve Act of 1913, which established the current central bank and the powers granted to that institution. Ultimately, national banks benefit the most from the existing monetary system and the creation of a leveraged money supply through fractional reserve lending, presenting a conflict of interest.

"It would be more beneficial to place this power in the hands of duly elected government officials, making it the direct responsibility of the United States Treasury Department. Congress chartered the Federal Reserve Bank, and the president appoints key positions in its leadership. All of this takes place despite the fact that the Federal Reserve Bank is not a government entity.

"That being said, I don't believe much can be done to reduce the power of the Federal Reserve. It's unclear what influences have sustained the central bank, but it has continued to reemerge and survive throughout American history."

"Wouldn't the potential for corruption increase if money became a direct issuance of the US government?" An unrecognized participant on the call posed this question, and Bo deemed it a valid one.

"It's not a perfect solution, but it provides more transparency and oversight as part of the public record."

Bo felt slightly unsettled. He didn't usually give away his position in its entirety. Yet he felt compelled to lay it all out. It might be his only chance to advocate for the reform he had long sought. He sensed he would never have a more influential audience than the one he had right now.

"Is there anything else you would do?" asked the participant whose voice Bo couldn't pinpoint. His head was spinning. *Why can't I recognize that voice? I've heard it before, and it's distinct from the others.*

"Yes, I would curtail the United States' involvement in major global financial and political institutions. If you think about it, the significant debt levels of many nations around the world can be traced back to these institutions. Although they present themselves as sources of assistance, they are, in fact, major holders of substantial loan notes. As a result, sovereign nations find themselves deeply in debt, with little hope of fully repaying these loans.

"This is particularly concerning for developing countries, where a large percentage of their GDP is allocated to servicing this debt. The funds used to pay off these loans could otherwise be directed toward improvements in healthcare, commerce, and other initiatives that could enhance the quality of life for their citizens."

"What about gold? What place does that have in this?" asked another participant.

Bo sighed. "The problem with gold is that it can easily be controlled by those who may not have the public's best interests at heart. For instance, many central banks and lending institutions hold a substantial amount of gold as collateral against the debts of various sovereign nations. It's important to keep in mind the golden rule: Those who possess the gold make the rules."

Bo recognized the next voice that spoke as Jack's.

"Thank you, Bo, for an informative and well-delivered presentation. I can assure you that my colleagues and I will discuss this at length in the days and weeks to come. I don't expect you to understand the full scope of the discussion today. Let's just say that your comments have served your nation well. All those years of research and insight you have labored to develop have not been in vain. These ideas are not entirely novel, but their application is both sensible and timely. We need ideas and answers, and we need them now."

Bo thanked them for the opportunity. As soon as he exited the meeting online, he breathed a sigh of relief. He felt that it went as well as it could have. More importantly, he hoped that he had, indeed, served his nation well today.

As he focused on transitioning back to his workday, one of the items on his to-do list was to identify the *mystery man* from the call. But first, he wanted to chat with Selby to let her know how the presentation went. He reached for his phone, which he had set to Do Not Disturb. He dialed her number, but she didn't pick up. *Must be on another call, he reasoned.* He would try again in a few minutes.

Meanwhile, he needed to check in with Spencer. Just as he stood up to make his way over to Spencer's office, he heard a knock at the door.

"Spencer saved me the trip," Bo said to himself as he opened his office door, expecting to see Spencer standing outside with a stack of client files.

"Mr. Parrott, we are so sorry to disturb you, but we must speak with you."

Bo took a step back. "Yulia? Dimitri?"

CHAPTER THIRTY-FIVE

Selby loved Christmas, and her favorite part was decorating the tree. When her twin daughters, Amelia and Alicia, were young, Selby would start decorating as early in the season as Bo would allow, with Halloween being the cutoff. Now that the twins were grown, Selby made it her goal to have the tree fully adorned by the time they and their spouses arrived for Thanksgiving.

Both Thanksgiving and Christmas brought back cherished memories from Selby's own childhood. Her parents had made the annual celebrations special with traditional meals and quality time spent with family. But it was Christmas that held a special magic for Selby, a feeling that lingered into her adulthood long after the anticipation of Santa's arrival stopped defining her excitement. The celebration of the mystery and wonder of the Savior's birth generated its own sense of anticipation as the weeks and days of the Advent season counted down.

Looking toward this holiday season, Selby was not sure how her treatments would affect her once they kicked into high gear. She'd had three so far, and they had left her feeling weak and depleted. She reasoned that she had more energy now than she would going forward. With that in mind, she went ahead and dragged the box containing the tree down from the attic to the living room. By the time she had set it in the stand and fluffed the branches, she felt exhausted.

"Time for a little pick-me-up," she said to herself as she went into the kitchen to grab a cup of coffee. When she did, she heard her phone buzzing from where she'd left it on the counter.

She looked at the caller ID. It was her doctor's office. She reluctantly answered.

"Hello?"

"Selby? This is Dr. McGill."

"Dr. McGill, what can I do for you?"

"There's something I'd like to discuss with you regarding your latest test results. Do you think you and Bo could stop by my office sometime today?"

Selby's stomach immediately twisted. She knew that whenever a doctor doesn't feel comfortable giving you results over the phone, the results aren't going to be favorable.

Selby took a deep breath. "That tells me that the news isn't good. To be honest, Bo has a hectic schedule today. It could be as late as tomorrow before we can coordinate our schedules. Can you just tell me over the phone and get it over with?"

Selby walked into the living room as Dr. McGill reluctantly explained the test results. By the time she was on her second sentence, Selby felt like Dr. McGill was talking to somebody else. She gently asked Selby several times if she had any questions, and Selby repeatedly replied that she did not. It wasn't that she didn't have questions; they just weren't questions her doctor could answer. *How was she going to tell Bo? How would they tell the children?*

Speaking of Bo, during her conversation with Dr. McGill, Selby saw that he was trying to call her.

When the call with her doctor ended, Selby walked zombielike over to where she had set up the Christmas tree. She crawled underneath it, stretched the cord over to the nearest receptacle, and plugged it in.

The tree came to life. She sat on the floor in silence as she watched the white lights twinkle cheerfully against the branches.

Christmas was her favorite season. This one would be her last.

She drew her knees to her chest and wrapped her arms around them. Then she rested her head on her knees and wept.

CHAPTER THIRTY-SIX

When Kathryn glanced at her phone and saw Lutz's number, her heart skipped a beat. He only contacted her secure line for critical, classified information. The last time he had done so was a few years ago to warn her about a bomb threat. This was back when her trust in him was far less strained than it was now. Such was the harsh reality of politics: Was it possible for anyone to wholeheartedly trust someone else?

Despite her misgivings about his character, she couldn't help but admire his remarkable strategic acumen when it came to military operations. His instructions today were clear, and Kathryn meticulously wrote down every detail.

When the call concluded, Kathryn used the same secure phone line to dial her military commander. After only one ring, he answered. Kathryn made sure to overenunciate every word to avoid any miscommunication.

"Authorize the air strikes on the port cities. Disable them, but do not destroy them. We want to preserve the assets to make the occupation effort worthwhile. This will send the message that we are emerging as a world contender." Her brow furrowed as she added, "It is moving faster than I had anticipated."

"Affirmative," the commander responded.

"Next, identify the loyalists who wave our flag. Let them know we have come to liberate them from a dreaded enemy. Flood the airwaves with our national pride and liberation message. We need our people behind us to continue the mission. Get footage of the loyalists smiling and embracing our soldiers once the areas are secured."

"Affirmative, Madam Premier. Let me know how else I can serve you."

The commander ended the call that had been on speaker and then paused for a moment. He turned to Simon and asked, *"On fait quoi?"*

Bo sat quietly in his office, trying to process the information he had just received from Yulia and Dimitri. His emotions were all over the place, and this was one time he couldn't give in to them. He had naively assumed that dealing with a crashing stock market, while watching his wife's health deteriorate before his eyes, would be all he would be required to handle. He now had to deal with the fact that not only had all his years of research fallen into the wrong hands, but the two people who facilitated this espionage-type activity had just apologized to him in a way that seemed remorseful and sincere. Even though he had been targeted for being intelligent, right now he felt anything but.

However, the task at hand required him to set his personal feelings aside. In the broader context, this wasn't personal. It was a matter of global concern, and Bo had to relay the information to someone who could act on it in a way that would best serve the United States, Europe, and, perhaps, the world at some point.

He took a deep breath and dialed Senator Prescott's number.

CHAPTER THIRTY-SEVEN

By the time December arrived, Bo and his team had reached out to most of the client base regarding the market downturn Bo anticipated. A significant number of clients had declined the reallocation strategy, choosing instead to keep their money in the stock market. Others had expressed dissatisfaction, believing they were missing out as they watched the markets rise.

Bo understood their frustration. A sense of complacency existed among investors, accompanied by minimal caution. Indicators—such as call buying, leveraged investing, price-to-earnings multiples, the percentage of client net worth invested in stocks, and consumer sentiment—were all elevated. In other words, all the signs of a market peak were evident. However, Bo knew that this *top* was about to *topple*.

In recent weeks, Bo and Selby had engaged in several tearful dialogues regarding Selby's prognosis. He still held out hope that a new treatment could become available that would turn things around for her. Anything was possible, but he knew the chances of that happening were slim to none. His line of work had conditioned him not to give in to wishful thinking, a principle he couldn't just leave at the office. In the past, his world with Selby had been a refuge where he could escape the stress he dealt with in the financial world. Now those two worlds overlapped, and both were crumbling . . . at the same time.

It became increasingly difficult for him to leave Selby each morning and go to work. At times, the guilt was unbearable. When he only had phone call appointments, he made those from home. But there were days when it was necessary for him to meet with clients in person, and he had no choice but to go in to the office. On those days, Alicia and Amelia alternated traveling to Wilson to be with their mom.

As Christmas, Selby's favorite holiday, approached, Bo became even more determined to spend as much time with her as possible. His demanding work schedule made this goal difficult to achieve. To make matters worse, he had received a notification about a seminar he was required to attend to maintain his continuing education credentials. This year, the event coordinators were hosting it at a local country club. Although it was only for one day, Bo regretted that it nonetheless took time away from being with Selby.

Looking for any silver lining in this otherwise ill-timed commitment, Bo reasoned that, at the very least, it would provide him with an opportunity to network with other advisors from the region and introduce Spencer to them.

Despite the seminar having "education" in the title, Bo wasn't certain how much he or Spencer would *actually learn*. In previous years, the material presented by the speakers lacked substance and was mostly fluff. But it did manage to encourage and inspire advisors to continue their efforts, and during long stretches of market volatility, that motivation alone made it worthwhile.

Another positive aspect was that the seminar schedule included an afternoon break. Bo knew that, after sitting in meetings all morning, he would need to use a portion of that time to return client phone calls. Afterward, he hoped he and Spencer could work in a game of tennis. The sport had taught Bo valuable life lessons as well as offering a healthy outlet for releasing tension. Since Spencer was also an avid player, perhaps they could take some of their recent stress and frustration out on a few tennis balls.

As Bo drove to the country club that morning, he reflected on his earlier conversation with Selby before leaving the house.

Selby was sitting in her favorite recliner, one that provided the best view of the Christmas tree. Bo took note that the tree looked more festive than in any other year he could recall. Amelia, Alicia, and their spouses had decorated it at Thanksgiving as an early Christmas present for Selby. Selby had commented that the only thing it lacked was a snow scene behind it . . . a real one!

"Are you sure you're going to be okay?" he asked her—for the third time.

Selby pulled up the red-and-green-checkered flannel blanket she had draped over her until it completely covered her shoulders. "I'm sure! The ladies from the church are delivering my dinner, and Erin across the street is on call for everything else."

"I feel bad for leaving you. If this seminar weren't mandatory, I wouldn't be going."

"It's okay! You need a change of scenery. And, while you're there, you and Spencer should definitely spend some time out on the tennis courts. Today's weather is going to be perfect for it. Go, and enjoy yourself!"

"Are you sure?"

*Selby waved him off. "I'll be here when you get back. In fact, I'll probably be **right here**! This chair is really comfortable!"*

Bo chuckled. Seeing Selby in good spirits made him feel less nervous about leaving. He only wished it lessened the guilt.

"Okay, if you're absolutely certain. I'll keep my cell phone on. And if you need anything or if anything changes—"

Selby nodded dramatically. "I won't hesitate to call you, even if it means interrupting a meeting, etc., etc." She cupped his face in her hands. "I know the drill. Now, get out of here so I can get some rest."

The seminar meetings continued throughout the morning, with a brief break for lunch, and concluded around 3 p.m. A complimentary dinner, featuring an inspirational speaker, would wrap up the event later that evening. By four o'clock that afternoon, Bo had finished his phone calls, just in time to make a court reservation for himself and Spencer.

The lessons Bo learned from tennis had far exceeded perfecting his serve or strengthening his backhand. It had taught him determination, focus, self-discipline, and timing, skills that had benefited him on—and off—the court.

Spencer, like Bo, had grown up playing tennis, and they occasionally ran into each other at a club where both had memberships. However, Bo was unsure about Spencer's skill level. Until he figured that out, he decided to take it easy on him.

After placing their rackets on a bench along the sideline, Spencer and Bo took a moment to stretch. The courts were quiet except for one game in progress, and Bo couldn't help but overhear the conversation between the two young men playing on the adjacent court. Based on their dialogue, they either worked in the finance industry or were investors. Either way, they sounded knowledgeable about the stock market. He discreetly motioned for Spencer to tune in.

The first player bounced a tennis ball several times before serving it over the net. When his opponent failed to return the serve, he announced the score and wiped his face with his shirt. His opponent then volleyed the ball back to his side of the court. As the first player bounced the ball again, he remarked, "You would think that the current market situation is favorable for investors looking to profit on the long side. However, more often than not, it may lead to gains for traders on the short side."

"You're right," his opponent replied as he lightly hopped from side to side, preparing for the next serve. "Those traders borrow shares of stock from their brokerage service and pay interest rates that are nearly double those of more conventional loans. More than likely, they're anticipating a decline in the price of the shares sold short."

The player bouncing the ball tossed it into the air and said, "If they're—" Just as his racket made contact with the ball, he exhaled while saying, "*WRONG*," and then waited to see if his opponent would return the serve. When, yet again, his opponent was unable to do so, he continued. "Not only will those traders owe interest, but they may also be required to cover any shortfall if the stocks go up."

"It seems counterintuitive to pursue a gain like this," his opponent stated. "But history shows that there can be significant rewards for those who get it right."

"Like those aces I've been serving?"

His opponent laughed and pointed in his direction. "Hey, don't get cocky. The game isn't over yet."

Bo looked at Spencer. "Did you learn anything from that?"

Spencer's eyes grew wide. "Sure did. Don't play against the guy who's serving!"

Bo chuckled. "For the most part, we work with traditional long-side investors. They often provide the feast, so to speak, for short sellers and programmed trades driven by algorithms. Which side of the court do you want?"

"I'll take the other side," Spencer said as he walked past the net and stood at the service line. Bo hit a warm-up volley over to him.

"But isn't that unethical?" Spencer asked as he returned the volley.

"Sometimes it's the winning strategy. It represents a more sophisticated type of weaponry in the battlefield of market activity."

Instead of returning the ball to Spencer, Bo caught it with one hand and walked up to the net. He looked around and said, "Just like these tennis courts, the marketplace is a competitive arena. Numerous skirmishes occur at various levels throughout the trading day. The constant fluctuations between the bid price and the asking price reveal the winners and losers in trading. It may seem quite docile when you casually place an order and receive the average fill price. However, the winners possess the killer instinct to execute their trades effectively and ultimately influence prices in their favor. While the outcome may seem unfair, they are, in fact, playing by the rules."

Spencer nodded and then, with a mischievous grin, he backed up to the baseline. "It's sort of like how I know that your right knee sometimes hangs up on you, and I'm going to hit serves that make you have to rely on that knee?"

Bo threw his head back and laughed. *So much for going easy on you, kid!* He tossed the ball in Spencer's direction and said, "There may be hope for you yet as a market trader. But on this tennis court? I'm going to destroy you!"

CHAPTER THIRTY-EIGHT

As Bo had predicted, the keynote speaker for this year's seminar provided a pointless—albeit highly emotional and lengthy—presentation. Bo likened it to a sugary drink that, while containing only empty calories, still gets you energized.

Bo could tell that Spencer was picking up on the speaker's lack of quality content. He leaned over and whispered to Bo, "Is this guy ever going to shut up?"

Bo whispered back, "I don't think so."

A few minutes later, the speaker ended his presentation, and the audience erupted in applause. One of the event coordinators, a well-dressed and attractive woman who appeared to be in her mid-thirties, stepped onto the stage. "Let's show our appreciation once more for Joe Houston's motivational speech!" Those in attendance clapped once more, and the session ended. Lively and upbeat music played on the sound system as everyone filtered out of the meeting room.

Bo was grateful that, if nothing else, the event had served to introduce Spencer to other advisors in the region. It turned out that the two gentlemen on the tennis court were financial advisors who managed a small-town practice near the North Carolina mountains. After Bo told them how much he and Selby enjoyed visiting that part of the state, they invited him to stop by on his next trip. In fact, if Bo could give them enough advance notice, they'd even arrange for a game of tennis.

As soon as Bo was able to excuse himself through the crowd of attendees chatting and exchanging business cards, he found a quiet spot and called Selby. He was relieved that she sounded upbeat and had enjoyed a restful day in the recliner.

Bo was about to put his cell phone back in his pocket when he felt it vibrate. The caller ID showed that it was Casey Balan. Bo pressed the answer button and said, "Casey, I can't believe you're just now getting back with me when free food was involved!"

Casey laughed and said, "It's not one of my prouder moments. After all, I have a reputation as a cheapskate to maintain. Unfortunately, I have been up against a publishing deadline. But since you brought it up, does that lunch offer still stand?"

"How does tomorrow look for you? Same place, same time?"

"Tomorrow it is! I'll see you at the diner."

Even though Bo was looking forward to seeing Casey, he knew this particular lunch meeting would be a departure from their normal, lighthearted routine. Instead of their usual banter over indigestion-producing cuisine, Bo planned to share with Casey the dream he had about the alligator and what he saw coming with the stock market.

More importantly, he planned to tell him about Selby.

CHAPTER THIRTY-NINE

"I can't get the alligator dream off my mind," Bo said as he watched the waitress set his and Casey's plates of food down on the table. He picked up a yellow plastic container. It made a gaseous noise as he attempted to squirt a line of mustard onto his hot dog. Only a yellow blob of water came out. He shook it again and, after spraying his hot dog—and a few unintended french fries— he offered to pass the container across the table to Casey.

"I had the dream back in October when Selby and I were in the mountains for a weekend getaway. The plan was for me to leave my work back at the office for a couple of days. But—"

Casey waved off needing the mustard and completed Bo's sentence, "Your work followed you to the mountains."

"Exactly," Bo said through a mouthful of hot dog.

"So, tell me about this dream," Casey said as he slid two ketchup-dipped french fries into his mouth.

After washing down the hot dog with a gulp of water, Bo wiped his mouth with his napkin. "There was a series of attacks attempted by a menacing alligator. With each one, the potential for harm increased. It began with the alligator lunging at a group of dogs, then at a group of children, then at an adult *and* a group of children. I was the one who had to intercept these threats."

Bo went on to describe the dream in detail and what he considered to be the interpretation, including the Elliott Wave Theory.

Casey shook his head. "It's one thing to recommend that clients like me reallocate their investments. But you had to tell aggressive-growth-profile clients to take their money out of a money-making market? That had to have been fun!"

"It was a nightmare . . . quite literally. But I think there's even more to the story."

"Go on."

"Let's assume that my interpretation of the dream, along with my research, is accurate. As we approach the low point of an upcoming economic cycle, numerous people will find themselves out of work and in need of assistance. Whenever the stock market experiences a significant decline, corporations typically tighten their belts. If the business outlook remains weak, there will be less capital expenditure, leading to a contraction in business and slower development. This situation results in *even more* individuals being out of work and seeking assistance. Corporations will require substantial funds to address these challenges. During times of crisis, government support is often requested and granted. And what does that lead to?" Bo asked.

Casey sighed. "It perpetuates the demand to increase the scale of government."

"Precisely. This swing of the pendulum toward an increased presence of centralized government is what certain groups in power are seeking."

"Such as?"

"Well, at the center of it all—as usual—is the Federal Reserve. The central bank is often at the center of economic turbulence. Do they really offer relief? Or does this same institution, that seeks to increase its intervention during a current crisis, *create* the crisis by earlier policy decisions?"

"Regardless of what side of the aisle you favor, that makes a lot of sense," Casey said as he dipped a french fry into a puddle of ketchup on his plate. "You're starting to sound like your hero, Milton Friedman. Another conservative. He had a lot to say about the Federal Reserve."

Bo nodded. "He was a sharp critic of the central bank. He believed that the advent of the Federal Reserve had escalated volatility and instability, rather than relieving it. He pointed out that a contraction of the money supply is involved for an economic depression to occur. Depressions occur because of the contraction of liquidity. All of this is at the direction of the Federal Reserve."

Casey took a sip of his iced tea and nodded. "We give place to this type of monetary policy seemingly without question."

"But what choice do we have? As they say, to challenge the Feds is like attacking the flames of hell with a water pistol."

Casey chuckled and then slid his plate to one side. He leaned back in his chair and folded his arms. "You know, Bo, not every battle is yours to fight . . . and certainly not yours to win."

Bo gazed off into the distance. "There's another battle I'm fighting right now, Casey, one that makes me feel even more frustrated and helpless."

Casey tilted his head to one side. "What are you talking about?"

Bo took a deep breath. "It's Selby. She has leukemia."

Casey's brow furrowed, and he shook his head. "I'm so sorry, Bo." He leaned across the table and grabbed Bo's hand.

Bo swallowed hard. Despite his best effort to hold back the tears, he could feel them trailing down his face. "She didn't respond to the treatments, and the test results showed that the disease had progressed much more aggressively than they had anticipated," he said as he wiped his face on his sleeve.

"Is there anything I can do?"

"You've already done it," Bo said, his voice cracking. "The day you spoke with Spencer and arranged that interview with Dallas for me? Unbeknownst to you, that was a difficult day for me. Getting that interview was a bright spot. Although when I heard the interview had been slated for that evening, on short notice, I wanted to throttle you!"

"It wouldn't be the first time!" Casey chuckled.

"Not only did the interview go well, but it ended with Dallas scheduling an appointment with me."

"So I heard," Casey said as he leaned back in his seat, as the waitress collected the plates from the table. "He asked you on the air during the interview!"

"Thank you," Bo said, looking up at the waitress and then back at Casey. "But what you *didn't* hear was, after the program ended and I was driving home, I received a call from Senator Jack Prescott. He also had listened to the interview and wanted me to provide my perspective on current economic events to a distinguished group of colleagues—so distinguished, in fact, that I don't even know who some of them were!

"What I'm trying to say is that I'm attempting to navigate one of the most challenging seasons of my life, both personally and professionally. I want to be able to fix Selby and fix the economy, but I can't do either." He raised his water glass as if toasting and said, "But being the sharp investigative journalist that you are, you already sniffed that out."

Casey smiled. "A writer does what he can."

Bo once again gazed off into the distance. "It goes without saying that I'd be willing to lose all the other battles if I could just help Selby win this fight against leukemia. Losing her *is* losing everything."

Once again, Casey grabbed Bo's hand. "How is Selby handling this? Is she in any pain?"

"No, thank God. She's just exhausted and weak. Typical Selby; she's keeping a positive attitude, or at least she's trying to. She has her moments."

"She's allowed those," Casey said as he raised his eyebrows. "And so are you."

Bo shook his head. "She's a lot stronger than I am."

Casey leaned to the side as he reached for his wallet from his back pocket and pulled out a few bills. "Neither of you should have to be strong right now. Let others bear some of the burden. I, for one, am here for you to help in any way that I can." Casey winked as he added, "And, unlike the government, I don't have a hidden agenda."

Bo couldn't help but chuckle. Then he saw Casey putting money on top of the tab that the waitress had left. "Hey, what are you doing? I'm treating today, remember?"

"You *were* treating. I've got this one."

"But you arranged that interview for me on Dallas's radio program . . . which led to one of the most rewarding experiences of my career."

"Bo, you've helped me with my investments for years. You've done a lot of good for a lot of people . . . with little recognition. I hope that changes. Meanwhile, I'm proud to call you my friend. Buying lunch is the least I can do."

Bo was deeply touched by Casey's kindness but decided it was time to lighten the mood. He couldn't let their lunch meeting end on such a sentimental note; it would go against tradition. He looked around and then leaned in toward the table. He lowered his voice and said, "But your reputation as a cheapskate? How will this affect that?"

Casey played along. He leaned in and whispered, "The way I see it? What happens at the diner stays at the diner."

Suppressing a laugh, Bo nodded reassuringly and responded in kind. "Your secret is safe with me."

CHAPTER FORTY

Bo couldn't believe how quickly Christmas arrived. The family had decided not to exchange presents but to simply enjoy the food, fellowship, and the one gift that had suddenly become precious and fleeting.

Time.

Bo and Selby's daughters and their husbands planned to arrive early tomorrow, which was Christmas Eve, and stay through New Year's. Their visits with Selby had become more frequent in recent weeks. Their presence was both needed and appreciated, as Selby had grown weaker and was no longer able to do as many things for herself.

In years past, Bo had worked the day before Christmas Eve, mostly making client phone calls. This year, however, he decided to take a break and channel that energy toward making Christmas as joyous as possible for Selby.

He awoke at daybreak and looked over at Selby lying next to him. She had lost weight to where the bed seemed to swallow her. No longer displaying just a few streaks of silver, her dark brown hair had turned mostly gray and appeared much thinner. He gently stroked her cheek. Gone were the pink apples that would get pinker when she got out in the sun. Her face now looked drawn and displayed a flat pallor.

Bo had to smile, though, as he straightened the covers around her and noticed that she was wearing a red-and-white flannel nightgown sporting a pattern of dancing reindeer. *Selby, you really are a kid at Christmas.*

As he stepped into the hall on his way to the kitchen to start Selby's coffee, he immediately noticed that the house felt colder than usual. He reached over and bumped up the thermostat. When he entered the kitchen, he saw something else. Even though the sky was overcast, a white glare came in through the windows.

"No way!" he said out loud.

He rushed back into the bedroom. "Selby," he said, gently shaking her shoulders. "Wake up!"

Selby groaned and pulled the covers up over her head. "What is it? Let me go back to sleep!"

"Trust me. You're gonna want to see this!"

Selby sat up in bed and mumbled, "What I want to see is the inside of my eyelids."

Bo stepped over and opened the shutters on the bedroom window, revealing a winter wonderland outside. If he had to guess, there were at least four inches on the ground, and more was coming down.

He watched as Selby's mouth dropped. She slowly swung her legs over the side of the bed. Bo helped her stand and supported her as they walked over to the window.

Selby's face lit up when she looked outside. And then she started to laugh. "I've been praying for Christmas snow for as long as I can remember. God was saving it as a present for me . . . for *this* Christmas."

It took all the willpower Bo could muster to stay in the moment. He wanted to sweep Selby up into his arms and say, "No! You're not going to die! We've got many more Christmases ahead of us." Instead, he responded, "So, was this present worth waiting for?"

He watched as Selby's eyes beamed with light. "It sure was!" Then, after a moment, her brow furrowed and she turned to Bo and asked,

"Did you know it was supposed to snow? Because I had no idea. Then again, I haven't exactly been keeping up with the weather."

Bo smiled sheepishly. "Me neither. I've only been tuning in to the financial news. Maybe God wanted it to be a surprise for both of us."

Selby leaned into him and put her arm around his waist. "Maybe He did."

"Now, milady," Bo said as he bowed dramatically, "would you like for me to prepare your morning coffee?"

"Not yet," Selby said softly, still gazing out the window. "Stay here with me for just a few more minutes."

"Of course," Bo said as Selby once again leaned into him. As they continued to watch the snow fall, Bo could feel her knees buckling.

"Why don't we move into the living room? That way, you can sit in your favorite recliner, sip your coffee, and look at the snow. I'll even plug in the Christmas tree."

"That's a good idea," Selby said, her voice now sounding just above a whisper.

Bo had an unsettling feeling he couldn't quite identify. It was scary, sad, and peaceful all at the same time. He made a quick trip to the bathroom while Selby's coffee perked. When he returned to the kitchen, he poured a cup from the carafe and delivered it to her in the living room. He set it on the table beside the recliner.

Selby's eyes looked cloudier than they had earlier. He watched her close them for a moment and then open them wide. She smiled and said, "It's beautiful! And it's *so* white!"

Bo knelt in front of the recliner. "Yes, the snow *is* beautiful. You finally got your white Christmas!"

But Selby shook her head as she looked off into the distance. "No, not the snow. This is much, much whiter. Wait," she paused and then exclaimed, "it's Him!" She reached out and took Bo's hand. "It's *Jesus*, Bo." She paused, took a breath, and then whispered, "And He's more beautiful than you . . . could ever imagine." Her voice trailed off as she took another breath.

He felt her hand go limp and watched as she closed her eyes.

"Selby? Please, wait! Don't go!" He leaned in closer, wrapping his arms around her. "Oh, my love, don't leave me!" he pleaded, his heart shattering into a million pieces. Clutching her tightly, he wept, desperately wishing that his embrace could somehow bring her back to him.

Then he felt something unlike anything he had ever experienced. It was love—powerful, holy, and unconditional—penetrating his entire being. The warmth only lasted for a moment, but the memory of it never faded. He never doubted who had sent it, or who Selby had seen that morning.

When he felt that he had no tears left, Bo wiped his eyes yet again with a tissue and braced himself for what was next. Unlike what he had planned for today, he would have to make phone calls after all.

A lot of phone calls.

CHAPTER FORTY-ONE

The following week passed in a whirlwind of activities for Bo. He worked on Selby's eulogy while mustering up the energy needed to engage in conversations with well-meaning people who either called or stopped by with food. The entire process was exhausting. In the rare moments when the phone or doorbell wasn't ringing, he took advantage of the quiet and allowed himself to grieve.

The most heartbreaking part had been breaking the news to Alicia and Amelia. The silver lining—if you could call it that—with a terminal illness is that the inevitable doesn't come as a surprise. It doesn't lessen the pain, but it provides more time to prepare for it. The family deemed it a bittersweet irony that Selby went to her heavenly home at Christmas, and a white one at that.

The distinct differences in the twins' personalities became evident as they assisted Bo in planning the memorial service. Alicia, who looked more like Selby, inherited Bo's attention to detail. She had already estimated the cost of the funeral in her head and came within a few pennies of nailing it. Amelia, on the other hand, resembled a female version of Bo, but with Selby's bubbly personality. She took over welcoming friends and family members, answering phone calls, and making sure everyone had enough to eat.

In the days leading up to Selby's memorial service, supporters sent an impressive number of holiday-themed arrangements and wreaths. The sheer volume of flowers prompted the decision to remove the first row of chairs at the front of the church to create space for them. There were so many, in fact, that Bo decided to donate a portion of them to a local nursing home.

After an opening prayer and hymn, Amelia and Alicia took turns sharing humorous stories about Selby, most of which had occurred during their teen years. When it was Bo's turn to speak, he picked up his notes and slowly made his way to the podium.

The first thing that hit him like an arrow through his heart was when he looked down at the front row and didn't see Selby. Not that he expected to, but the memories of how she had consistently been there to support him flooded his mind. In particular, he recalled how she had beamed with pride after his presentation at the Carolina Economic Forum.

Selby had always expressed an admiration for Bo's mathematical and analytical acumen. At times, he suspected this admiration bordered on tolerance, but Selby never would have disclosed that. Yet it was those abilities that had catapulted Bo into a career in finance, enabling him to decipher and even predict movements in the stock market.

However, as he stood behind the podium, those talents and skills suddenly felt useless. Even the intricate workings of the stock market paled in comparison to the complexity of the task before him. He swallowed hard as he prepared to say goodbye to Selby Ann Brookstone Parrott.

After collecting his emotions, he glanced down at his notes. Folding them in half and setting them aside, he looked over the sanctuary where every seat was full. Taking a deep breath, he began. "I had jotted down a few key points of what I wanted to say this afternoon. But to truly honor Selby, the best way for me to do that is to share from my heart.

"I'm sure that everyone here, especially those sitting up front, can smell the cedar and pine in the lovely floral arrangements surrounding the altar. Christmas was Selby's favorite holiday, and part of what she loved was the fragrances associated with it. Yet, when I think of Selby, I don't think of these seasonal greeneries, but rather a flower that blooms in early spring. It happens to be my favorite, as it reminds me of Selby.

"The flower I'm referring to is wisteria.

"Wisteria's blossom is so delicate that it can fall apart at your touch. Yet, it possesses the fortitude to thrive almost anywhere, from manicured lawns"—Bo swallowed hard as his mind flashed back to when he and Selby had stopped for gas while traveling to the mountains that Easter weekend—"to roadside dumpsters. In this way, it tends to show up unexpectedly, not only to provide beauty but also a powerful fragrance that lingers long after the blossoms have faded. For wisteria is a flower that graces the world only a little while, and then it's gone.

"Selby had a tender side to her, yet she lived life with a strength and resilience that helped her face challenges head-on, and that included her illness. And she certainly had a way of showing up unexpectedly, beginning with the first time I met her.

"It was my senior year of college, and I had forgotten my lunch that morning. I stopped at the first diner I came to, not knowing that I'd meet someone who, like wisteria, would bring beauty and fragrance into my life, forever changing it for the better. I was so taken with Selby Ann Brookstone that I left that diner without my lunch." Bo paused as the room erupted in laughter. "But I made sure I had something even more important: Selby's phone number."

Once again, laughter rippled through the crowd. Bo paused and then continued, "Today we have gathered to celebrate the life of someone who brought beauty and fragrance to every life she touched. I think we can all agree that having known Selby, our lives have been forever changed for the better."

Bo glanced down to pick up his notes and then, when he looked back up, he could see Selby sitting in the front row, beaming with pride. Was it his imagination? He knew she couldn't be there physically, but perhaps she was there in spirit. He smiled as he considered that, if she were with him today, maybe she always would be.

CHAPTER FORTY-TWO

In the days following Selby's memorial service, Amelia and Alicia played a crucial role in helping Bo tidy up around the house. This included making sure that the home-cooked meals provided by neighbors were either eaten or safely stored in the freezer for later use. They also took the time to write and mail thank-you notes. Before leaving to return home, they divided the remaining flowers between themselves and Bo.

As Bo watched their cars pull out of the driveway, he felt a sense of sadness. However, he appreciated the quiet moments of reflection that followed. He found comfort in knowing that Selby's celebration of life had truly been just that: a celebration.

Now came the challenge of living his life without her, something he knew he would have to tackle one day at a time. Getting back to work would help, at least in establishing a sense of normalcy. But his first day back was anything but normal.

"Damn this market!" Howard Lanning exclaimed over the phone. "We're getting killed!"

Bo wanted to retort by saying, *"I told you so!"*

Bo had contacted Howard several weeks ago to suggest reallocating his portfolio to become more conservative. Unfortunately, Howard had dismissed the recommendation and said he wanted his money "to work for him all the time." Bo complied, and the investment positions remained aggressively allocated. Then the early January Santa Claus rally ended, resulting in a sharp downward movement of the market. Unfortunately, Bo saw it as merely the first wave in an extended series of downward adjustments.

Bo finished the call with Howard that ended with, "Thank you, Howard . . . the flowers you and Patricia sent were lovely . . . I appreciate the prayers . . . talk to you soon."

Bo then turned in his chair to face Spencer. This was the first chance they'd had to catch up since Bo returned to work that morning. It was also the first time he'd seen Spencer since Selby's memorial service.

Bo watched as Spencer fidgeted and shuffled in his chair. After a couple of awkward moments of nervously gazing around Bo's office, he blurted out, "You really did receive a lot of beautiful flowers. People think highly of you, Bo. I hope that brought you a measure of comfort."

Bo managed to smile. "People thought highly of *Selby*. And, yes, the support meant a lot."

Bo could tell that Spencer didn't really know what to say. Then again, who does in a situation like this? Words feel so inadequate when people are grieving.

"So, Howard Lanning is less than satisfied with his account performance?" Spencer asked in an apparent attempt to change the subject.

Bo responded in a businesslike manner, hoping it would put Spencer at ease. "It's challenging to get clients to depart from a more traditional approach of stocks and bonds and go along with alternative investment positions. But what's unnerving me now is that the first leg of a downward trend is often followed by subwaves of market movements. This current development may only be the first of five waves, if the Elliott Wave theory is indeed applicable. If the pattern persists, we could see a year of prolonged negative market movement."

"That doesn't sound good."

"No, it doesn't. I found this report online and printed it out. Here is your copy." Bo handed Spencer a one-page printout. "It shows how consumers feel about current economic issues. The statistics indicate that consumer sentiment is declining rapidly. However, consumer confidence—measured by what consumers do rather than just how they feel—hasn't decreased all that much. Despite feeling more pessimistic, consumers' actions have remained largely unchanged."

"All the technical jargon aside, we can simply say that navigating this current market is a royal pain in the ass!"

Bo laughed. "I'd say that sums it up quite well. It's an ongoing learning process. My lack of market savvy has gotten the best of me more times than I'd care to admit. As the saying goes, 'The market makes fools of us all.' It's humbling but enriching at the same time."

Spencer pointed to the wall-mounted flat-screen television by Bo's desk, where the financial news channel was on. A popular news anchor was interviewing a high-profile commentator. "What about those guys?" Spencer asked. "They're only predicting gloom and doom."

Bo raised his eyebrows. "Ah, yes. The flamboyant market prognosticators who are wrong until they aren't. They're like a broken clock that is eventually correct at some point. Meanwhile, they play on people's fears and predisposed inclinations. That is not to say that some of what they are saying isn't true; it just isn't the whole picture. And sensationalism is always good for ratings."

"So, ignore them?"

"Just chew up the meat and spit out the bones, as my father-in-law used to say. On another television network, you might get a completely different viewpoint from a different type of financial professional."

"Such as?"

"The more traditional figures. Their message routinely comes across as calming and reassuring. They often represent established institutions and don't want to appear extreme. They also work with long-side investors who seek to make money when markets go up. They can't afford the indiscretion of talking against their books."

Spencer rubbed his chin, "It sounds like everybody has an angle, so to speak."

Bo nodded. "Everybody does. So, the listener must use discretion. Now, I hope you didn't celebrate too much at New Year's. Because, until the year closes out, we're in for a bumpy ride."

CHAPTER FORTY-THREE

As the weeks and months dragged on after Selby's death, it took all of Bo's physical and emotional energy to reestablish a sense of normalcy. Even market turmoil and difficult client conversations offered a reprieve from the overwhelming sadness that continually engulfed him. Nothing could ever fill the gaping hole in his heart, but at least work had provided a distraction, and for that he was grateful.

Likewise, time, which had become a foe during Selby's illness, became a friend again. It was through the passage of time that Bo experienced healing that helped him feel more like himself. He began to believe that, even though he still had a long way to go, perhaps he would make it after all.

Bo was finishing up a phone call when Spencer lightly tapped on his open office door. He motioned for Spencer to come in and have a seat.

After the call ended, Bo set his cell phone on his desk. "Spencer, it's after three o'clock and I haven't had lunch yet. Have you?"

Spencer shook his head. "I'm afraid not. I've been on the phone for hours."

Bo stepped over to a mini refrigerator located on the other side of the room. He removed two plates covered with plastic wrap. Holding them in front of him, he turned toward Spencer and announced, "Carrie sent me home with these the other night. I'm going to heat one for me and one for you."

"How is it you have my wife's amazing dinner leftovers, and I was going to pick something up from Billy's Burgers?"

"Probably because these were the only leftovers, you know, left over. Carrie's cooking gets gobbled up fast."

"That's a valid point! I'll take you up on the offer."

"Now, what's the overall mood of the clients you've spoken with?" Bo said as he popped the first plate in the microwave.

"Initially, we had clients concerned about potentially missing out on market opportunities after shifting to a more conservative approach. Some questioned our recommendations, while others expressed seller's remorse. However, today, none of those clients has anything negative to say. We may not have handled every situation perfectly, but I don't think we could have tried any harder."

Bo retrieved the first plate from the microwave, placed it on his desk in front of Spencer, then stepped over to place the other one in the microwave. When the timer beeped, he placed the second plate on his desk in front of his own chair. He opened a desk drawer and retrieved two sets of plastic forks and napkin combos wrapped in plastic, handing one to Spencer and keeping the other one for himself.

"Wow, I feel like you provided the food and, hey, you even set the table!"

Bo smiled as he sat back down. "Don't forget this food was from a meal from where you hosted me in your home. I really appreciate how you and Carrie have been there for me these past several months."

The plastic covering over his fork and knife made a crinkling sound as Bo pulled it off. "It's hard to believe I'm at the halfway mark of the first year since Selby's passing. Our daughters live several hours away in different directions and make the trip home as often as they can. But it's been nice to be able to drive a couple of blocks and spend time with folks that *feel* like family."

Spencer's eyes filled with tears. "We consider you to be family, too. And we'll continue to be there for you. Like you said, it's only been six months."

Looking over toward the window, Bo's eyes squinted. "You know, sometimes it feels like it was years ago. Other times, it feels like yesterday. But most of the time? It simply doesn't feel real."

Spencer nodded. "I understand. Please let us know if there's anything we can do . . . besides provide you with leftovers, that is!"

"It sounds like you've been doing it with all the client outreach. What's the latest update?"

Spencer took off his glasses and rubbed his eyes. "Right now we're focused on those who have suffered losses and are living on a fixed income, such as retirees. I've started an outreach effort specifically for those clients. The advisory team remains vigilant in reaching each of them so that no one slips through the cracks. Speaking of the team, hiring Emily Dodson was a smart move. She's been a big help."

"I'm glad to hear it. Jacob Wiley took Polly Dunnigan, but we snatched up Emily Dodson. I'd say that evens up the score. Good work, by the way," Bo said as he plunged his fork into a heap of steaming lasagna. "I didn't see the bear market affecting fixed income as clearly as I saw it affecting equities. I also underestimated the Federal Reserve's zeal in slowing down the economy. If they continue to implement intense monetary policy changes so rapidly, I'm concerned it will result in unintended consequences."

"What have they implemented so far?" Spencer asked as he slid his chair closer to Bo's desk and removed the plastic wrap from the plate Bo had set there for him.

"The current tightening measures have led to sharp and consecutive increases in interest rates. Tightening involves allowing the current balance sheet to roll off as existing bonds mature, stopping the purchase of bonds on the open market, and selling mortgage-backed securities on the open market.

"An inverted yield curve occurs when the yield on a ten-year Treasury note is lower than that of a ninety-day Treasury bill. This situation often signals a potential recession, indicating a decline in economic activity, even though the economy may still appear somewhat robust. Such a recession could be deep and prolonged."

Spencer rolled his eyes as he wiped his mouth with his napkin. "It seems every market analyst and economist has an opinion about what the Fed should do. Why doesn't anyone ask why the Federal Reserve has been given such preeminence in the first place?"

"I, for one, have asked it numerous times. In fact, last night I was once again reading Milton Friedman's writings. I know I've quoted him before, but his words bear repeating. He said that the role of the Federal Reserve appears to *increase* instability rather than decrease it. The irony is that, following the stock market crash of 1929, the Federal Reserve continued to raise interest rates as the Great Depression of the 1930s worsened. Could history rhyme once again, here? I think we're watching it do just that."

Bo and Spencer paused to look at the business news report on the screen. The headline read "Market Officially Enters Bear Market Territory."

"Wait," Spencer said as he looked more closely at the screen. "Did the market close?"

Bo nodded. "Yes, it's what's called a *limit-down* day."

"I remember it from the securities licensing exam. Remind me of when that occurs?" Spencer said as a piece of lasagna fell off his fork and onto his pants.

"That," Bo said as he reached for an extra napkin from his desk drawer and handed it to Spencer, "is when the breakers trip after a certain high percentage of downward movement occurs in the market. There are also limit-up days when the market advances too rapidly in an upward direction. Today, the market is down. There will be a brief pause in trading until it resumes."

Bo took a sip of water from a plastic bottle on his desk and then continued, "Another breaker is in place to halt trading if the market movement reaches the next lower level. When that happens, trading is suspended longer than during the first limit-down stop. If there were more time left in today's trading session, I could see that occurring. You remember the alligator dream, right?"

"I do. Are you seeing another phase of it play out today?"

"Humor me while I quickly recap. In the opening scene, I discovered an alligator with its prey hiding in the floor. It lunged but then went back into hiding. Then it attempted to attack a group of dogs, but I rescued them. There was a brief respite, and then the alligator launched an assault on the children. Finally, the alligator tried to attack the children *and me*. Regarding the current activity in the market? I sense it's more like the second assault scene in the dream—more intense than the first. Therefore, we need to implement a more concentrated rescue effort."

"Sorry to interrupt," Spencer said as he pointed to the television screen. "The market reopened a few minutes ago, and now it's closed."

Bo looked on and nodded. "It closed at the regular time without further decline after reopening. That's a good thing. But think about it; it's springtime, and we're only at wave three in a potential Elliott Wave pattern."

"What are you saying? Whatever it is, I have a feeling it involves more work."

"The temporary boost in the market starts with the corporate earnings season in early April. The typical increase on the first trading day of the quarter tends to be short-lived and often sets the stage for a subsequent decline. If a five-wave pattern appears in June, we may see the most significant movement yet to come."

Spencer gently laid his plastic fork on top of his plate. Without blinking, he stared ahead and said, "I'm going to be making these phone calls for the rest of my life, aren't I?"

Bo smiled. "The rest of your life, no. The rest of this market cycle? I'd say the chances are good."

After Spencer left his office, Bo sat in his desk chair and closed his eyes. He had to organize his thoughts, something he remembered doing the first time he met Selby as he calculated the cost of a cup of coffee. Even then, he was a torchbearer of economic good sense. He would give anything for that to be the extent of his concerns today.

Besides losing the love of his life in the past year, he'd also lost his friend and mentor, Edmond Brockett, to a tragic accident. While Selby's passing was closer to home and more heartbreaking, at least hers made sense. Edmond's still didn't.

Beyond that, his dream about an alligator attack had symbolically begun to play out in the stock market, detail by detail. Then there was the matter of his research and market study now in the hands of the United States government and, according to Yulia and Dimitri, the Russian government as well. All these events took place against the backdrop of an impending stock market crash.

Bo felt a little like Dorothy in *The Wizard of Oz*. He was leading his band of sojourners on a quest to find solutions for complex problems. As the pressures mounted with peril seemingly around every corner, the only thing to do was to persevere and keep going.

As Bo's analytical mind shifted into overdrive, he sorted through all the possible scenarios that could result, and none was favorable. If anything, they were catastrophic. He opened his eyes and looked around the room, his heart racing. Somehow, he had to muster the courage and faith to keep moving.

He had frequently prayed when Selby was sick. It didn't alter the outcome but did provide him with a measure of strength and comfort. In this moment, he needed both.

With his office door closed, he knelt on the Oriental rug in front of his desk. Then, he offered a supplication from his heart, known only to God and himself.

He lingered for a moment. It remained a mystery how such an obscure act could somehow alter the course of world events. But Bo believed it could. It was also a way for him to unburden himself, like a child allowing his father to carry a load too heavy for him to bear. Bo had just released this weight to his Heavenly Father.

Now all he could do was wait.

CHAPTER FORTY-FOUR

Stock market streaming quotes dominated the financial media coverage as the negative numbers moved across the bottom of the screen. The color red was everywhere, indicating the transition from a collapse to a crash. Bo was glued to the commentaries as media mogul after media mogul appeared in succession to trowel out the bad news.

Then another flash of red appeared on the screen, this time to alert viewers of breaking news. A female reporter, dressed in a gray wool coat, stood outside in the dark as the wind forcibly blew her hair. Behind her, workers in hazmat suits carried stretchers to ambulances idling with their back doors open. On cue, she positioned the microphone closer to her mouth and said, "A large explosion occurred at 5:37 a.m. Eastern Standard Time here in central Asia. No group has yet taken responsibility for the bombing, and there is no current death toll. We will get those details to you as soon as we receive them."

Bo and Spencer exchanged glances of disbelief. Then the network news anchor adjusted his earpiece and said, "I've just received word that the United States Secretary of State is about to make an announcement."

The screen immediately switched to an undisclosed location at the White House. A tall, clean-cut man in a navy suit stood behind a podium flanked by what Bo could only assume was a team of Homeland Security officials.

He leaned into the microphone. "We can confirm that there has been an explosion in central Asia. We just learned that the death toll is twelve. We are still gathering intel as to the source and motive behind this bombing. That's all I have for now."

Spencer blinked hard. "What? Did he just say only twelve people died in the explosion?"

Bo heard his cell phone ring. He checked the caller ID and saw that it was Senator Jack Prescott. He answered, "Senator Prescott?" He mouthed to Spencer, "I need to take this in private."

Spencer raised a hand, indicating that he understood, and quietly closed Bo's office door behind him.

Evidently, the senator had no time for niceties or decorum. He immediately started talking. "Bo, I'm certain that you—like the rest of the world—have seen the news this morning. I'm calling to let you know that what you had to say on the conference call a few weeks ago proved to be most insightful, not to mention the intel you provided from your anonymous European source. Our most capable tactical teams traced a supply stream of money back to a powerful clique of the world's influential players. What you're seeing on the news was a failed attempt on their part to cause global destruction."

Bo couldn't believe what he was hearing. He sat down in his desk chair. "Are you serious?"

"We uncovered this plot along with a vast network of associates and covert operatives—a crime ring that has existed for centuries. This consortium was connected to some of history's greatest benefactors. For years, their activities had occurred in plain sight, but they made sure to cloak them with indistinction to avoid detection."

The love of money, Bo thought as his eyes grew wide. "How did my recommendations about what to do about currency and debt help to accomplish that?" he asked as his heart raced.

Jack responded, "You put the puzzle pieces together for us regarding how the current money system had evolved over time and, more importantly, who benefited the most from it. You know the old saying, 'If you want to understand something, follow the money trail'? This case serves as a compelling example, as well as a sobering reminder, of the power that money can wield—for good or evil."

"So, this explosion, it was supposed to bring global destruction. Then why were only twelve people killed? The loss of any human life is always regrettable, but why such a small number?"

"The twelve individuals who died were not mere victims; they were the architects of a catastrophic global event they had orchestrated. Unfortunately for them, their scheme unraveled in the most devastating way imaginable. Burrowing into a bomb shelter designed for their protection, they unwittingly sealed their doom, becoming trapped in the fallout of their own explosion. That shelter, meant to offer them safety, became their tomb. As the only casualties, they inadvertently saved countless lives. In a chilling twist of fate, one can argue that justice was not only served but delivered with a notable element of irony."

Jack continued, "Also, Bo, your economic plan has found a home, at least domestically. We intend to implement sweeping reform to the monetary system. You were absolutely right; it is crucial that we establish a sovereign national currency."

Bo couldn't believe what he was hearing. "You mean that debt creation won't be synonymous with money creation?"

Jack chuckled. "The central bank will serve primarily as a clearinghouse, while regulatory authority will remain with the federal government's Treasury. Treasury dollars will replace central bank notes on a one-to-one basis, ensuring stability in the money supply. Furthermore, bank regulations will impose restrictions on fractional reserve lending."

Unable to contain his excitement, Bo quickly added, "By adopting this strategy, we can significantly reduce the risk of overleveraging during both economic downturns and upswings, enabling us to manage the fluctuations of the business cycle more effectively."

"Exactly. Let me be clear that none of these reforms will happen overnight. After all, we are talking about government agencies in Washington, DC."

Bo laughed. "But they will be on the table, which is a first step."

"And while the plan may not carry your name, your timely input was what brought it about. As I mentioned earlier, you served your country well, and your service will not be forgotten. The president will be conducting his State of the Union address in a few months. There is a good chance you will be invited to attend. I'll be in touch."

Jack ended the call before Bo had a chance to respond.

His eyes grew wide. *Did he say I might get invited to the State of the Union address?*

CHAPTER FORTY-FIVE

Regina Brockett balanced a cup of coffee in one hand and used the other to pick up the morning newspaper from her front porch. As she read the headline on the front page, she gasped. She hurried back inside the house and into the den, where she turned on the news. As she listened to the horrific details of the predawn attack, her breath quickened.

Whenever international incidents like this one occurred, Regina's thoughts immediately went to Kathryn. This morning, the usual questions swirled through her mind and demanded answers: Was Kathryn involved? Was she one of the twelve who died in the explosion? Until the media outlets disclosed who the victims were, Regina would have to wait like everyone else.

A benefit to Kathryn holding such a high-profile position was that any news regarding her well-being would be made known in short order. Yet, with Regina always seeing Kathryn as her daughter first and a world leader second, even that amount of time would feel like an eternity.

Kathryn stood outside the abandoned warehouse. The cold predawn hours carried with them an icy wind that felt like shards of glass hitting her face. She knocked on the door. She could hear footsteps approaching from inside, then the sound of a lock clicking. The door slowly creaked open.

"I've been expecting you," Simon said. The frigid outside air blew his hair back. Though clothed only in a cotton T-shirt, he seemed unfazed. "Come inside."

Simon offered to take her coat, but she shook her head, brushed past him, and quickly headed down the stairs to the basement. She walked over to the table where some of the most influential people in the world had once convened. She sat down in one of the chairs and looked over at Simon. "So, Lutz, Min Yun, Dominick, everyone? They're gone? Just like that?"

Simon's eyes displayed no emotion. "Yes, just like that." He raised his left hand in a loose fist and then dramatically released his fingers. "Poof! They're out of the picture."

Kathryn's stomach felt sick at what she deemed to be a pointless loss of life. She swallowed hard and then asked, "What happened to their assets?"

"Like the outside air this morning, they are frozen. Those associated with them will also find themselves in a financially unfavorable situation. While they anticipated that their put options would protect them against market declines, these options will ultimately expire without value, leaving them with no returns. Moreover, those who followed their advice for short-selling equities will be required to repurchase shares at higher prices to cover their short positions, which will result in further losses."

Kathryn sat up straight. "'Those associated with them'? You mean there were others? What has happened to them?"

"Well, they're not dead, obviously," Simon said matter-of-factly. "But you know the old saying, 'Smite the shepherd and the sheep will scatter'? Let's just say they've scattered. They turned on each other. Singing like canaries and cutting plea bargain deals at lightning speed."

"The news coverage made it sound like the good guys won," Kathryn said as she leaned back in her chair and folded her arms. "A global crime ring was broken up. *And only the twelve people who had planned mass destruction died in the explosion. The pit they dug for others, they fell into themselves.*" She scoffed, "We both know that part isn't true."

Simon's lips curled into a smile. "What is truth?"

She paused and then leaned forward in her chair. "Why did you do it?"

Simon shrugged his shoulders. "It was time for a reset, as they say in the financial world. We still have the money that The Circle provided for their pathetic little plot. That nest egg will jump-start a better—and dare I say flawless—plan. My plan. By the way, how does it feel to sit at that table, my Kathryn?"

Kathryn didn't want to give in, but she couldn't resist. She smiled broadly as she leaned in and caressed the smooth, wooden surface. "It feels wonderful."

"Doesn't it? I prefer it to the rugged and splintery finish that's so often associated with, how do they say it, *redemption?*" Simon visibly shuddered, and his eyes grew dark before he walked over to where Kathryn was sitting. He stood behind her chair and rested his hands on her shoulders. He leaned in and whispered in her ear, "I knew you would love sitting here. But my dear, you are in the wrong seat."

He took her hand and led her to the head of the table and pulled out the chair for her. Once she had sat down, he gently pushed it forward. "This is your place now. You will do much better than Lutz."

Once more, Simon rested his hands on Kathryn's shoulders. He wistfully looked off into the distance. "They only think they've won, but it's not over yet. No, it's far from over."

Then he laughed, a laugh that struck Kathryn as both enticing and hideous. It contained an air of authority she felt powerless against. But by surrendering to it, she felt as if an inky blackness had gained entrance into her soul. Going forward, she would do Simon's bidding, no questions asked.

However, she did have one condition. "Before I take over Lutz's position, I first must do something that I've been wanting to do even longer than I've wanted to be the leader of The Circle."

"I can read your mind, Kathryn. Take your trip, but then get ready to *roll up your sleeves*, as they say."

Looking up to make eye contact with him, Kathryn said, "I understand. We have much work to do."

"Yes, we do. Rest assured, my plan will come to pass. However, it will take time. You may not be here years from now when it comes to fruition."

He smiled and whispered, "But I will be."

CHAPTER FORTY-SIX

The online call organized by Jack Prescott, where Bo shared his insights on strengthening the economy, remained at the forefront of his mind, especially as he navigated the ongoing turbulence in the investment markets. Occasionally, he also found himself wondering about Dimitri and Yulia. Had they returned to Europe? How had they reacted to the bombing? Did they know any of the people who lost their lives? Bo had no way of reaching either of them, which he suspected was intentional on their part. Despite what had defined Yulia and Dimitri before they arrived in America, he admired their courage in making a fresh start. Ultimately, he wished them well.

As a matter of national security, Senator Prescott had urged Bo not to disclose how his input would be used to help revamp the American economic system. The senator stressed that the government could not afford any leaks to the press, as the process was still in the planning stages and would take time to implement.

Meanwhile, with the arrival of the month of June, Bo had to deal with a stock market that appeared to be in a steady decline. The question on everyone's mind had been asked more times than he could count in recent days. Right now, sitting in Bo's office and looking weary from the whole process, Spencer was the one asking it.

"This has to be the bottom . . . right?"

Bo sighed. "If my calculations are correct, this is the bottom of the last down move of the market, but it's not the *bottom of the market*. I anticipate a brief seasonal rise in July, followed by a resumption of the final downward move. For the anticipated upward move, I'm affirming new positions to add to client portfolios in pursuit of a modest gain. I've heard a few commentators advocate stock-picking in this market. They assert that this is a *market of stocks* more than a general *stock market*."

"Which ones are safe?"

"A few story stocks continue to show resilience. While investors typically favor growth stocks, they are currently cautious about those that rely on momentum and the potential for future profitability instead of current profitability and dividend distributions. Cyclical and interest-rate-sensitive stocks have experienced significant losses, as their long-term profitability projections depend on an optimistic outlook—something that is lacking in the market."

Spencer leaned back in his chair and folded his arms. "Do you still think the Federal Reserve is in the middle of it all?"

Bo scoffed. "To me, it's as plain as day. What I see coming is a contraction in the money supply, which will likely lead to a downturn in the stock market. As you well know, such downturns often occur before an overall economic decline. This can result in a slowdown that may lead to job losses and a decrease in commerce across various sectors." Bo dramatically leaned forward as if he were bowing and said, "All brought to you courtesy of the United States Federal Reserve."

The arrival of the summer season typically lifted Bo's spirits. He enjoyed the warm temperatures, long days, lush foliage on the trees, and the aroma of neighbors cooking steaks outside on the grill.

During the spring months, winter can still make an encore appearance, much like a nearly healed patient experiencing a relapse. But June seemed to be the time when winter fully released its chokehold on Mother Nature, allowing the color to return to her cheeks. All of creation seemed to burst forth with new life.

This year, however, summer's arrival would only make Selby's absence feel more pronounced. Bo would miss the walks they took at sunset, their drives to the beach for a long weekend, and how they rode out thunderstorms on their screened-in porch as they sipped a glass of wine.

Regarding the market? All the indicators told him that the worst was yet to come. At this point, he just wanted to keep his head down and keep going.

And that's what he did. July went by in a blur and, before he knew it, August did as well. Labor Day was fast approaching, and countless stories would swirl about the market moguls' lavish parties out at the Hamptons and the Cape. Of course, they all had left their subordinates behind to staff the trading portfolios, and not by coincidence. The market action around Labor Day was akin to cleaning toilets.

For this reason, Bo and his advisory team contacted the brave clients who had reentered the market at the beginning of the third quarter, encouraging them to exit once again. The strategy was to be cautious and favor defensive allocations. Typically, the firm's compliance department disapproved of this kind of trading activity as it deviated from established protocols. Furthermore, both systematic portfolios and individual customized accounts had seen a higher frequency of reallocations this year, and the year was not yet over. However, given the current market conditions, they made an exception.

Bo looked down at the long list of phone calls he still had to make. As he'd done numerous times in recent months, he sighed and started dialing.

CHAPTER FORTY-SEVEN

"Are you sure everything is in order for an afternoon meeting?" Kathryn asked as she absentmindedly twisted the pearl necklace she was wearing.

"Yes, I am certain. How many times must I reassure you? Now relax and perform that last-minute primping thing you do whenever you have an important engagement."

"I don't do that *every* time," Kathryn said, pretending to be defensive. "Okay, maybe I do," she said with a smile: a *genuine* smile. Not a perfunctory smile for the cameras, a diplomatic smile, or the one she displayed when she felt broken and weak but wasn't allowed to show it. This one was different, as it didn't originate from her facial muscles, but from that all-important muscle beating frantically in her chest.

Unzipping her purse, she retrieved her makeup compact. It made a clicking noise as she opened it and, while looking in the mirror, she applied a touch of powder to her nose. Closing it and placing it back into her purse, she smiled once again and said, "You are right, PaPa."

She looked out the window as the limo driver maneuvered through a maze of winding streets that emptied into a private estate secured by a large iron gate. As he inched the car closer, the gate creaked open automatically. Kathryn took in the scenery as the limo made its way up a long, paved driveway lined with meticulously manicured bushes on both sides.

Cresting the hill, she spotted a French Tudor–style house. The limo driver slowly pulled into a circular driveway and stopped the car at the entrance to the house.

"We have arrived, Madam Premier," the driver said, and then stepped outside to open Kathryn's door.

"Viktor, do I look okay?" she asked before getting out of the car.

The driver looked amused and responded, "Lovely as always. No need to be nervous."

But she *was* nervous. For years, she had only dreamed of this moment. And now, finally, the day had arrived. Her heels clicked against the brick steps as she ascended them. She glanced back at Viktor, who nodded and then pointed to the front door. When Kathryn turned around, she saw Regina standing there.

The first thing Kathryn noticed was how much they looked alike and that Regina, also, had her makeup perfectly applied and every hair in place.

Kathryn's eyes filled with tears of joy. *This, indeed, is my birth mother!*

Regina opened the door, took Kathryn's hand, and led her inside. Without speaking, Regina took Kathryn's face into her hands and studied it in detail. Then, as if she had the same epiphany, her eyes filled with tears. The two embraced for what seemed like an eternity, but even that wouldn't have been long enough.

Regina finally stepped back and reached for a tissue box from the foyer table. Pulling out two tissues, she handed one to Kathryn and used the other to wipe her eyes.

Through her tears, she laughed and said, "Our makeup is running!"

After serving her tea and hors d'oeuvres and talking about everything and nothing, Regina gave Kathryn a tour of the house. When they arrived at Regina's and Edmond's bedroom, Regina stepped over to her vanity, opened the drawer, and pulled out the photo of a baby girl.

Handing it to Kathryn, she said, "This was the last photo we took of you before . . ."

Regina paused, her eyes welling with tears. Her voice cracked as she said, "Of course, we have photo albums *filled* with pictures of you when you were an infant. I pulled them out of storage so that we could look through them, if you have time, that is."

Kathryn looked down at the tear-stained, faded photo and then at Regina. Perhaps for the first time, she took in the enormity of the sacrifice her birth parents had made so she could train in the best schools in Europe and rise to the position of power she currently held. Yes, she was premier. But she was also someone's daughter.

Kathryn swallowed hard as she carefully set the photo on the vanity. "I don't know how to thank you."

Regina shook her head and took Kathryn's hands into her own. "No, my love, you don't need to thank *me*. I protested it with every fiber in my being." Her eyes narrowed as she briefly looked away. "It was your father who was responsible."

"How did you do it, day in and day out? You must have missed me terribly."

Regina shrugged her shoulders. "How do we do anything that seems impossible? The only way I could cope—and this may seem silly—was to compare releasing you to how Moses's mother set him afloat in a basket down the Nile River. She not only wanted to save his life but also give him one greater than what she could provide. I had to trust that the same was true for you."

Kathryn turned back toward the vanity. She picked up a framed picture and pointed to a man standing beside a set of golf clubs. "This is my father, yes?"

"That was taken a few years ago." Regina's face softened. "You have his smile."

Kathryn's face lit up. "I can see that! It is a nice photo of the two of you."

She started to set it back on the vanity when Regina stopped her. "No, you keep it."

Kathryn put her hand on Regina's shoulder. "Thank you . . . Mother."

Regina sighed. "You don't have to call me that. Yulia and Dimitri raised you, and I am grateful for how well they cared for you."

Kathryn shook her head. "No, I call Yulia *MaMa* and Dimitri *PaPa*. You are *Mother*."

Regina's shoulders shook as she burst into tears. Kathryn pulled her into a hug. "You will always be Mother." She paused and then added, "And I am so sorry for what happened to Father. A terrible accident."

Regina pulled back and looked intently into Kathryn's eyes. "It wasn't an accident."

Kathryn's jaw dropped, and she sat down on the corner of the bed. Looking up at Regina, she said, "You knew?"

Regina nodded.

Kathryn's eyebrows snapped together. "Rest assured, the person responsible will be held accountable."

"That will never happen," Regina said softly as she sat down on the bed and faced Kathryn. "If there's anything I've learned from this quasi-clandestine life we have lived, it's that justice is rarely served to those who truly deserve it. Edmond's death, like all the others, will soon be forgotten."

Kathryn took her hand. "But *we* will never forget."

"No, we will not," Regina said as, once again, she looked away for a moment. Then, focusing back on Kathryn, she smiled and said, "Why don't I freshen up your tea, and we can look through those photo albums?"

"That sounds like a wonderful idea!"

From her seat on the couch in the den, Kathryn looked at her watch. "I can't believe it's already nine o'clock! I should have just planned on staying here tonight."

Regina's heart warmed. "You are still welcome to do that."

"I appreciate the offer and your warm hospitality. But I have already made other arrangements, and my security detail is waiting for me. Perhaps next time?"

"I would love for there to be a next time, but under one condition."

"Of course, Mother, what is it?"

"That you bring Yulia and Dimitri along. It's important that we meet. Even though we have lived on opposite sides of the world, we have shared a common interest . . . and love."

Kathryn smiled. "You may not have to wait long for that to happen since they are currently *not* on the other side of the world. They are in the States and plan to stay for a while. I will make sure they contact you."

Regina's face beamed. "I would like that very much."

"One day, I want you to visit *my* country." Her smile faded, and her gaze fell to the floor. "But today is not that day. There is much unrest, and I am afraid it is only going to get worse."

Regina put her hand to her chin, nodded, and smiled. "Someday, then."

From her seat on the couch where she sat next to Regina, Kathryn turned to face her and took Regina's hands into hers. "You know, today was a *someday*: the day I would finally meet my birth mother."

Regina tilted her head to one side. "Was it everything you had hoped it would be?"

Kathryn shook her head and squeezed Regina's hands. "No . . . it was better."

CHAPTER FORTY-EIGHT

Regina and Kathryn chatted nonstop as they gathered Kathryn's belongings. In addition to the picture of Regina and Edmond, Kathryn now had an entire box of photo albums to take with her.

It had been unrealistic of Regina to expect that she and Kathryn could catch up on decades of missed conversations in just a few hours. However, there was one piece of parting advice that Regina wanted to share, especially since she wasn't sure when the two of them would see each other again. She just hoped Kathryn would listen.

As they stood by the front door, Regina rested her hands on Kathryn's shoulders and took a deep breath. "I know that you are surrounded by brilliant minds that counsel and advise you."

Out of the corner of her eye, Regina spotted the headlights of Kathryn's limo approaching the house. Though she and Kathryn had exchanged many heartfelt words that day, none held the profound significance of what Regina was about to express. With time running out, she felt the weight of the moment and the urgent need to convey her thoughts as clearly and concisely as possible.

"In your position of power," she said as she glanced from Kathryn to the door, "you can't afford to give in to your emotions. You must think logically and strategically. But there are times when you must listen with your heart. As a woman, you have God-given instincts. If something inside of you is telling you that situations or people aren't as they appear, pay attention to that voice. It won't fail you."

Kathryn's eyes filled with tears, and she embraced Regina. "That is the best advice you could give me."

Regina watched as Kathryn's driver escorted her down the steps and then held the door open as she got into the limo. While the driver stepped around to the other side of the car, Kathryn rolled down the window, blew Regina a kiss, and waved. Regina raised her hand as if to catch the kiss. Kathryn giggled and rolled up the window.

Regina fought back the tears as she imagined similar moments she would have witnessed while Kathryn was growing up. She envisioned a snaggletoothed version of Kathryn getting on the bus for elementary school, followed by a blushing teenager leaving for her first date. Then, she pictured a more confident young woman posing for photos before her senior prom. Regina's heart ached at the thought of having missed all those milestones. Yet, at the same time, her heart was full. Like Kathryn, she felt that today's visit was more than she could have hoped for.

It was not surprising that her time with Kathryn today had produced a stampede of emotions. However, anger no longer led the herd.

Her anger had been satisfied.

As Regina watched the limo disappear from view, she closed the front door and clicked the lock into place. She then stepped into the kitchen, uncorked a bottle of cabernet, and poured herself a glass. After turning off the kitchen light, she made her way through the den. As she passed by the window overlooking the side porch, she noticed the kerosene heater. She hadn't moved it since the first responders had set it there after inspecting it.

For years, Edmond had pleaded with her to get rid of it, noting that it was dangerous and useless.

Dangerous? Yes.

Useless? Maybe not.

"Oh, Eddie," she said as she took a sip of wine. "You didn't allow me to live a natural life, so why should I allow you to die a natural death?" She paused and smiled. "I knew that old heater would come in handy someday."

She checked the lock on the den door, turned off the lamp, and went to bed.

Riding in the limo to her hotel, Kathryn found herself reflecting on Regina's parting advice. It had prompted her to pause and consider what ultimately guided her decisions. Specifically, when was the last time she had paid attention to that quiet, inner voice Regina mentioned?

Her thoughts were interrupted by the sound of her phone ringing from inside her purse. The caller ID displayed Simon's name. Once again, she could hear Regina's words echoing in her mind. As she stared at her phone, an unsettling feeling began to stir in the pit of her stomach.

What if Simon wasn't who he appeared to be?

She watched as the phone continued to ring.

But wait, wouldn't I have seen it by now? Or have I seen it and turned a blind eye? What is so powerful about Simon's hold on me that it renders me helpless to resist it?

She sat up straight in her seat. Perhaps she was not meant to resist it. If anyone could turn her dreams into reality, it was Simon. Didn't Dimitri and Yulia teach her to aim for the stars and take risks to achieve her goals? If Edmond and Regina had raised her, she might not have developed such a fearless mindset. But they didn't, and wasn't that fate? If it was fate, then she was simply fulfilling her destiny and had nothing to feel guilty about.

In an instant, as if she had come back to her senses, she picked up the phone.

"Simon, how are you?"

As she and Simon talked that evening—sharing ideas and aspirations—the uneasy feeling in her stomach began to dissipate. Before long, it had vanished entirely.

One day, years into the future, she would feel it again. But by that time, it would be too late.

CHAPTER FORTY-NINE

"The market is down over thirty-five percent for the year."

Bo was sipping coffee in his study and watching an early edition of the financial news, one that zeroed in on the current turmoil in the stock market. A high-profile financial analyst had just used the word "depression" twice. If Bo hadn't been fully awake before, he was now. October had arrived, the month in which the market crashes of both 1929 and 1987 had taken place.

The question weighing heavily on Bo's mind was undeniable: *What would October bring this year?*

He watched as a panel of so-called experts bemoaned the market's performance over the past year while, at the same time, expressing wistful optimism. When the network went to a commercial, Bo rolled his eyes, picked up the remote, and turned off the television. "You're all wrong," he said out loud as he took another sip of coffee and then headed downstairs to get dressed for work.

Today was scheduled to be yet another day of back-to-back appointments, with client phone calls filling in what little time existed in between. However, based on what he had just seen on the newscast, he wondered if it would be just *another day* after all. He was keenly aware of how pressure builds in the stock market during October. In years when declining stocks outnumber advancing ones, stocks tend to sell off more readily as investors seek to capitalize on losses for potential tax savings.

In contrast, during years of market gains, investors often delay selling to avoid realizing taxable gains. Many financial institutions close their fiscal years in the autumn, which can lead to more significant sell-offs. This creates opportunities for short sellers who profit from falling stock prices. Consequently, panic selling may erupt among frustrated investors disheartened by the market's overall performance.

This activity signals the critical point where market bottoms form. Although this juncture offers valuable buying opportunities for knowledgeable investors, it will, unfortunately, cause others to suffer substantial losses. The formation of the market bottom marks the final capitulation, a key moment in the fifth wave downward, consisting of five subwaves. When this development occurs, the completion of subwave E could lead to a significant turnaround, indicating a long-awaited market recovery.

As Bo drove to work, he felt his stomach churn as he thought about how his research had suggested that the market might have one more decline before stabilizing. This could lead to a *kitchen sink* moment, where a broad sell-off occurs, marked by crescendo of market activity. Margin calls at brokerage firms, along with heavy selling, would likely lead to the liquidation of both well-performing and underperforming stocks. Consequently, this situation could create opportunities for *bottom fishing*, where investors look to uncover valuable gems in the market. At that point, stockholders will be ready to throw in the towel and sell at any price.

Bo made his way into the office and pushed through two morning appointments. When he finally got a chance to check the news, his breath caught in his throat.

The market was limit-down. Volatility had spiked, and wild swings had occurred throughout the morning, indicating a crash. It was all Bo could do to remain calm. He knew that a handful of his clients were still in equity positions. Thankfully, most were patiently awaiting the conclusion of this dark stretch of market activity.

He looked up from his laptop as he heard Spencer step into his office. The panicked look on Spencer's face told Bo that he, too, was concerned about what was happening.

Spencer swallowed hard. "I didn't know if I should have interrupted your last appointment or not. Please tell me this isn't what it looks like. Because, to me, it looks a lot like 2008."

Bo motioned for Spencer to sit down. "There are similarities. The difference is, this time, the federal debt is massively out of control—not just for America, but for nations around the world." He gazed out the window and let out a heavy sigh. "Perhaps, the can has been kicked down the road . . . and the road has reached the end."

"I've been getting calls from clients all morning. They want to know if they should consider other investments."

Bo furrowed his brow as he examined the chart on his laptop screen. "I recommend waiting on those investments as well. Not only are stocks and bonds risky, but other asset values are also declining. Even the sectors that have performed better than most are now showing signs of weakness."

"When will we know that it's safe to invest again?" Spencer asked, taking off his glasses and rubbing his eyes.

"I foresee a scenario much like the grand finale of a fireworks display, characterized by an intense buildup and a whirlwind of activity that signals the conclusion. This moment will represent the capitulation point or a blow-off bottom, where we'll see a dramatic spike in volatility indicators. It's a daunting time, as panic selling reaches its zenith. Following this peak, I anticipate that the market will struggle to perform for an extended period, yet without any sharp declines."

"So, this is what it looks like?"

Bo nodded. "I'm afraid so. However, our main focus should be on demonstrating strong leadership early in the recovery process. We need to assist our clients in finding value in share prices that are likely to be thirty to fifty percent lower than they were at the beginning of the year."

"When do you anticipate that happening?"

"Christmas could mark the time of that market low, or it may occur sometime next year. Either way, it's approaching. At that time, picking up the phone to call clients will be an absolute joy."

"Until then?"

Once again, Bo sighed. "Unfortunately, there is more pain to come in the short term."

Spencer leaned forward in his seat. "What will this market look like as it starts to recover?"

"Good question. I think a smoothing of movements will occur. With less artificial support and stimulus, the algorithms will return to smaller and more traditional-size movements that characterize a classic and orderly market.

"Think of it like a high-performing athlete coming off performance-enhancement drugs. His body will experience stages of withdrawal as it recovers. The process is painful and drawn out, but it results in restored health. That's where we want to go with the market. Continued patience will be required as money is still working its way out of the system. In the long run, it will lead to better investing."

"In other words, there's light at the end of the tunnel?"

Bo nodded and once again glanced out the window. "But it's going to be one long tunnel."

***

When the market reopened, trading was soon limit-down again due to a further sharp decline. There were no buyers for the stampede of sellers who rushed to unload their holdings.

The market was in a free fall.

The crash Bo had both dreaded and predicted was happening before his eyes. Seeing the numbers plummet made him feel like a storm tracker watching a monster tornado level everything in its path. He pictured the aftermath as being similar, as recovering those losses and rebuilding those assets would take time. Even those who got out of the market wouldn't be unaffected. The financial destruction left in the wake of the crash would affect everyone and all sectors of society.

Sure enough, in the weeks that followed, reports abounded of financial institutions on the brink of collapse. Unemployment rose sharply for the quarter, as did crime rates. Reports circulated that loan defaults were snowballing. Those who had purchased property—as well as assets of nearly every other category—realized they had paid too much.

Interest rates were historically low, which meant money was cheap. This made monthly payments affordable, but without work, there's no income. And without income, borrowers can't make payments and, as a result, lose their property. This domino effect results in the economy buckling.

In response, key regulatory agencies began to take extreme measures. The Federal Reserve halted its money-tightening campaign and announced a policy reversal. Interest rates were further reduced, not raised. Bond purchases for Treasury instruments resumed. The US Treasury vowed to do whatever was necessary to stabilize the markets.

Finally, the president made a speech to reassure the nation. He was new to the office, having just been sworn in a few weeks earlier in January. It was his first speech, brief but calming. Bo was watching the broadcast on the television screen in his office when, suddenly, something registered.

That voice . . . I've heard it before. Then it dawned on him. It belonged to the "mystery man" on the call months earlier, the call Senator Prescott had asked Bo to join.

Bo's jaw dropped, and he said out loud, "I was talking to the next president of the United States!"

CHAPTER FIFTY

Bo yawned as he shuffled down the hall and into the kitchen. From his view out the window over the sink, he could see the sun starting to peek over the horizon. Looking over at the brick patio, he also noticed that a decent amount of pollen had arrived overnight, covering the furniture on the patio like thick yellow chalk. Bo reached up into a cabinet and, after moving a few items aside, retrieved his allergy medicine and placed it on the counter beside a row of vitamin supplements.

The filtered water dispensing from the refrigerator door made a hissing sound as Bo filled the coffee pot carafe. He leaned down, opened the freezer, and retrieved a bag of dark roast. After adding a couple of scoops to the filter in the coffee maker, he clicked the brew switch.

As the machine gurgled to life, Bo picked up the television remote from the counter and turned on the wall-mounted flat-screen television. He clicked the stations until he arrived at one of the financial news channels. To his surprise, there were no glaring headlines of further downward market movement. He clicked the remote to another financial news channel.

Nothing.

He made his way upstairs to his office and, after keying in a few prompts, six monitors came to life. Bo took the mouse and began scrolling through different reports. The yearly chart was still showing a decline. The quarterly and monthly charts were pointing down but were starting to flatten. The weekly chart had now formed a white candlestick, indicating a move higher in the current week.

He switched between different time frames as he examined various changes on the screen. While studying the broader charts, he noticed a shift: the alligator jaws, which had previously appeared to be widening, now appeared to be narrowing. The upper line had dropped to a new low, while the lower line was higher than in the last snapshot. It took him a moment to accept that a bullish divergence might finally be developing. This phenomenon occurs when the price line dips to a low point, yet the market indicators reveal a newfound strength beneath the surface. This divergence suggests that resilience is building within the market, priming it for a potential rebound.

He reflected on his dream about the alligator. Everything had come to pass, including the third and most aggressive assault against Bo and those with him, which he believed symbolized his clients, friends, and family. Despite an attack against their well-being and livelihood, they all had survived.

Bo had seen wealth disappear in the last few years without a clear trace of where it went. Of course, he was convinced that it didn't disappear; it just changed hands.

He focused intently on the chart displayed on his screen, and what he saw confirmed his suspicions: There was a shift in the lower standard deviation movement line. This dynamic pattern suggested a significant change on the horizon, one that warranted immediate attention and action.

Bo ran downstairs and located his cell phone. He dialed Spencer's cell number. After a few rings, Spencer answered.

"Good morning, Bo," Spencer croaked. "What can I do for you that doesn't require my brain to function on all cylinders? I've only had a few sips of my first cup of coffee. Emphasis on *first* cup."

Bo had no time for small talk. "What time are you getting to the office?"

Spencer sounded more alert when he responded, "The usual time, but I can get there earlier if you need me to."

"The usual time is fine. But please start emailing the clients on the cash list as soon as you arrive. We have a record amount of cash on the books for our clients, as we've been moving away from equities for the past several months. The indicators suggest it's time to change that strategy. Small-cap stocks tend to perform well in a baby bull market, offering significant growth potential. While it may feel awkward to invest millions back into equities, that's what we need to do. And we need to do it now."

Spencer responded, "Wait, are you seeing something that looks like we're finally headed into recovery territory?"

Bo couldn't believe the words that were coming out of his mouth. "We've been experiencing market contractions for months. It's been a long and painful delivery. If I'm seeing what I think I'm seeing, the baby bull's head is starting to crown."

Spencer shouted, "YES! Thank God! It's about time."

"I'm thinking out loud, but *emerging markets* can also offer lucrative opportunities for clients. The manufacturing sector has the potential for rapid growth, and lower-cost production hubs can expand quickly. Furthermore, large companies in the technology sector can gain traction as demand returns and innovation takes center stage once again.

"Remember that the stock market is often a leading economic indicator. Just as it led the way down before the damage to the world's financial system was visible, it may be showing the beginning of the move up in advance of oncoming economic improvement for Wall Street . . . which could also lead to financial gain for Main Street."

Spencer sounded wide awake now. "This is great. It also means we're going to be back in the trenches making phone calls, but we'll be delivering good news instead of bad news."

Bo chuckled. "That's right. However, you need to understand that clients who have sworn off stocks may be reluctant to reenter the market. It's like Mark Twain said, 'If a cat sits on a hot stove, that cat won't sit on a hot stove again. That cat won't sit on a cold stove either.' This serves as a contrarian indicator, contrasting with how investors were eager to jump into the market earlier in the cycle."

Spencer responded. "To quote a stockbroker named Bo Parrott, is this the time to be 'greedy when others are fearful'?"

Once again, Bo chuckled and said, "I've taught you well. Now, let's get this party started!"

"You must be joking. Have you looked at the news lately? Record unemployment, crime, suicide, bankruptcy—record *everything terrible.*"

These were the words of the same investor who, a couple of years ago, challenged Bo when Bo suggested reducing market exposure. Now that Bo was calling to *increase* market exposure, he was getting the same response. Bo knew this was a good sign, so he remained calm. Theodor Reik's quote came to mind about history not repeating but merely rhyming.

The rhyme was becoming apparent.

Even with a few clients responding negatively, nothing could extinguish the joy and anticipation that defined this outreach campaign. Bo wasted no time marshaling the team and organizing a systematic approach. It was a window in the market that was opening quietly and was somewhat camouflaged, like the alligator hiding in the floor. But now what was hidden didn't represent destruction and loss, but restoration and gain.

"The stock market always makes you work for it," Bo told his advisory team. "What we're doing is a little bold, but we're on a mission for full deployment of capital. It's time to make up for lost time!"

Over the following days and weeks—client by client—positions were added as portfolios were reallocated back to more traditional percentages of equities to fixed income. As a result, the current project had a slight overweighting toward equities. While a few clients expressed trepidation, most were hungry for something more than conservative allocations.

Within a few short months, the financial news feed began to thaw out. Discredited pundits kept low profiles for a while. When the networks eventually featured them for interviews, they appeared a little more seasoned—and a little less avuncular.

Among the fallen was none other than Jacob Wiley, who was arrested and charged with insider trading. Bo wasn't all that surprised. While he was glad that Jacob had been *taken off the streets*, so to speak, he felt compassion for those he had deceived and cheated. Specifically, he wondered if he'd be hearing from Polly Dunnigan in the coming days. Time would tell.

Regarding the market, Bo considered how its lessons must be learned repeatedly every eight to sixteen years as cycles played through.

If we could only remember those lessons and not have to learn them all over again.

CHAPTER FIFTY-ONE

"Well, it's about damn time!"

The words came from Bill Corey, the founding partner and president emeritus of the firm.

Bo interpreted the growling comment as a compliment from the eighty-two-year-old cigar-chewing golfer who used to wear his soft-cleat golf shoes to the office. Perforation marks on the floor tiles were still visible from the days he wore the more rigid ones.

For years, he had looked to Bo for investment leadership. While never one to dole out accolades, Bill could not thank Bo enough that his account was only down 6 percent from the high, far better than the 58 percent drop in the overall market that Bill's peers and competitors had endured.

Bo shook Bill's hand and led him back to his office. After offering him a cup of coffee, which he declined, Bo watched as Bill slowly eased into the chair across from Bo's desk. He removed his golf cap and placed it on his right knee.

His gaze fell to the floor as he said, "Bo, I blew up at you on our last phone call." He raised his right palm in the air and said, "There's no excuse for my behavior, but my wife's health wasn't good at the time." He paused and then looked up at Bo. "You know she passed away a year ago this July." He shook his head. "All of that was happening, *and* the market was crashing. I had a lot on my mind, and I took it out on you. I hope you can forgive me."

Bo had to will his eyes not to grow wide; this behavior was completely out of character for "Big Bill Corey." Evidently, life events had changed him. Bo knew firsthand how they had a way of doing that. And he considered that Bill might not have been aware of Selby's health condition at the time.

He didn't hesitate to respond. "It's alright. We were all doing the best we could."

Bill's eyes became misty. "Looking back, I realized that, when I lost my temper with you because of the difficulties I was dealing with in my life, you were dealing with the same difficulties in yours. Selby was also terminally ill and then passed away, too. You showed me deference when I least deserved it, and I won't soon forget it."

"Thank you, Bill. That means a lot."

"Now, if it is not too late, would you consider taking on another client?" Bill winked.

Bo chuckled. "I think I can find the time. When would you like to meet?"

"Are you busy now?" Bill asked.

Bo grinned. "Why don't you take me up on that cup of coffee and wait in the conference room? I have one phone call to make, and then I'll be available."

Bill reached down to the floor beside his chair and picked up several thick white envelopes. Standing, he placed the envelopes on Bo's desk. From where Bo was seated, he recognized these envelopes as containing account statements.

Bo knew that Bill had several million dollars in liquid assets. He had it invested in ten accounts spread across ten different brokerage firms. He liked playing one broker against another to see who had the best ideas and was willing to work the hardest. Bo was only one of the ten.

However, his jaw dropped as Bill looked over at him, nodded, and with a slight smile said, "They're all yours now."

After finishing the client phone call, Bo walked down the hallway toward the conference room. He was eager to rekindle an old client relationship, one that, until today, he concluded had ceased to exist.

As he spoke further with Bill, Bo felt a renewed sense of collaboration. As the investment markets improved, client accounts would follow. The six to nine months of leading economic indicators for stock market activity would correspond to an improvement in the economy during that period. Jobs would return. Crime would decline. The rest of the investment community would eventually need to get on board, a requirement for any sustained rally that was broad and meaningful.

Money wasn't everything. But when people maintained a viable sense of well-being, everything worked out better. Money played a big part in that.

For the first time in months, Bo was enjoying his work. He no longer braced for the worst when the phone rang. With a healthy market, he had fresh ideas. Except for Selby not being with him, his world finally felt like it was back in balance.

As Bo drove home that evening, he remembered a favorite excerpt from nineteenth-century poet Walt Whitman. In an interview in 1888, Whitman commented on the avid participation in a newly reemerging culture and economy of that period.

"Open up all your valves and let her go. Swing. Whirl with the rest. You will soon get under such momentum, you can't stop, if you would." The Gilded Age was well underway at the time. The emergence of modern industrialization and innovation ushered in a sustained period of prosperity that buoyed American sentiment.

Bo wondered. He was vaguely aware of a lost sense of patriotism that characterized much of the contemporary mood. Was it possible that the nation—and possibly the world—now stood at a new vantage point for advancement? One that was satisfying for participants and possessed lasting value? Perhaps hope could find its way back into the national psyche. It could become stylish once again to exude optimism and belief that what can be imagined can be achieved.

When people have hope, they generate new energy. When energy is generated, achievement is maximized. Generosity is spurred by success, and charitable nonprofit organizations flourish as donors have the means and the confidence to give more liberally.

Key players learn valuable lessons from past mistakes on the world's stage. Those who have lived long enough know that this won't last forever. But for now, it was a welcome relief.

CHAPTER FIFTY-TWO

Bo could feel his phone vibrating. He sat up in bed and fumbled for his glasses on the nightstand. Putting them on, he looked to see who was calling him at this hour. The clock on his phone displayed 12:17 a.m. The caller ID displayed the name "Senator Jack Prescott."

"Senator?" Bo answered. With the lateness of the hour, he wondered if Jack had accidentally dialed him. Then he heard Jack's voice booming on the other end.

"Bo Parrott, I didn't wake you up, did I?"

Bo was about to respond when Jack laughed. "I'm certain I did, and I apologize. But I didn't want to wait until tomorrow to deliver a very special invitation to you, albeit one delivered over the phone."

Bo had become wide awake as soon as he saw that the call was from Senator Prescott. "First of all, it's no problem. That whole idea of beauty sleep is just a myth anyway. What kind of invitation?"

"Do you remember our last phone call several months ago when I mentioned that you would not be forgotten for the information you provided to not only bolster the economy but also spare the nation—and the world—a serious calamity?

Bo's heart skipped a beat. "Yes, I remember."

"Well, I just got out of a meeting here in Washington. That's why I'm calling at this late hour. We received the guest list for President Grantham's first State of the Union address. And guess whose name was on that list?"

Bo jumped to his feet. "You've got to be kidding me!"

"In Washington, we don't kid about this sort of thing. The one caveat is that it's on short notice. The president's address is scheduled for two weeks from this Thursday. I'll email you all the details, including your flight information. It's all been arranged; you just need to show up."

Bo sat back down on the bed. "I don't know what to say!"

Jack chuckled. "How about that you'll attend?"

"Of course, I'll be there. Thank you, Senator. This is a great honor."

"I look forward to seeing you then. Take care, Bo."

Bo ended the call and then fell back on the bed. Looking up at the ceiling, he started laughing. He felt like a kid at Christmas. The market was up, clients were happy, and he was going to Washington for a once-in-a-lifetime event. After so many months of gloom and despair, he couldn't believe how things had turned around. Then it dawned on him.

What does one wear to a State of the Union address?

He had purchased a new suit for his presentation at the Carolina Economic Forum. That should do. Maybe he'd even get a new tie.

He stretched his arm over his head to Selby's side of the bed and looked over to where she had always slept. He thought about how excited she'd be for him.

And she'd insist he purchase that new tie.

———

Thursday morning dawned with clear skies and temperatures in the mid-sixties. Bo's flight wasn't scheduled to take off until after lunch, so he spent the early part of the morning catching up on client phone calls.

When his plane touched down in Washington, DC, later that afternoon, he grabbed his carry-on suitcase, slung his book bag over his shoulder, and took the escalator down to the ground transportation level. There he saw a clean-cut young man, possibly a college undergraduate, holding a professionally printed sign with Bo's name on it.

"Hello, Mr. Parrott?"

Bo smiled and extended his hand. "Yes, I'm Bo Parrott."

The young man made eye contact and gave Bo's hand a firm, quick shake. "My name is Carter, and I'm Senator Prescott's page. I'll be riding with you to your hotel."

Carter took Bo's suitcase and began rolling it toward several sets of double doors. He talked as he walked, and Bo had to hurry to keep up with both his steps and his words.

"After we drop you off at your hotel, we'll have the kitchen staff deliver a meal to your room. You'll have the rest of the afternoon to eat and get dressed. The next shuttle will arrive at your hotel promptly at six. I'll call you two minutes before it pulls up to the front of the hotel."

As they stepped through a set of automatic double doors, Carter and Bo approached a black sedan idling outside. The driver quickly stepped out of the car and circled around to where Bo and Carter were standing. Almost in one sweeping motion, he opened the back passenger's side door, picked up Bo's suitcase, and put it in the trunk. By the time Bo and Carter had sat down in the back seat and buckled their seatbelts, the sedan was already exiting the airport.

When they arrived at Bo's hotel, the same thing occurred, but in reverse order. Before he knew it, Carter had handed him his business card in case Bo had further questions, and the sedan sped out of sight.

Bo checked in at the front desk and then took the elevator up to his room. Upon opening the door, he could see that the room was nice, but not extravagant. He reasoned that the executive office wasn't necessarily cutting corners. After all, this was downtown Washington, DC. Any hotel room would be pricy, even the modest ones.

Just as Carter had said, Bo received a phone call at exactly 5:58 p.m. He made sure he had his room card in his wallet before shutting the door. He had taken a few steps down the hall when he realized that he'd forgotten his coat.

He sprinted back to his room, grabbed his coat from where he had draped it over a chair, and hurried to catch the elevator before the doors closed.

Arriving downstairs in the lobby, he could see the same black sedan idling in front of the hotel. This time, the driver didn't get out to open the door for him. Bo slid into the back seat and immediately apologized. "I'm sorry for the delay. I left my jacket in the hotel room and had to go back to get it."

Looking straight ahead, Carter stated matter-of-factly, "If you had forgotten it, we could have provided a loaner for you."

"A *loaner?*" Bo asked.

"Yes, we have a closet full of men's navy and black suit jackets—all sizes." He briefly glanced in Bo's direction and displayed a slight grin. "It gives a new meaning to the term *coat closet.*"

In a few minutes, Bo could see the Capitol building just ahead. The driver pulled up to a side entrance where a security guard stood. Carter walked with Bo up to the door and swiped a card on a small electronic machine that the security guard was holding. When he did, the side door beeped open, and the guard led Bo inside.

Bo was mesmerized by the historic glamour of the architecture as he followed the guard to a large door that led to the balcony seating.

The guard turned to Bo and pointed up the stairwell. "This is where the guests sit. The ground level is for the elected officials."

After Bo and the guard had ascended a carpeted staircase, they walked a short distance until they had reached the middle section of the first row of seats. He pointed to a chair and motioned for Bo to sit down. "This is your seat, Mr. Parrott."

Bo didn't know what to say. *A front row seat! And how did he know my name?* Then he reasoned that when Carter swiped the card, it probably displayed Bo's name as a guest.

The balcony quickly began to fill up. Bo checked his watch. There were only a few minutes left before the president would enter the chamber. Bo wondered what issues he would focus on. The stock market crisis, of course, was number one on Bo's list.

Bo watched as the television camera crew downstairs tested their equipment and took their places. He looked over toward his right when he heard a group of ladies talking as they walked up the stairs. One, an attractive woman who appeared to be in her late forties, walked over to where Bo was sitting and pointed to the seat next to him. "Is this one taken?"

Bo clumsily stood to his feet and stuttered, "No ma'am, First Lady, Mrs. Grantham . . . ma'am."

He waited until she had sat down and then leaned over and said, "Can I try that again? I sort of butchered it the first time. It's just that it's such an honor to be in your company!"

Still facing forward, she leaned over toward Bo and said, "I could say the same thing about you, Mr. Parrott."

Bo wanted to ask her how she knew his name but noticed that the television crew had started the countdown. Within seconds, the double doors at the front of the House Chamber opened, and the sergeant at arms announced in a loud voice, "Mr. Speaker, the president of the United States!"

The crowd jumped to its feet and applauded as President Calvin Grantham entered the room. Bo's heart warmed as he stood and watched the leader of the free world shake hands and exchange friendly backslaps with senators as he made his way to the podium.

After the president had officially greeted the vice president, the Speaker of the House, senators, and distinguished guests, he began his speech.

"While there are numerous topics that I want to address tonight, I want to begin with the economy. I'm certain we all remember that fateful morning a year and a half ago when an explosion took place in central Asia: an explosion that could have ended with millions of lives lost instead of just a few. Our homeland security team had received information that not only helped them avert a global catastrophe but also dismantle a vast network of international criminals who were intent on creating havoc worldwide.

"Now, you might be wondering, where did they get this data? Was it from the CIA or some top-secret government envoy?"

Bo felt his heart begin to flutter. His palms started to sweat. *"Oh my God . . . is he . . . really?*

"No, this information came from an American citizen who, for years, has applied himself to studying—in detail—the rich history of our great nation and, specifically, the history of our economy. He has also devoted hours of analytical study to the stock market. Due to his dedication to his field of expertise, one of our senators contacted him, curious about what he saw that needed to change to improve the current economy. That answer, supported by all those hours of research, put the pieces of the puzzle together, allowing them to discover a nefarious network trying to manipulate the system and weaken the global economy.

"This citizen also foresaw the stock market crash—and the ensuing period of economic depression—before most of the rest of us did. Because of his timely intervention, he prevented numerous people from losing their investments . . . and their shirts."

The president paused while the audience laughed.

Bo's eyes welled with tears. The First Lady reached over and took his hand.

"The First Lady is currently sitting beside this distinguished American citizen. He's an investment advisor from the great state of North Carolina, and his name is Beaufort Hardy Parrott III. His friends and family know him simply as Bo, which is a good thing: That name is a mouthful!"

Once again, the crowd laughed.

The president smiled as he said, "Bo, would you please stand?"

Bo took a deep breath and wiped the tears from his face with the back of his hand. His knees were shaking, but somehow, he managed to get up from his seat.

"Selfless dedication to our craft—whatever that may be—is something we, as Americans, take pride in. But selfless dedication to our nation? That is something we reward. Bo, tonight we are awarding you the Presidential Medal of Freedom for your tireless work and service to your clients, this country, and the world. Congratulations."

Bo felt as if his heart would burst. His untold hours of studying the stock market had served him well in predicting what was coming. But this? He never saw this coming.

He smiled, nodded toward the president, and said, "Thank you."

The next thing he heard was the First Lady whispering, "Now you hold still while I snap this into place!"

Bo turned so that his back was to her and then felt the weight of the medal on his chest . . . just above his heart. He touched it, smiled, and then waved. The crowd stood to their feet in a roar of applause.

Back at his hotel room later that evening, Bo gingerly placed the medal on the dresser beside a Polaroid picture of the president shaking his hand. A print of the official photo would be mailed to him in the coming days. He then checked his phone, which had been charging on the nightstand. The tears returned when he saw that he had forty-five missed calls and over 500 text messages.

He was still in shock over what had just occurred. Following in his grandfather's footsteps, he hadn't chosen this career for the accolades or recognition. Instead, his true passion was to empower individuals to thrive and take control of their financial futures. Whenever that happened, he felt rewarded.

He had never experienced such an honor for his life's work, and probably never would again. Especially since he had planned to finally submit his retirement notice at the end of the year. He would work another year after that and then transition into a consulting role.

Weathering the recent market depression had taken a toll. The circles under his eyes, coupled with fatigue that didn't improve with a good night's sleep like it used to, were glaring indicators. His age was catching up with him. The timelines were beginning to show.

He was at peace with his decision. He had had a good run. Tonight was a way to go out on top in a way that he never could have imagined, a true swan song.

He had experienced several dreams over the course of his career that provided him with insight and clarity, dreams so vivid that they felt like reality.

Tonight was just the opposite. It was reality, but it felt like a dream.

CHAPTER FIFTY-THREE

The next two years flew by faster than any that Bo could remember. He couldn't decide if it was because he was enjoying his work so much, or because he knew the end was in sight. His focus had been on preparing his team for the transition of leadership. Spencer would be stepping into Bo's role, something Spencer was approaching with much trepidation. But Bo saw that he was much further along than he was at that age and felt grateful to be leaving the practice in such capable hands.

Today would mark his last day of work. He got dressed as he had done each morning for the past forty years. However, on this particular morning, as he buttoned his shirt and tied his bow tie, he reflected on what he had experienced over the past four decades.

In short, he had seen it all. Several booms. Several busts. He had felt like a hero. He had felt like a failure. Sometimes he had gotten it right; more times than he cared to admit, he had gotten it wrong. Right or wrong, he had given it his best every day.

He had considered other worthwhile pursuits earlier in his educational career but had chosen this one. Stockbroker. Investment advisor. Although he worked within the financial industry, his responsibilities extended beyond investing in stocks and bonds. It had been defined by investing in people's lives, which, in his estimation, was the most worthwhile pursuit of all.

He finished tightening his bow tie and made his way to the garage. He placed his lunch provisions in the trunk of his car in the same place he had placed them for decades. The only difference was that this time . . . would be the last time.

Today, he wouldn't need to schedule a morning meeting with his advisory team to organize the day's activities. Instead, all he had to do was show up, smile, and genuinely take it all in.

As he drove up to the office building, he couldn't help but marvel at the number of cars in the staff parking lot. His practice began with only two: Bo and one other associate. They started from virtually nothing. Yet, somehow, it became something. To Bo? It became something special.

He grabbed his jacket and headed for the employee entrance. As he readied his key to unlock the door, he took a deep breath and stepped inside the building. He had cleaned out his desk a week ago and turned it over to Spencer. Bo treasured the early days of his career that the desk represented. And he appreciated Charlie Randolph's help in getting a rookie broker off to a running start.

And the race had continued . . . for the next forty years.

Bo was speechless as his team of advisors greeted him in the conference room with an elaborate spread of food. A vase filled with lilies and roses graced the center of the table. In a brief speech, Bo thanked everyone for their individual contributions over the year. Whatever they had accomplished, they had done so as a team.

Bo took the time that afternoon to speak with each one. He could recall past instances when the older advisors had received similar retirement send-offs. Now it was his turn. It had all gone by in a flash. But, tomorrow, the sun would rise as it always had, and Bo would rise with it—and start a new season of his life.

As late afternoon approached, Bo packed the gifts from well-wishers into the trunk of his car. His favorite was the one from Spencer: the game of Monopoly. Bo thought it most appropriate because it teaches the most valuable lesson about money: it doesn't last forever.

Nor does this life. As Bo arrived home at nightfall, he thought about how, despite the joy the day had brought to his heart, it still felt incomplete without Selby. He knew that, in the days ahead, he wouldn't have his work to distract him and would feel her absence more than ever.

The following morning, Bo's phone alarm woke him up at 6:30 instead of 4:30, now that he was retired. He would set it for the same time the next day, and the day after that. He was determined to maintain a schedule to help him remain disciplined and productive.

As he walked into the kitchen, he opened the door leading out to the patio. He immediately noticed that the fresh spring air carried with it a familiar floral scent—wisteria. The smell was so enticing that he decided to look for its source.

He ambled through the yard, peering under bushes and shrubbery until he discovered a vine bursting with blossoms underneath a magnolia tree. He picked a generous number and carried them back inside. After rummaging under the kitchen sink in search of a suitable vase, he selected one that had displayed Selby's anniversary flowers a few years ago. He filled it with water and arranged the wisteria.

As he stood there, he thought about this purple flower. It produced a soft fragrance and delicate blossoms, yet it possessed the fortitude to grow and flourish in the harshest of environments. It reminded him of other enigmas in life that transcended human reasoning, such as the power of a simple prayer or a moment of divine inspiration.

There were many things that he would never completely understand, at least not on this side of heaven. And of anyone, Beaufort Hardy

Parrott III was familiar with seeking knowledge and understanding. He had spent his career deciphering complex charts, diagrams, graphs, and mathematical probabilities. Even with all his analytical skills and decades of research, there remained mysteries surrounding the stock market that he still couldn't explain.

And for the first time in forty years, he didn't have to.

ABOUT THE AUTHORS

Billy Hemby is a managing director with Level Four Financial, a division of CRI Advisors, PLLC, and has over thirty years of experience in the financial services business. With multiple books in publication, Jan Hemby is an award-winning novelist and a regional featured speaker. The two are native North Carolinians with deep roots in Southern culture. Their goal is to bring to life money dynamics, global events, and local culture in story form that engages both experienced investment enthusiasts and casual readers alike.

www.ingramcontent.com/pod-product-compliance
Lightning Source LLC
Chambersburg PA
CBHW070850160726
48004CB00003B/1012